OVER

BY THE SAME AUTHOR

FICTION

Dame's Delight
Georgy Girl
The Bogeyman
The Travels of Maudie Tipstaff
The Park
Miss Owen-Owen is At Home
Fenella Phizackerley
Mr Bone's Retreat
The Seduction of Mrs Pendlebury
Mother Can You Hear Me?
The Bride of Lowther Fell
Marital Rites
Private Papers
Have the Men Had Enough?
Lady's Maid
The Battle for Christabel
Mothers' Boys
Shadow Baby
The Memory Box
Diary of an Ordinary Woman
Is There Anything You Want?
Keeping the World Away

NON-FICTION

The Rash Adventurer:
The Rise and Fall of Charles Edward Stuart
William Makepeace Thackeray:
Memoirs of a Victorian Gentleman
Significant Sisters:
The Grassroots of Active Feminism 1838–1939
Elizabeth Barrett Browning
Daphne du Maurier
Hidden Lives
Rich Desserts & Captain's Thin:
A Family & Their Times 1831–1931
Precious Lives
Good Wives?
Mary, Fanny, Jennie and Me, 1845–2001

POETRY

Selected Poems of Elizabeth Barret Browning (Editor)

Over

Margaret Forster

Chatto & Windus
LONDON

Published by Chatto & Windus 2007

4 6 8 10 9 7 5 3

Copyright © Margaret Forster 2007

Margaret Forster has asserted her right under the Copyright,
Designs and Patents Act 1988 to be identified as the author of this work

First published in Great Britain in 2007 by
Chatto & Windus
Random House, 20 Vauxhall Bridge Road,
London SW1V 2SA

Addresses for companies within the Random House Group Limited can be found at:
www.randomhouse.co.uk/offices.htm

The Random House Group Limited Reg. No. 954009

A CIP catalogue record for this book
is available from the British Library

ISBN 9780701181253

The Random House Group Limited makes every effort to ensure that the papers used in
its books are made from trees that have been legally sourced from well-managed
and credibly certified forests. Our paper procurement policy can be found at:
www.randomhouse.co.uk/paper.htm

Typeset by Deltatype Ltd, Birkenhead, Merseyside
Printed and bound in Great Britain by
Clays Ltd, St Ives plc

1

I HAVE to start somewhere, trying to understand.

*

We lived on a noisy road, on a hill. Our house was at the point
of the hill where cars change gear. The house was a bargain,
when we bought it. It had a long, narrow garden at the back,
with a gate in the hedge giving access to the tennis courts be-
longing to a local club. We didn't play tennis, but we thought
the children might, later on. It was easy, because of the silence
at the back of the house, where we slept, to forget about the
constant traffic at the front, though sometimes, if a very heavy
lorry was labouring up the hill, the whole house trembled. I
worried about this, but he never did. The house was old. He
said it seemed to him that it had survived worse things than
lorries groaning past. Four houses down from us, there was a
gap where a bomb had dropped in the Second World War. Our
house had stood firm then. He had confidence in it. We had a
survey done before we bought it and no structural faults had
been revealed. But I worried.

In all the years we lived there, the happy years, there was
only once talk of moving, to somewhere quieter. He suggested
it. We all objected, for different reasons. The twins were eight
and were horrified at the thought of moving schools, and Finn,
three years younger, had just become best friends with the boy

next door and couldn't imagine life without him. I'm not quite sure why I resisted the idea as strongly as I did. I liked the house, but it wasn't perfect. I could have liked another, perhaps even more. He took us to look at the area he was thinking of. It was very attractive, not quite suburbia, but plenty of greenery, lots of wide, tree-lined roads, no noise. Most of the houses were detached, built in the 1930s I think, solid-looking but without much character. I shook my head, wrinkled my nose. I think I complained that there was no atmosphere. Our hillside location had cafés at the foot of the hill, and a row of small, useful shops, and there was no dull uniformity – the buildings were a satisfying mixture of old and new.

He didn't try to persuade me. He said if it was a case of four to one, then we would stay where we were. It was good of him to give way like that, but he was – is – that kind of man, decent, understanding, anxious to be fair. We got our wish, the children and I, and he never made us feel guilty at thwarting his own desire to move.

*

Why I have begun with the house I can't imagine. The house was of no consequence whatsoever. I suppose I am trying to find a beginning and that describing where we lived when it happened helps me to start. But though there was a beginning, there is, as yet, no ending. That is what he wants, and he will never get it. I can see that, everyone else can see that, but he can't. He remains single-minded, in pursuit of the truth. This, he says, has nothing to do with any desire for revenge. He wants to discover the truth and see justice done, in so far as it can be done. An admirable man. None of us can match up to him. He makes us feel unworthy, cowardly, feeble, ashamed. All we want to do is forget. Not forget *her*, as if we could, as if we would want to, but forget *it*. We want to recover, and we can't, so long as he continues with his impossible quest.

The thought of actually recovering is something I think he

2

cannot bear. To recover would, for him, be the greatest betrayal of all.

*

It is strange living on my own again, though I don't know why I say 'again' when I've never truly lived on my own. That's odd, too, I suppose. It makes it sound as though I went straight from living with my parents to living with him, with Don, when we got married. But that's not the case. There were years in between when I was training as a teacher, either living in a college hostel or in a flat with other girls. But all that time I never had my own room. I don't remember minding this. Until recently, I've always liked company, I've always got on well with people. I'm still friends with Lynne, Pat and Ruth, the girls I shared with for three years. We meet at least once a year, have a little reunion, though it's hard for Pat to come to London. We send each other birthday cards, and ring each other up if one of us has heard some news about one of the others which needs to be passed on. They all rang me, when it happened. They read about it in the newspapers. They kept on ringing too, they didn't fade away – and my tears, and then my silences, didn't embarrass them.

*

I teach Reception, the babies. Teaching Reception is not easy. Margot Fletcher, the headmistress, wondered, when I came back afterwards, whether I was up to it. She said it was won- derful to have me back but maybe ... and she left her sentence hanging in the air, waiting for my reaction. I said I would be fine. She nodded, said she trusted me to tell her if I found I was struggling.

Struggling? Of course I was struggling. But without the chil- dren the struggle would have been lost.

*

I have a helper in Reception, a teaching assistant called Jeremy. He is sweet. He looks like a young Jesus Christ, with his long hair and beard and his soulful eyes. He feels like my son though he is nothing like Finn. Half the time he is in a dream and he has to be programmed to do what needs to be done, but he takes direction well. He isn't lazy, just vague and lacking in energy. I can't imagine him in charge, sole charge, of a class.

I wasn't sure at first whether Jeremy had been told about me. I loved the idea of working with someone who knew none of my recent history, but I thought it unlikely that he hadn't heard something. There are quite a few people on our staff who enjoy passing on dramatic information, though I'm sure never in a malicious way. A word in young Jeremy's ear may have been irresistible. But if he did know anything he didn't show that he did – there wasn't that look in his eyes, when he met me, that I had grown to recognise and dread. All he said was that everyone had told him he was lucky to be with me and he'd have no problems. That was clever, and flattering.

He is good with the children, gentle, affectionate and yet managing not to get too involved. I am pleased with him, on the whole, though his occasional trance-like state can be irritating. One or two of the girls have already started to boss him about, and they are only five years old. In fact, one of them, Paige, realised straight away that Jeremy would take orders. It was 'Hang up my coat, Jeremy' and 'Wash my hands, Jeremy' when, of course, she was perfectly capable of doing both herself and should have been told to do so. But he was amused, and hung up her coat and washed her hands, and her triumph registered with her. She is an attractive child, tall for her age. Like Miranda.

Luckily, there isn't much time for nostalgic ruminating in Reception. We started term with ten children and now another five have been phased in, soon to be followed by the final five, to make the class complete. They take some settling in, most of them. Even though nearly all have been to nursery school, this is 'big' school, and feels very different. We have a lot of tears, a lot of wanting of mothers, lots of wet pants. Some of the parents are more of a hindrance than a help – hovering at the door after I've closed it, peering anxiously through its glass panes, or managing to leave the building but then unable to resist trying to look through the windows (we are on the ground floor). I have to be firm. Pleasant, sympathetic, but firm. And I am.

There are plenty of hugs from the children. I am generous with hugs in return, though I don't let the children become clinging. A few moments on my knee, while I hear whatever the tale of woe is, and then eyes are wiped and the child lifted down. But they are good for me, the hugs.

*

So, I am living on my own, in a flat, quite near to the school, a ten-minute walk away. It is a first-floor flat in a modern block, with a view of the park and in the distance of the canal. Finn decorated it for me, glad to be doing something positive, I expect. Don told me to take whatever I wanted from our house, so I did. What I wanted was very little. The furniture I did bring looks strange in the flat – it hasn't yet grown accustomed to its new surroundings. I thought the sofa from our old kitchen was small but here, in this room, it looks suddenly bigger. And shabbier.

*

Stopping and starting, bits about houses, about schools, about where I'm living – it's no good. I sit here, at my little desk which – no, I won't describe the desk or I'll be off again, stuttering, putting off really getting to grips with why I want to write down anything at all. But I do. I want to have it all on paper, a record, from my point of view. I don't expect anyone to read it. I don't feel any obligation to posterity. Nothing so self-important. And as for grandchildren in the future, it will be Don's version they will be more interested in, and there will be plenty of sources

5

for them to use, if they want to. His photograph was in several newspapers. He appeared on television once. It got to the point, locally, when he was recognised in the street. People, complete strangers, stopped him and told him how they admired him and thought what he was doing was right. They wished him good luck, told him not to give up. As if he ever would.

So I sit at this desk and try to be ... I can't think of the word. I try to concentrate on the point of this exercise. The point is ... the point is, he didn't seem to hear me. He didn't seem to know how cruel he was being. He didn't seem to realise how much worse he was making things for the rest of us. And I kept silent, first through grief and misery, afterwards because I was exhausted, numb. I had the other two to think about. I couldn't afford to do what he did. And I suppose, too, that for the first few months afterwards I thought he was right. I agreed with him. It couldn't have been an accident. Someone was to blame and that someone should be called to account, exposed. Yes, I thought he was right. I wanted him to act the way he did. What I can't remember is exactly when I stopped caring about who was responsible. When did it become irrelevant? When did we part company on this?

*

It was a little girl called Lola's birthday today. Her mother, she's a single parent, brought in a cake she'd made herself, dripping with chocolate icing that hadn't set, and we all had some. The mother had provided five candles but the cake was so soft the candles wouldn't stick in properly and Lola cried. Jeremy got some plasticine, and made a cake shape and stuck the candles into that and lit them, and we sang 'Happy Birthday', but Lola went on sobbing. She was still weeping when it was home time and her mother came to collect her. I explained what had happened, taking care not to criticise the cake, stressing how delicious it had been, every crumb devoured, but the mother's face collapsed and she started crying too. 'Nothing I do is right,' she said. 'I can't even make a cake properly.' I gestured to Jeremy to see to the other children being collected, and sat this young woman down in a corner, with Lola on her knee. By then Lola had stopped crying, fascinated by her mother's tears, or maybe alarmed by them. I talked to her. I said how well Lola was doing, how willing to learn, how popular with the other children. I said, she, the mother, must be doing something right, to produce such a well-behaved, responsive child. The mother dabbed her eyes, and smiled, thanked me. She said she expected she was just tired. I said I expected that she was. Then she said, 'She's everything to me, see. She's all I've got. I want things to be right for her, I want to do my best.' 'We all do,' I said.

*

This year the date has come and gone as, of course, it is bound to every year. There is no point in trying to forget it or ignore it. That's impossible. But I refuse to commemorate it in any way. I never mention the date. This year it was a Wednesday.

On the first anniversary, afterwards, we received cards. Several of them, some from people we did not know very well. I imagined a lot of care had gone into choosing them. They were tasteful, either with a simple flower on the front, the colours pale, or else a peaceful view of hills. The messages inside were more or less identical – 'Thinking of you on this sad day' vied with 'Always in our thoughts'. It would have been silly to be upset by them, and I wasn't. I think I even smiled slightly as I passed them to Don, who immediately scrunched them up and threw them in the wastepaper basket. 'They were only being kind,' I murmured. 'Kindness does no good,' he said.

Doesn't it? I know what he meant: kindness does not get to the root of what happened. This is true, but nevertheless for everyone except Don it did, and does, help even when it makes the tears come. Finn appreciated kindness. He said over and over how kind people were to him, what consideration the boys and teachers at school showed. For a while, a short while, he couldn't speak. He was literally mute with shock, couldn't answer a single question of the most ordinary variety. 'Potatoes?' the server at the school canteen would ask, spoon poised, and I was told that all he could do was nod. In any situation where a nod or shake of the head wouldn't suffice, he was panic-stricken, but he said his friends spoke for him. Then later on, when he could speak again, he knew he often sounded rude and brusque, but he was never told off for it.

Finn was the first of us who actually said to Don that he wanted to forget. One evening, at supper, when Don was in the middle of recounting his latest interview with someone who had sailed the same kind of boat, Finn got up, leaving his plate almost untouched, and left the table. 'Finn?' Don said. 'This is important.' 'I don't want to hear it,' Finn said. Don sat motion-less, knife and fork poised in his clenched fists over his plate. When he began eating again, he cut the meat very carefully, as though he was worried about hurting it. There was no scene. He didn't call Finn back, or get angry. I wanted to help him and asked him what he had been about to tell us that was important. He shook his head, and said, 'Not now, later.'

Finn began to separate himself from Don. It was managed in small, unobtrusive ways, an indication, I thought, that he was aware of how upset his father would be that he no longer wanted to hear any news of his 'investigations'. Finn was trying to limit the damage, I'm sure. The moment Don began on anything connected to the accident, Finn would leave the room, saying he had to go and phone someone, or he was late for football practice, or he'd forgotten something. The reason for his exit was always plausible, there were no more abrupt departures in the middle of meals, or outspoken announcements. Sometimes, if he was caught unexpectedly, he hummed, very quietly, till he could escape. He would stare into the middle distance and I knew he was chanting 'I'm not listening, I'm not listening' in his head.

I tried, in those days, early on, to defend Don. 'He wants to find out the truth,' I said to Finn. 'Surely you can understand that? Don't you want to know exactly how it happened? Don't we owe it to her?' Finn frowned, and rubbed harder at the boots he was cleaning, then began picking the lumps of mud off the studs and breaking them up with his fingers.

'It was no one's fault,' he said. 'The man said so, at the inquest. It was an accident.'

'But your dad doesn't believe that. He wants to find out ...'

'But she's *dead*, Mum, it doesn't make any difference. Even if he finds someone to blame, it won't bring her alive, so what's the point?'

'I've just told you what the point is, finding out the truth is the point.'

'But why doesn't he believe the police?'

'He's gone through the statements they took. He doesn't think they asked the right questions of the right people.'

'I know all that.'

'Well, that's your answer, Finn. That's why he won't let it rest. He can't let someone get away with this, and maybe some other person die because of some kind of mistake or laziness.'

Finn shrugged. 'I don't believe it,' he said. 'It was an accident.'

'Maybe. But there's always a possibility that –'

'I don't want to hear any more, Mum. I don't want to have to go over and over it all, I'm *sick* of it.'

He was shouting by then, red in the face, the football boots thrown to the ground. I put my hand on his arm, meaning to be sympathetic, trying to show that I understood, but he shook me off and crashed out of the kitchen, and I heard the garden gate slam.

It exhausts me even remembering it.

*

We are doing a Healthy Eating project in Reception R (R is for my name, Roscoe). Each child has to draw a picture of what they like to eat best of all and write their name (with help) underneath. Paige had trouble writing bubblegum. Lola did a very good drawing of an apple and managed to write the word clearly. At least half the class listed some sort of sweet or biscuit, but I suppose that was inevitable, considering the question. We had fun learning about what makes children grow, what makes their teeth strong and their bones sturdy, and we stuck pictures of all the appropriate foods onto sheets of coloured cardboard. Then Jeremy measured them all and we made a chart of heights too. This led, naturally, to some boasting about who was the biggest. 'Biggest is best, Miss, isn't it?' Paige said. I said no, being big didn't mean you were better than someone smaller. Being healthy was what mattered and small people could be just as healthy. Paige didn't believe a word of it. We moved on to talking about how food is grown. They knew apples grew on trees but they thought potatoes and everything else did too. 'If you don't eat carrots,' Paige said, 'you go blind.' She had other gems of a similar nature. Corrected, she came up with: 'Anyway, if you don't eat the right food you die. Don't you, Miss? You die, and they put you in the ground and worms crawl over you.'

*

Don phoned. I was just sitting here, staring into space, as I so often do, and the phone rang and I answered it instantly. His voice surprised me. He doesn't usually ring. Since we parted, he uses e-mail to tell me anything he thinks I need to know, and we occasionally meet, though it is a few weeks since we last did so.

We met last time to discuss the house, where I was still living. We were selling it, and splitting the proceeds so that we could each buy something separately. At least, I was going to buy this flat, but Don needed some of his share to fund his 'investigations'. He said he hadn't time to search for a property to buy so he had rented a bedsitter. At his age, in his position – a bedsitter. It is pathetic, but he doesn't seem to see that. We met in a café, one that we used to frequent often as a family, which made the encounter a little upsetting – at least for me – but Don suggested the venue and it was convenient, and I couldn't think of anywhere else.

He was business-like, and in rather a hurry. We ordered the soup we always used to have there – it's very good, a meal in itself – and that was all. Don wanted my agreement to an offer just made for our house, and I gave it at once, eager to buy this flat which had just come on the market. He talked about the mortgage and how much we would each get once the sale went through. I asked how long that was likely to take and he estimated six weeks or so. I was worried about what to do with the furniture and contents but Don had little interest. That was when he told me to take whatever I wanted. After that, we were silent. The noise we made supping our soup seemed indecent, but once we were finished neither of us wanted to talk. I was startled when after a lengthy pause during which we both stared at our empty bowls Don suddenly said, 'Do you want a divorce?'

'No!' I said, and then repeated it in a less indignant tone. 'Why would I want a divorce, Don? It's never entered my head.'

'Well,' Don said, 'we've parted, because you wanted to, and we're selling our house … I just assumed …'

He looked at me then, and I returned his stare. I like to think quite steadily.

'Sorry,' he said, and put a hand over his eyes, rubbing them. Then he tried to smile. 'How are you, anyway? I haven't asked you. You look well, relaxed.'

I couldn't reply. Relaxed? He'd paused a fraction just before he said that word and I knew he'd been going to choose 'happy'. I wasn't supposed to be able to look happy ever again. Smiles, laughter – they were banned. Afterwards, whenever the children and I laughed together, at some joke, or more often at something on the telly, we all felt such a rush of relief – we were *laughing*! – but it would be followed by a nervousness which wasn't quite guilt but came near to it. We got into the habit, if Don was in the house, of closing the sitting-room door firmly if we were going to watch a comedy programme when we might, just might, guffaw loudly.

When I still didn't reply, Don said, 'How's the teaching? Still enjoying it?'

I nodded. Enjoyment was another feeling that I knew he could no longer remember. Except that is not quite true. He enjoys his 'investigations'. The longer they go on, the more complex (and pointless) they become, the more he enjoys them, I'm sure. He gets excited, still, about 'leads', microscopically small pieces of new information he reckons he has discovered. He writes everything up, very neatly, and puts it in his files.

That was one of the first indications of what was going to happen. Afterwards, he went out and bought a filing cabinet. Storing information on his computer apparently wasn't enough. It was a big, ugly steel thing he'd got at some sale of antiquated office furniture. It took two men to carry it into the house and up to his study. There was nowhere really for it to go. His study was tiny, a mere box room, with a desk and a bookcase and a single chair taking up most of the space. It was a struggle to wedge the filing cabinet into a corner, but he was so pleased to have it. When I asked him what he wanted it for he said, 'I'll need it. Everything must be filed, every last thing. It's the only way.'

Next, he bought a tape recorder. We already had one, but he wanted a much smaller model which would tuck neatly into a pocket. Hours, he spent, researching the different makes, and then he was off to Tottenham Court Road and spent a whole day testing them. That evening, he came as near to smiling again as he was ever to do. After supper, he told us to sit still a minute, he had something amazing to demonstrate. We waited, expectant, but wary. He put his hand in his jacket pocket and produced what looked like a tiny transistor radio, about 10 by 4 centimetres, and then he pressed a switch. All our conversation during supper was faithfully and clearly reproduced.

'See?' he said. 'None of you knew I was doing it. It's so sensitive, this machine, and so powerful, it can pick up sound even when it's in my pocket, muffled. Extraordinary.'

It was Finn, of course, who realised first. 'Dad,' he said, 'it's dangerous. It would be getting evidence under false pretences. I've read about it. It would be inadmissible – I think that's the word.'

'I'm not worried about that,' Don said, impatiently. 'The point is, it will help me get to the truth. People are frightened to tell it, but if they think it's in confidence, and there's no microphone around, and I'm not taking notes, then ...'

'They can say anything,' Finn said. 'Anything they know you want to hear. What use is that?'

*

His voice sounded strange on the telephone, as though he had a bad cold. 'Don,' I said, 'are you all right? You sound hoarse.'

'I want you to come with me,' he said.

'With you? Where to? When? Why?'

'To Holland. I need a witness. There's no one else I can ask.'

'But Don, I teach, I can't just take time off, you know that.'

'Saturday then, Saturday morning. I'll come and get you.'

'But Don, we've been through all this, I've told you, I don't want to be mixed up any longer in your investigations. You know what I think about them. It makes me feel ill, I just can't be involved.'

'Louise, don't you want to find ...'

'Don, I'll hang up if you say it. Please, leave me alone. Ask one of your friends to be a witness to whatever it is you want to do. Not me. I helped all I could. I don't believe in investigating any more.'

'You disappoint me. I thought, in spite of everything, that I could count on you in an emergency.'

'I'm sorry,' I said, my voice sounding harsher than I intended. Then I hung up.

An 'emergency'. He knew he could 'count' on me. It amounted to a kind of blackmail, which he perfectly well knew. Two years ago, he wouldn't have needed to resort to it. I would have been with him without needing to be asked. But not now. Now, I have to be tough. What has overtaken him is a sort of madness born of grief, and yet he doesn't recognise this. He remains absolutely convinced that he is going to discover a culprit. Some poor piece of workmanship, or some lax checking will be traceable to one person, and he will expose them and demand that they admit their guilt and they will say they are sorry and then they will be punished. 'And then, Don?' I asked, the last time he outlined this scenario, 'And then, what?' 'I will have done my bit,' he said. 'My duty to her will be over.' 'And your duty to the rest of us?' I asked. 'You're being melodramatic,' he said. 'You disappoint me, Lou,' and he hung up.

I 'disappointed' him. How cutting he made that sound. Once, Miranda had disappointed him, though he never told her so.

*

Miranda shoplifted. A sweater, nothing special, just an ordinary red sweater, probably didn't cost more than £30, from Top Shop. It was the first sign that she had a reckless streak in her, or if not reckless exactly then a wish to take risks, be daring, just for the excitement. When I found this sweater I knew at once that it had not been paid for in the normal way. She was only thirteen and though she had pocket money, and could have saved it to buy the sweater – and she did love clothes and spent most of her money on them – I knew that if she had *bought* it, she would have worn it immediately. But it had never been worn. The price tag had been half torn off and it was rolled up and shoved inside one of her boots. It was October. I was thinking of buying a pair of boots for myself and remembered this pair Miranda had bought but I couldn't recall the shop she'd got them from.

14

I'd meant to ask her, but had forgotten, and I went to her room to have a look. I found them in her cupboard and picked one up to see the make. They were from Office. And then I saw there was something in the boot and I pulled out the sweater.

It was normal enough. I knew that. Lots of teenagers do it. It's a kind of showing off. I thought I wouldn't confront Miranda. I thought I would just leave the sweater on her bed and mention that I'd been looking at her boots because I fancied a pair like them. I hoped she didn't mind my copying her taste. She blushed furiously. No more needed to be said. The sweater disappeared. I don't know what she did with it. When I told Don, half laughing – though I knew there was nothing funny about it – he was horrified. He wanted to tackle her, confront her. 'It's stealing,' he said (rather unnecessarily). 'Why does she have to steal, a girl like her? She disappoints me.' I told him to calm down. I asked him if he had never nicked anything when he was a boy, but he said no, he hadn't. I believed him, it fitted. I said I'd keep an eye on Miranda, but I was pretty sure she wouldn't do it again. Don went on thinking about what could have made her do such a thing, harping on about it. He wondered if she was being led astray. He wouldn't have it that it was her own idea and that she wasn't quite the good little girl he imagined.

*

Molly sends me e-mails regularly. She phones me once a month, if she can get to a phone, six o'clock on a Sunday evening. These are self-imposed routines and I'm always telling her that she doesn't need to be so conscientious, but she says she worries about me. I beg her not to – it's awful to think of being a worry to one's nineteen-year-old daughter. She hasn't been in touch with her father for a long time. This doesn't please me. Don, I know, will be bitterly hurt and won't begin to see it is his own fault. When Molly left, he was devastated. He couldn't bear the idea of her being in a foreign country, so far from home, so far from his protection. He accused me of encouraging her. He was right, I did. She had to leave us, put some real distance between ourselves and her, for her own sanity. There he was, trying to keep Miranda alive every single minute when she was dead, and Molly was struggling to face up to it. It was Miranda, Miranda, Miranda all day long and for her twin this was unbearable. Go, I said to her, get right away.

Molly was always the plump twin, Miranda the slender one. Molly took after me, Miranda after Don – it was perfectly plain to see. They weren't identical, which I think made them happier twins. Their identities were never confused. There was no rivalry between them, they were very close, devoted to each other. So often, with twins, there is one who seems, as it were, the poor relation, literally, but not with my girls. Everything was evenly balanced. Molly was plump, and wished she wasn't, but she had the best hair and teeth. Miranda was thought to be prettier and she was athletic, excelled at all sports, whereas Molly was useless but this was balanced by Molly's greater academic ability. It was like that with all their different talents – neither was the more favoured, they each had something the other didn't. They were a good team, endlessly supportive of each other, the other's champion.

Molly was always stronger, though. Miranda leaned on her more than she did on Miranda. Neither of them was shy, but Molly was always the one who took the initiative even if Miranda seemed the more forceful. It was interesting to observe. Don and I used to discuss how the twins operated in certain situations and he could never quite see how crucial Molly's approval was to Miranda. I'd cite examples of what I meant and he'd be surprised and have to concede I was right. He wondered what would happen when they formed other partnerships – would Molly's opinion still be as vital to Miranda when she had a boyfriend who was also influencing her? We were just beginning to find out.

*

16

The other day, when I was on a bus, there was a photograph on the front page of the newspaper the man in front of me was reading. I didn't want to stare at it, but again and again I kept coming back to it. It was of a happy-looking young woman. I could only see one part of the headline, which read: 'Body Found in River'. Then the man folded the newspaper the other way. I wondered what river it was, and then caught myself and was horrified that I could be so callous, when a woman had drowned. But still my thoughts went on; I couldn't stop them. How had this woman drowned? Was it suicide? Was it an accident? I hated my own curiosity, but it was there. It is always there. Exactly how ... why ... on and on. Never ending, never over.

2

THERE IS a blackbird hopping its way round the edge of the garden – this block of flats has a communal garden – towards a tree where it has its nest. The bird always goes along the same route, as though trying to shake off a pursuer. Then, in a sudden rush, it flies up into the branches of the tree and, I suppose, to its nest, though no nest is visible. When the bird leaves, it flies straight out, at terrific speed.

I watch it for hours, or what seems like hours. I sit absolutely still, pen in hand, taking in the bird, the grass, the tree. This is what it must be like being old or very ill, and I am neither. It's a steadying thing, watching birds. Such frail creatures – but no, not all birds are frail, there goes a crow, terrifying my neighbour's cat, beating its black, black wings as it swoops down and comes to rest just ahead. Shouldn't it be the cat chasing the bird?

More diversions ... but I need them. They help.

*

I was trying today to remember exactly when I returned to teaching – difficult when remembering anything about those weeks is what I do not want to do. Because it all happened at the end of July, there had already been five weeks in which to start to pull myself together before term began. Finn went back to school in September, and Molly started attending an induction course before preparing to go off to Africa. She'd always

18

intended to do this in her gap year anyway. Once the house was empty for most of the day it became an unbearable place. I became afraid of my own head, of what went on inside it, of the clamour that shrieked away in there with no way out. I wanted to go back to teaching then, but Don wouldn't hear of it – he said he needed me at home, to help him, so I stayed away from school for half a term. It was the worst thing to have done. I didn't help Don. I couldn't see how I could – when he was at home he was either on the telephone or the Internet all the time. All I did was listen. I listened to a lot of technical detail about boats, which I didn't begin to understand. Something to do with a certain type of engine and with the metal this certain type of engine was made of. Don, when he started on his investigations, didn't understand either. He has no mechanical knowledge or aptitude – he's a creative person. He was a man who had no idea how his car worked – he turned the key and the engine started and that was enough for him. But, afterwards, he made himself study the engine that was in that boat. He even went to the factory in Sweden where these engines are made and he was allowed to follow the manufacturing process all the way through. He was away a week that time. While he was gone, Finn started bunking off school. This was easy to do. He knew it would take a while for anyone to realise. But I happened to see him, from the top of a bus, walking along the road with two other boys, all of them eating something out of those small polystyrene containers. I knew he should be having double maths. When he came home that day I didn't play any mind games. I hadn't the energy. I just told him that I'd seen him and I asked him what happened to double maths. He didn't play mind games either, didn't make up any excuses or offer likely explanations. He said he hadn't felt like maths. He couldn't be bothered. I relayed this to Don when he rang from Sweden but he hardly paused in his description of what he'd seen that day. I repeated what I'd said, cutting into his little lecture on fuel-supply systems and cooling systems and other information he'd newly learned about engines and that meant nothing to me. He simply wasn't interested. If Finn was bunking off school because he couldn't be bothered to go to lessons he didn't care. 'I'm trying to tell you something important, Lou,' he said. 'Are you listening?' I was, but he wasn't.

Don expected me to be just as interested as he was in how the boat's engine might have malfunctioned. He was in a passion about the possibility, asking me if I understood how vital such information was. He said that if he could prove that one of the parts was not properly made or not properly checked, or fitted, or that part of the engine was corroded, then we would have cracked it. I asked what it was we would have cracked. 'Why it happened, for God's sake!' he shouted. I asked if that would make him feel better. He raged at me, saying that feeling better was not the point, it was establishing the truth of what happened that mattered, exposing shoddy workmanship and calling to account those who were responsible for it.

It was painful and somehow embarrassing, listening to him rant like this. I had an image of him in some enormous factory where row after row of men in overalls were standing in assembly lines fitting screws to – what? I hadn't the faintest idea. All I realised was the clear impossibility of tracing the workman who made or checked or fitted some tiny part wrongly – if indeed they had. If it hadn't been so sad, it would have been ludicrous. And the coroner had stated clearly at the inquest that there was no proof of engine failure.

Don discovered nothing of any importance or use at that factory in Sweden. I don't know how they put up with him. He came back despondent but not defeated. He never even mentioned bunking off to Finn.

*

Lynne rang just then. She was in John Lewis, looking for a wedding present for a friend. She suggested that I should meet her in the café there. 'It'll do you good,' she promised. The idea of sitting in a café in John Lewis doing me good ... But I knew

20

Lynne didn't mean that. It's seeing her that always does me good, for the time I'm under the influence of her energy and confidence. I quite enjoyed getting ready to go, changing my clothes – Lynne is always immaculate and we all try to live up to her (and fail) – and putting on some lipstick. Lynne, when she came to comfort me, always concentrated on my appearance. I would feel better if I let her wash my hair. I would feel better if I got out of those awful trousers. I would feel better if I did some yoga exercises with her. I would feel better if I straightened my back and walked tall ... 'Walk tall', when I could hardly crawl, but she pushed me, and for the time she was with me, I let her. When Lynne left, her energy always left with her, and I collapsed again.

The first thing she said to me, as I walked towards where she was sitting, at a table in the window overlooking Cavendish Square, was 'Louise! You look wonderful!' She insisted on standing up and holding my face in her hands. 'Lovely!' she said. 'Those pretty plump cheeks are back, the lines have gone ...' I told her to stop it at once, she was being absurd, but I liked her enthusiasm all the same. She has so much of it that she carries me along and I feel buoyed up for a while. Don found her totally exhausting – if he knew she was going to visit, he always made sure he was out of the house. He wondered, aloud, how on earth she could have become my friend. Afterwards, he dreaded Lynne descending upon us – he didn't want to see anyone at all, no relatives, no friends, but most of all no Lynne taking charge of me. I don't truly know how I felt. Did I want Lynne? She didn't ask me if I wanted her. She just came, and held me, and answered the phone for me, and made food none of us ate. But she only ever stayed a day and a night each time. Don made his hostility towards her quite obvious and she withdrew, respecting his right to exclude those towards whom he felt such antipathy. I remember that once when she left, she said, 'He frightens me, Lou. Don't let him frighten you,' which at the time, in my numb state, I thought strange – what did she mean?

Lynne's life, since we were all together at teacher training college, hasn't been entirely happy, but nobody would think so. She is absolutely determined to see a good side to every misfortune. This annoys some people – Pat, for example – but I find it touching. I admire her for it. She can't have children, but she doesn't moan about it, though she adores children. Once she knew for certain that there would be no children for her and Eric (after the hysterectomy to cure her endometriosis), she concentrated her maternal instincts on nieces and nephews, and godchildren, and became a popular aunt, never forgetting a birthday, regularly appearing to offer treats. My three love her, especially Finn.

We swapped teaching news at first. Lynne is the headmistress of a primary school in Surrey and is in her element. It's a different school from mine – no immigrants, no black or mixed-race children – but we have a lot of the same problems to do with all the wretched testing and assessing that goes on these days. Then Lynne showed me what she had bought for the wedding she was going to, and we discussed what kind of shoes and bag she would need and whether a hat was, or was not, necessary. But all this was only a preliminary. Lynne never ducked the questions others feared to ask. On our second cup of coffee, she took my hand across the table and fixed me with what Ruth used to call her 'ancient mariner stare' and said, 'So. How are you managing without Don?'

'Fine,' I said, trying to withdraw my hand, but failing.

'Really fine, or doing-as-well-as-I-can?'

'I think really fine. But I worry about him.'

'Do you still love him? Is that why you worry?'

'For heaven's sake, Lynne.' I looked round the now crowded section of the room we were in. The tables are very close.

'Nobody is paying us any attention,' Lynne said, firmly, 'and I want to know. It's important. Do you still love him?'

'I'm not going to answer that.'

'There you are then.'

'Where am I? It's just that I don't like him. I don't like who he has become.' I was whispering, head down.

Lynne put a finger under my chin and lifted it up. 'I can't hear properly, you're muttering,' she said.

I wasn't going to repeat it. 'Shouldn't you be getting on with your present buying?' I said.

'Why don't you come on holiday with me?' Lynne suddenly said. 'In the spring half-term. Somewhere in the sun, somewhere different.' She'd suggested it before. Afterwards, about a year afterwards, she'd suggested we went to Madeira. I wasn't even vaguely tempted, to Don's relief. But now, I was. She could sense it in my hesitation. Things had changed.

'I'll organise it,' Lynne said, 'and if there are any money problems ...'

'There aren't,' I said, quickly. 'That's one problem I don't have.'

'Good. Then we can be extravagant?'

'I'm not sure about that.' Lynne was renowned for her extravagance.

We tried to have a holiday about six months afterwards, before Molly went to Africa. It was partly a way of avoiding the horror of Christmas and New Year at home. Don was against the idea – the thought of anything as frivolous as a holiday appalled him – but I pleaded with him, saying that we needed to be together, going on a normal family outing, and he finally agreed, if still reluctantly. There was some pleasure in choosing the destination, a village in Austria, and in packing, but I think I knew before ever we arrived that the holiday was not going to be a success.

The trouble was, we were *not* together. Going away as a family hadn't made us as together as we had once been. We each remained in our own little, painful world, hardly communicating in any real sense at all. Everyone skied except for me, but they didn't ski on the same runs. Don was a competent skier but now it was Finn who chose the black runs while Don

23

held back. As for Molly, she was not much better than a beginner. Miranda had been the skier. But we should all have been able to enjoy each other's company in the evenings. The hotel we stayed at was perfect – enormous log fires, hearty, nourishing food, comfortable sofas to sprawl on, and plain but spacious bedrooms. The other guests were families like us. And yet not like us, not as we were then. We withdrew, every evening, into a corner where we sat silently nursing our glühwein, eyes lowered, avoiding all overtures to friendship. There seemed to be a competition to see who would say goodnight first and retire to bed. We all kept announcing, how tired, how exhausted we were, the skiers because of the strenuous skiing, me because of the tough paths I'd walked, trudging through the hard packed snow. On Christmas Eve, scarcely able to bear the festivities, Don and I were in bed at nine o'clock. On New Year's Eve we all, except Finn – I don't even know what he did – went straight from dinner to our rooms. Don was asleep, or feigning sleep, it comes to the same thing, before I had undressed.

Yet that day, I'd felt hopeful. I'd walked to Inner Alpbach on the back road, as far as I'd ever gone, and as I turned to retrace my steps three people came out of a farmhouse onto the balcony and they lifted trumpets and blew a fanfare which echoed exuberantly all around. They saw me and waved, and one of them shouted something – I think it was the German word for 'practising'. The sun was brilliant and hit the snow-covered waves of mountain peaks with such glittering force that I couldn't look back at them even wearing sunglasses. Everything seemed so clear and clean and immaculate, that my spirits rose in response to my surroundings – and I'd arrived back at our hotel smiling. One by one, when the others came to join me, I tried to explain to them how the scenery and the weather and the laughing trumpet players had made me feel, but I was met with dull-eyed boredom and blankness. Molly struggled to be interested, but not for long. Don said he was glad I'd had a good day, but in a voice so funereal that it sounded like

24

a mournful comment. Finn said he couldn't imagine enjoying such a dull walk – it sounded pathetic to him, and he felt sorry for me.

In the morning, New Year's Day, I felt sorry for myself. I woke early, dressed, and then slipped out of the hotel. It was still dark but there was an early-morning mass in the church so it was lit up and the light spread across the churchyard warming the bleakness of the ice and snow. The graves had little lights on them and I saw black-dressed women with shawls over their heads standing in front of some of the stones and crossing themselves before hurrying into the church. I wanted so badly to be with them.

*

We are buying a goat to send to Africa. By 'we' I mean our school, of course. Each class has to fundraise to find the money to do it. 'Where is the goat?' Paige wanted to know. 'Can we see it first?' The aim is to send twelve goats. 'Will they be friends or relations?' asked Paige. Dutifully, I explained what had been explained to me: the goats will be sent through an organisation called Farm Africa. The families who get the goats will be very grateful because a goat will provide sustainable support. I didn't tell my class that bit, since 'sustainable support' would be meaningless to them. Easier to say that a goat can be milked. 'So can a cow, and a cow is bigger and the milk is nicer,' said Sophie, who has an uncle with a farm. That led on to a discussion about which animals can stand the heat. They all know Africa is hot. I said that my daughter was in Africa, in a country called Zambia. I told them that she was living in a grass hut and helping the villagers to build a mill. Paige asked if she had a goat. I said no, but she had mentioned that she had seen some goats and some chickens and a pig. Then Sita suddenly asked if my girl's skin had turned black with the sun. I said no. She kept out of the sun as much as she could, but anyway her skin would not turn black. 'Or she might die,' Paige

25

said. No, I said, she wouldn't die. And then we began drawing goats.

*

Every time I see, or hear, from Lynne I seem to hear from Pat and Ruth. I don't think this is a conspiracy. Maybe at first, afterwards, they discussed me with each other – in their place, I would definitely have rung the other two – but not lately. I like them phoning now I am living alone. Before, with Don there, I felt uneasy, in case he thought either that I was shutting him out or that I was telling my friends what I might not be telling him. I couldn't really enjoy their calls if he was around, and they could tell that I wasn't relaxed. The calls went on for ages, another thing that exasperated Don if he was within earshot. He would remark that for the last forty-five minutes I had repeated myself endlessly, and that what I had repeated was trivia. He said if the other end of the conversation was as banal as this end then he doubted the intelligence of both parties. He used to say this indulgently, finding my chatter quite amusing, rather liking this image of me as a fluffy empty-headed female when he knew I was nothing of the kind. But afterwards it annoyed him. He became contemptuous. 'It's Lynne,' he'd say, when he'd answered the phone (or Pat, or Ruth). 'I'll go to my study, I'm sure you'd rather be private.'

Ruth is the one I hear from least, but in many ways she is the one I am closest to, even after all these years, when 'close' doesn't mean the same. She isn't at ease on the telephone, always sounds hesitant, and I seem to do most of the talking. She listens, carefully. Sometimes there is a long silence when I've finished unburdening myself, and then she will come up with an opinion, or a comment that surprises me with its insight. Ruth didn't phone, afterwards. She wrote. At the time, I hardly read her letters – they meant no more than any of the others and I couldn't be bothered with any of them. But I kept them, and when I finally read them, preparing to reply, which

I felt was a duty, I was struck by how Ruth had expressed her grief and sympathy. There was not a cliché or a crass remark in the pages she wrote, and I appreciated her sensitivity.

Ruth is an English teacher, head of department in a big comprehensive. She works very hard and has little spare time so we hardly ever meet. When our children – she has two, both boys – were young we used to make the effort to get together at weekends and try to talk above the chaos of five children playing. Now, it tends to be only about three or four times a year, and I go to her more than she comes to me. She was calling to suggest that, for a change, she should come to me after an appointment she had at the Eastman Dental hospital, which is only a bus ride from me. She's coming tomorrow. Another excuse to stop this.

*

Ruth's face was numb – she'd just had root canal treatment. She looked worn and tired, and I don't think this was all due to her dental troubles. It felt good to be concerned about someone, extending instead of receiving sympathy for a change. I enjoyed fussing over her, though she didn't want me to. There are never any searching questions from Ruth, à la Lynne. She just waits, and because she waits I eventually fill the chasm with the sort of confessions Lynne longs for.

'I miss Molly,' I found myself saying. 'I want her to stay where she is, but I miss her.'

Ruth nodded.

'She had to get away, it was the right thing to do, I encouraged her, and she loves it there, but ...'

'You need to see her, to check she's managing as well as she tells you she is,' Ruth said.

'Don was appalled that she was going.'

'He didn't see he was part of the reason she needed to leave?'

'No.'

Then I told Ruth that Don had not forgiven Molly for going off to Africa. There had been such an awful scene when she broke the news that she was going ahead with her original plan to work, unpaid, for a charity in Zambia. Don hadn't liked the idea anyway, when she first came up with it, but then, afterwards, he was shocked that she still intended to go. He couldn't understand how she could even think of going so far away. He asked if she didn't realise what she would be putting us through – the worry, on top of everything else we were suffering, would crucify us. She wouldn't be safe, he said, she'd fall ill, with malaria or typhoid, or some other tropical disease. Molly said she wouldn't. She would have all the vaccinations, take all the preventative drugs, be very careful what she ate and drank. Don said that wasn't the point, surely she understood how *we* would feel. She didn't reply. I told Ruth that I'd never forget how she turned and looked at me, so beseechingly, and I'd told Don I thought she needed to get right away and that we should not try to prevent her. She was old enough to make her own decisions. 'Dad,' Molly said then, 'I have to get away. Somewhere completely different.' 'It won't help,' Don said, 'you can't run away from what's happened. You'll take it with you, it will be worse on your own with no one near you to understand.' Molly said that was what she wanted, no one knowing about her. She said she had to believe she could start again, and be happy. He said she could learn to be happy again with us, and then I told Ruth how he'd added, 'If happiness is possible, which I doubt,' and Molly said, 'Exactly, Dad,' and left the room.

There were other scenes, though, mercifully, I couldn't remember them in detail. Don kept on and on at Molly, telling her how she was disappointing him, and that he would have thought that she, of all people, would have wanted him to establish the truth of how Miranda was murdered. Molly couldn't bear the word 'murdered'. She told him that he was the only one who couldn't accept that the whole tragic thing had been an accident, with no one to blame except Miranda herself. When she said that, Don was so furious he trembled with rage. I told Ruth how frightening it had been to have to witness these exchanges before Molly left.

I'm sure she had no idea how upset her father was during them. All she saw was his anger, not his distress. But I knew that Don's rage hid the real depth of his emotion – he was simply terrified of losing another child. So was I, but I at least knew there were more ways than one of losing them. He had turned Molly and Finn against him through his obsession with discovering what he thought of as 'the truth'. They didn't want to hear him any longer. They thought he was mad.

'I think,' Ruth said, 'he probably is, don't you?'

I was shocked. 'No,' I said, 'he's not *mad*. It's just that his mind has become one-track.'

'Isn't that a kind of madness? Monomania?' Ruth said.

She thought Don might need treatment. It was fortunate that he wasn't there to hear her say this. We had been offered counselling, afterwards. Our GP said she could recommend a psychotherapist. Don was livid. He told her that no therapy in the world would help to expose the truth of why and how his daughter had been killed and it was an insult to suggest that it would. All that would cure his blinding headaches was getting to the bottom of what had happened. The doctor gave him a prescription, and left it at that. He never went back, though the headaches continued.

But that night, after Molly had said what she did about Miranda being to blame, Don was more distressed than I had ever seen him – more distressed, in fact, than when we were told about Miranda's death, because then he simply hadn't believed it. He didn't weep openly that night, when Molly had gone to bed and we were still up, but his voice wavered and I knew he was almost afraid to speak at all in case he lost control. 'What is wrong with me?' he said. 'Why does she have to leave? Why does she have to say things like that about Miranda?' And I lost a perfect opportunity to enlighten him. I couldn't bear his misery, and so I comforted him, and told him there was nothing wrong with him, he was a wonderful father. I said it was natural that Molly should want to go abroad – it was exciting, she would have wanted to go off whatever had happened, probably would have gone sooner, before now. I even said it had nothing to do with her twin dying (and I didn't take up what she'd said about Miranda). But I did at least manage to point out that he had hurt Molly by saying that she'd disappointed him; and he had the grace to acknowledge this and be ashamed. In the morning he apologised. Molly said, 'It's OK, Dad. I understand.'

And I think she did. I suspect that after all she understood more than I did, at the time, about her father.

*

Pat has written to me. Not the same day that Ruth visited, so soon after I'd met Lynne, but the same week. Of the three of us, Pat writes most, though every now and again there'll be a long catch-up phone call. I don't actually see her often. She lives too far away to be able to come to London more than once a year. She lives in Scotland, near Perth. Since she left teaching, she's done a variety of jobs – they seem to change every time I hear from her, but they are all to do with being outdoors, working as a ranger, or an instructor at a sports centre, that kind of thing. Pat skis, rock-climbs, runs. She's fantastically fit, even now.

No one expected Pat to stay in Scotland. The attraction seemed to be the landscape – she loved the mountains, the wild coast, especially the coast. She sailed. She knew about boats and engines and storms at sea. Don had several long telephone conversations with her, afterwards, which I'm sure were a great trial to her, but she put up with them for his sake. They exchanged letters, too. Somehow, Don was not pleased with whatever Pat wrote. I didn't read her letters to him. He tried to get me to, but I said they would be too technical for me, and Don must have thought I was right because he didn't press me. In her letters to me, Pat never mentioned anything she was sharing with Don. All she wrote, once, was that she feared he was 'barking up the wrong tree'.

Pat rented a cottage in Dunblane for a short time, when she was working at a fitness centre in Gleneagles. It was odd, seeing the postmark on Pat's letters. Impossible not to associate it with the senseless deaths of those children. I remember how, at the time, Don seemed to find my appalled fascination with the whole terrible story repugnant. 'How can you watch this?' he asked, as I sat, stunned, in front of the television, as it showed parents, mostly mothers, running towards the school, fear tightening their faces. He pointedly left the room. And when he heard me tell a friend that I knew someone who used to live in Dunblane, he was disgusted, asking why on earth I had to mention that. He said it was as if I were boasting, straining so hard to make some connection, and the connection anyway was so tenuous as hardly to exist. His own attitude was one of sympathetic detachment. 'The man was clearly mad,' he said, 'and no one can guard against the random actions of that kind of madman.'

But I know that if Miranda had been one of those sixteen children Don would not have accepted that nothing could have been done to control Hamilton and prevent the murders. He would have been ruthless in searching out which person or system was to blame, and in establishing how a man so clearly deranged could have escaped detection. The moment the campaign was launched to control licences for handguns, Don would have been at the forefront, speaking and writing and agitating – as others did – until our gun controls became the tightest in the world. Once it was revealed, as I believe it was, that there had been *three* police reports in existence detailing that Hamilton had struck children at camps he helped to run, and yet no prosecution had taken place, there would have been no restraining Don. He would have had his target and would have pursued it relentlessly: someone would have been called

31

to account. And then his rage would have found some outlet, and because Hamilton had killed himself there would have been some kind of end to it all.

I don't know if it would have helped that other parents would have been sharing his misery. I doubt it. There would have been no comfort in that sort of solidarity for Don. Maybe for me, though. To have other women experiencing the same agony, weeping together, knowing others truly could say they understood. And for me, if not for Don, there would have been comfort in joining in things that were done afterwards. I remember stained-glass windows were designed with symbols – I think snowdrops – for each child, a beautiful memorial to them. I would have liked that. I wouldn't have wanted the attention those stricken parents received, the arrival of the politicians and the media, but afterwards, to have been able to band together, have an aim ... I am appalled at the way my mind runs and yet I cannot always control it. I *am* maudlin, I *am* morbid, I *do* think these things. I am always terrified that I will betray myself and reveal such sickening thoughts. The shame would be unbearable.

*

Pat is coming to London next weekend, my first guest in this flat. She is coming to attend a meeting on Friday about the Olympics – she's very active on all kinds of sports committees. Her event, when we were all at college, was hurdling, though she's too old now to think about competing. She was brilliant at it, a sight to see, flying down the track, leaping over the hurdles so effortlessly. We used to go to all the events she entered and cheered like mad, knowing that none of the rest of us could have cleared a single hurdle.

People (not us) used to wonder if Pat was gay, but she wasn't, isn't. Her clothes don't help the general impression. Tracksuits may have been popular at one time, but not the sort Pat wears, the strictly professional type. At our wedding, Pat was a bridesmaid, together with Lynne and Ruth. The bridesmaid thing was a bit of a joke at first but as my mother began seriously planning the wedding it became less and less of one. She wanted the bridesmaids to be 'proper' bridesmaids, in long dresses and with flowers in their hair. I'd thought they could just wear a summer dress of their choice, maybe in the same colour, but Mum wasn't having it. Since the whole church wedding lark was to please her – I did a staggering amount of things in those days to please her – I found myself giving in. Lynne and Ruth didn't mind (in fact Lynne definitely liked the idea) but Pat was worried. 'I'll look a fool,' she said. I said, Nonsense, of course she wouldn't, but the truth was that she did look uncomfortable and awkward, and I felt guilty. I'd chosen pale yellow – 'primrose', my mother corrected – as the colour, but the style was suggested by Lynne, and I agreed, since she was the fashionable one. I don't think Lynne was being malicious, but the Empire line, which she and Ruth wore gracefully, did not suit Pat.

We talk a lot about Pat, wondering whether she is happy. I think she is. Ruth thinks she would have loved children. Afterwards, when Pat wrote, the first letter I got, she said that to lose a child was the worst thing in the world. She'd tried to imagine it, and couldn't. It seemed to me an unusual thing for a childless woman to say. What did she have to compare it with, to make it the 'worst'? How could she understand an emotional tie she had never had? But then she wasn't claiming, as so many others did, to understand anything at all except the pain we felt. Hers was one of the few letters Don could bear to read. He'd always thought Pat 'sensible'. Of my three close, old friends she was the one he liked best. He never thought her the least bit 'butch' either, saying there was nothing more feminine than Pat's complexion, and it was Don who pointed out to me how elegant Pat's hands and wrists were, something I'd never noticed. I wanted to pass his compliment on but I thought I might sound patronising or that it might embarrass her, so I didn't.

33

We went on a school outing today, the entire Infants, in three coaches. I'm never sure that these trips are achieving what they are supposed to achieve for the very young children. The excitement is tremendous but so is the tension – who will sit with whom, and all that. And then many of my children have never been in a coach, or even a bus, some because they are taken everywhere by car and some because they walk everywhere, with 'everywhere' being a strictly limited area between flats and shops and sometimes the park. Coaches are quite scary for some of them and bewilderment can overcome the most timid. Hussain is terrified. I don't think he has ever been in any kind of vehicle. It's amazing that his mother gets him to school at all, and she took some persuading that it is the law and that he must come.

Paige, of course, has been in aeroplanes as well as buses, cars, and coaches, and gave us all an account of her travels as we waited to board. She stands head and shoulders above the other five-year-olds – God knows what her mother feeds her on. The other children are intimidated by her and yet at the same time they admire her and want her to be their friend. She's a bully in the making but she won't have everything her own way. Sita will challenge her before long, and Sita is cleverer though smaller. I sat Sita beside Lola, who needs a protector. Paige sat with Jeremy, which she didn't like one bit. I gave no one any choice. Choice would only have led to arguments and then to tears, with those who haven't made a particular friend left out and in a panic.

We went to see a pantomime at the Hackney Empire. Gorgeous theatre, beautifully restored and renovated, not that any of my class appreciated the décor or architecture. But they did appreciate the plush seats and the glitter of their surroundings. 'Is it a palace?' Sita asked. Some of them had been in cinemas, and several in churches or mosques, but none of them had been in a theatre to see a live show. The noise really was exactly like the sound a flock of birds makes, starlings, when they are clustered together on a building and take off in a crowd, but when the orchestra tuned up and the lights went out, it stopped, except for rustlings and shufflings. It was touching looking along my row and seeing the little faces literally rapt with the wonder of it all.

That was during the first fifteen minutes or so. After that, a measure of boredom set in among some of them, and the fidgeting began and the whispers, and I had to do some fairly fierce shushing. Jeremy had to take Yusuf out before the interval – he'd wet himself, laughing at the Ugly Sisters. The interval was a strain rather than a relief, with half of them thinking the whole thing was over even though Cinderella had not yet been fitted with her slipper or found her Prince. It was a long show, over two hours, much too long for their age group. On the way back to school, some of them fell asleep and didn't wake up when the coach stopped. Jeremy and I had to carry them into the classroom. I carried Lola. She's small and light. Her little body in my arms felt so fragile. I wanted to hug and kiss her, and had to restrain myself. I was careful not to look at her face as I cradled her head in the crook of my arm. It would have undone me.

I knew what that was about, and was able to deal with it. It was obvious. Almost everything is.

*

Getting my spare room ready for Pat's arrival, shopping for things, was a pleasure. It had been months before I could go into any shop other than a supermarket for food. The whole idea of having fun *shopping* was almost disgusting. The first time I timidly went into a proper shop, Heals, looking for a present for Ruth, who had just moved house, I had difficulty coping with all the goods on display. I went from department to department, picking items up and putting them down, not seeing any of them properly, and this dreadful feeling of use-lessness washed through me – this was *useless*, buying things, it was irrelevant, I couldn't be bothered. I bought a wooden salad bowl in a great hurry and left the shop. But furnishing my flat, I was able to concentrate. I was efficient and organised again, and I enjoyed it.

That was before Don moved out of our house. I came home cheerful, determined not to let him spoil my mood. 'I've been buying stuff for my flat,' I said, 'while the sales are on.' 'Ah,' he said, 'the sales, yes.' And that was all. He showed no interest in my purchases, but then he rarely did. He used to like me being what he called a shopaholic, teasing me about my 'addiction', but never complaining about the cost. But there was an element of what I chose to interpret as unpleasant sarcasm in the way he said 'Ah, the sales', a touch of contempt. It annoyed me. Maybe I was looking for a fight, so that I could get rid of so much that I wanted to say. 'What's wrong with taking advantage of the sales?' I asked. He just sighed. I should have left well alone, but I was tired of doing that. 'It isn't the sales that you disapprove of, is it? It's the shopping itself. Go on, say it, how can I bear to shop?' He looked straight at me, and said, 'No, I won't say that. I know very well how shopping helps you. It's good that you can take pleasure from it again. I'm glad.' He said it so quietly. I was ashamed that I'd been defensive, and unfair, but I didn't apologise. If, at that moment, he had taken me in his arms ... A laughable idea, by then. There was no room in Don's arms for anything but the bundles of papers amassed during his ever ongoing investigations.

I suppose, when he began trying to establish what exactly had happened to Miranda and the boat, I thought it might all be over in a month or so. Maybe Don himself thought that. Surely there was only so much that could be investigated, only so many avenues to explore. But no. Everything seemed to take ages. The simplest enquiry involved dozens of phone calls, dozens of letters going backwards and forwards. And Don was working, trying to hold down his job at the advertising agency at the same time. His job is not easy. The competition is intense, and the agency had just lost an account to Ogilvy & Mather – hard for Don to accept, not just because he'd been in charge of the campaign they'd been running but because he started off at Ogilvy & Mather and felt the blow personally. I've never understood all the rivalries but I know they exist. He worked long hours co-ordinating a new campaign – it was something to do with a sports personality, and he was pitching to one of the big sports-wear firms – determined to win the account to balance having lost the other. I appreciated this, but what I resented was how he spent his so-called leisure time. All his weekends and all his holidays, except for one, were spent in Holland or Sweden or Germany following up 'leads'. When he was at home, it was as though he was studying for a university degree as he pored over instruction manuals to do with engines and boat construction, and studied maps and tides. I couldn't follow any of it and soon he stopped expecting me to.

There were piles of yachting magazines on the floor of his study, most with yellow post-it notes sticking out of them. The covers all looked the same to me – unsurprisingly, photographs of yachts in full sail skimming across the waves. The top magazine had such a photograph on the front, beside it a red box with white lettering and the words, 'Going Solo made Simple'. I turned to the correct page, helpfully marked, I could see, by Don. 'Sound seamanship is the key to successful solo sailing' was the heading. There was a story about a man who sails a boat called the Contessa 32. His character as a single-hander had been forged on a smaller yacht. When the rudder stock (?) sheared off leaving him without a tiller he didn't call for help but worked his way back to port using an outboard and a 6-inch adjustable spanner. Don had underlined '6-inch adjustable spanner'. He had also marked the box labelled 'Preparation' on the same page. Ropes had to be to hand, winch handles ready, sail ties put where they were needed … 'It's preparation, preparation, preparation.' Or in Miranda's case, not.

In the middle of this magazine there was a double page spread entitled 'The tools for the job'. How long had Don spent trying to establish what had been in the toolbox of the yacht Miranda sailed? Weeks. And why? She wouldn't have known how to use putty knives and 'circlip pliers' and 'rigging knives' and all the other 'essential' stuff, even if there had been time. But the information most heavily highlighted by Don made more sense: the radio. He was always convinced that Miranda must have radioed for help and that the fact that no message had been received must mean the boat's radio was faulty. She should have had on board a VHF radio which was DSC compliant, whatever that means. It can apparently send and receive routine call alerts. The radio needs a Short Range Certificate ('Did it have one?' Don has written on this page.) But even if there was such a radio, and it had been licensed and programmed, had Miranda been taught how to use it? The magazine said the instruction course lasted a day. Would she have been on one? Unlikely. She was only crew for Alexander. But more weeks followed, inquiring about the radio – pointless. No detail was too trivial or irrelevant for Don. He became lost in a labyrinth of pointless information where I couldn't follow or find him.

3

'YOU'VE NO photographs around,' Pat said, looking thoughtful. I told her I managed better without them.

It's true. Photographs of those who have recently died tell of times that are over, and make me long to have them back again, and that is no good. And I don't need photos to conjure up the faces of the living. Images of my children are in my mind all the time. I tried to explain this to Pat. 'And Don?' she asked. 'What about Don?'

Don's face, his image, is a different matter. Sometimes I think I've lost him for good. The wrong face appears before me when I think about him now (and that is still very often). I persistently see a younger man, his complexion healthy, his eyes bright, his chin clean-shaven, his hair combed. I always loved his hair, not exactly blond (though Judith told me it had been white-blond as a child) but very fair and thick. When I met him (I was twenty-two) I thought he might be younger than I was – he has one of those broad, square faces with strong cheekbones that don't age quickly. At forty, he still looked nearer thirty. But now, at nearly fifty, he looks more like sixty. When I think of him as he was, he smiles at me. I smile back. Then I blink, and the comforting image disappears. Instead, I see a caricature of the man, the skin grey, and lined, the eyes dull, the stubble thick, the hair wild. I don't know him, or maybe it is that I don't want to know him, or have anything to do with him, so I banish him. I tried to tell

Pat this, but it was too difficult. I ended up simply shaking my head, and she said she was sorry she had asked.

She wanted to know what he was doing at the moment, how he was managing on his own. I said I didn't know much about his new circumstances. He'd stayed with his sister for a while but that hadn't worked out. Pat asked why. It was difficult to explain. They didn't argue or anything like that. They never have done. But Judith creates around her an atmosphere of, well, heartiness, I suppose, which Don can't stand. She's a bit like Lynne, she wants everyone always to be happy and having a good time and she tries to make sure that they do, which is kind of her – she *is* a very kind woman – but she panics in the face of misery or depression, and this makes her uncharacteristically nervous. She becomes jumpy and agitated when confronted by long faces – she needs anyone who's feeling low at least to pretend that things are improving. 'You could try to smile a little, Don,' she once said quite soon afterwards. 'It wouldn't hurt.' She followed this by saying she'd read somewhere that the act of smiling itself released some hormone, 'or something', which actually did make even wretched people feel a little happier.

Pat said she could understand how Don felt, if this was how his sister dealt with his unhappiness. It would be enough to drive anyone out. She asked if I had an address for Don at least. I told her I had his mobile phone number and an e-mail address. 'Do you think I should call him, and maybe go and see him, or meet him somewhere?' I shrugged, said she could do what she liked, but that probably she'd find Don had gone off on some new wild-goose chase.

'You sound bitter, Lou,' Pat said.

'I am bitter. No, I'm beyond bitter.'

'And what does that mean?'

'Worse. I'm worse than bitter.'

'Is that fair?'

'*Fair*?'

'Well, it isn't Don's fault, all this, he can't help what's

happened, and how he feels. I feel sorry for him, for the mess he's in.'

'I feel sorry for him, too ...'

'You don't sound it.'

'But I feel more sorry for Molly and Finn and myself. He's made the whole tragedy so much harder to bear.'

Pat was frowning by the time I said this, and I knew I sounded resentful and hard and that any minute now she would wonder aloud where the old Lou had gone. She seemed to have forgotten how she herself had become exasperated with Don when he'd tried to enlist her help. 'Let's not talk about Don,' I said. 'It's too distressing.' I was feeling agitated, annoyed by Pat's attitude, her concern for Don. I wanted her to be more concerned about me, or Molly, or Finn. She seemed different, a touch judgemental, which she had never been before. 'I'm not criticising you, Lou,' she said. 'Honest, I'm not. It's just that I always liked Don, and it breaks my heart to hear of the state he's in, and I wish I could do something and ...'

'Nobody,' I said, 'can do anything for Don.'

I was saved, at that point, by a call from Finn, one of his quick calls, made from his mobile while he was walking along a busy street, and the reception was appalling. The rest of the evening we talked about Molly, which was a pleasure. There was plenty to talk about and all of it easy. I got a map out and showed Pat where she was in Zambia, and where she would be going, to a village called Nambo, and, though I had no photographs of her displayed round my flat, I had packets of snaps she'd sent and I produced those. There was no more tension, thank God. But I was glad when Pat left. Something had altered between us and I hadn't felt completely at ease with her. She'd disappointed me, let me down. Our old friendship, which I'd thought strong and solid, suddenly seemed threatened. I'd wanted something from Pat and whatever this was – I didn't know myself – she hadn't been able to give. I felt, in a childish way, that she had taken Don's side against me.

41

I wonder if she has gone to visit Don?

*

We've been working on families. Jeremy ran off a sheet of A4 for each child. They wrote their names at the top (or he wrote them), and then affixed a snapshot of themselves. Getting the photos was a bit tricky. Some children didn't have a single one, but I brought my camera in and we solved that problem. Most of the photos were of the children as babies, which is what we'd asked for, and they loved looking at themselves. Then they had to draw and name their family. Great care was taken by me to emphasise that 'family' could be anyone close to them and could include people not their relatives. Sita had so many people on her sheet that she had to squash them in, but she knew the names of all the aunts and uncles and cousins. Lola drew her mother and that was that. Yusuf drew a row of six women then put a black cross through three. 'They passed over,' he said. Hearing him tell me this, Paige said that meant they were dead and if they were dead they couldn't be his family, it wasn't fair. Before I could say anything Yusuf said they were in the next world and they were still his family. He looked to me for support. I said of course they were still his family but, because they were not living in his house now, he didn't need to draw them. It didn't mean he'd forgotten them. Rather sadly, Yusuf rubbed out the three crossed relatives. Paige's nod of satisfaction was hard for him to bear. She now has more members in her family than him though I'm quite sure they don't all live with her. Both sets of grandparents figure prominently. She has uncles who are twins. She took great pains to draw them exactly the same.

*

Pat wrote as soon as she got back home. She did meet Don. She rang him, on his mobile, she said, and he was 'surprisingly friendly'. He told her he was very busy, and about to go to Holland yet again, but that it would be good to meet up for

42

a drink or something. She asked him to suggest somewhere because she hardly knows London, and when he heard she was catching a train back to Scotland the next day he proposed a café opposite the station. He was there before her, but she didn't recognise him and went to sit at an empty table. He had to come over and identify himself, which made her uncomfortable. But then they chatted quite happily. He was very pleasant, as he always used to be – no sign of the madness or aggression or neurotic behaviour I had described. He asked where she'd been staying and she told him and he seemed 'very concerned about you, Lou'. He wanted to know how I seemed, what she'd thought of me. She told him I seemed to be 'managing better' and he was glad. They were getting on so well that she decided to bring up the subject of his own behaviour. She started off by saying she'd been so shocked to hear that he and I had parted and sold our house. Don said this wasn't his doing. I had chosen to distance myself from him and couldn't bear the sight of him or the house, and had insisted on him moving out. He thought *I* was 'deranged' and it was for the sake of my mental health that he had agreed to what I wanted.

I hardly cared to read on after that, but I did. Pat wrote that she took a deep breath and accused Don of having neglected me and his children in his search for what he persisted in thinking was the hidden truth about Miranda's so-called accident. She told him that I'd said he thought of nothing but his investigations, that she'd heard he hadn't time for anything else. He had looked offended, and frowned, and told her he had only been doing what had to be done and he expected me to share his determination to find out what really happened to cause Miranda's death. If he had alienated me with his determination to establish the truth (which he thought the inquest certainly had not done), I had alienated him with what he wrongly labelled my 'head-in-the-sand' attitude. The real blow was in Pat's last bit: 'He said you always had worn rose-coloured spectacles faced with anything nasty, just like his sister.'

I am nothing like Judith. What he has told Pat is absolutely untrue. It indeed is Don who cannot face up to what is very 'nasty'. Miranda, who had never sailed on her own, took out a boat and could not cope with the violent freak storm, which came out of nowhere that day. And she drowned.

*

It is hard, looking back (and I don't want to look back, though I'm doing so all the time) to describe what those days afterwards were like – I mean, the exact *feel* of them, as week succeeded week and what is called 'normality' returned. It often struck me as incredible the way we obeyed the simple demands of the body – we ate, we moved, we excreted, and when our hair grew we cut it, and when our nails grew we had to cut them. We bathed, we dressed, we functioned. But we did all this in different ways. I did it for the sake of Molly and Finn. Every time I wanted just to stay in bed and howl, I was disgusted with myself. I had to show them that life, our lives, *their* lives, would go on. I make myself sound like some kind of martyr, but I was not. I was making constant bargains with myself: if I managed to cook a favourite family dinner and we all sat down together and chatted as we ate it, then I was entitled to shut myself in my bedroom in the afternoons when the house was empty and weep. I *had* to try, and I did. So, in their different ways, did Molly, before she went to Africa, and Finn. I recognised their efforts. I saw the dreadfully strained faces in the mornings, the way they moved about as though they were not quite sure which way to go, and I was touched by the little gestures they made – the pats on my back as they passed me, the squeeze of my hand when I gave them something – though they almost undid me. On and on we went, forcing ourselves to control our grief for the sake of each other until in time it began to lessen in degree.

But Don did none of this. He sealed himself off from us. When he sat with us at the table – and I had to beg him to join

44

us – he either gave a monologue on whatever line of investigation he was currently pursuing, or he sat quite silently, head bowed, flinching if any of us laughed or became too animated. 'I am suffering', his attitude said, as though we would not know about this. It took me a long time, months and months, to begin to think that I did not have to endure this. It shocked me when the first glimmer of the idea that I did not have to live with Don entered my head. But then I let it hover there and it grew and grew until it was like a blinding light – I could, if I wanted, be free of this weight oppressing me. It felt dangerous to consider the possibility of breaking out of what I felt to be a stranglehold, but the danger attracted me. Worse: it excited me. Even thinking about it, my heart would start to beat more rapidly. If Don was in the same room at the time, I would have to leave it. He never once asked me why I'd made such a hurried exit, but then he was so much in his own world he probably didn't notice. I couldn't have told anyone any of this.

*

Extraordinary, but after that outburst, I slept well. Any morning when I wake up and realise that I have slept well, I feel triumphant. It's such a glorious feeling to open my eyes and not have a headache and for my face not to feel stiff. I treasure it, luxuriate in this victory. And of course my whole being is transformed by this good night's sound sleep – I feel cheerful and well and more than able to face the day. That ghastly creature who cowered under the covers, aching all over, barely able to open one sore eye, is banished, and so is the memory of the ghost-like spectre wandering in her nightdress from room to room, never able to settle for five minutes even though she was exhausted, weeping with fatigue as well as misery. It makes me shudder to remember those weeks and weeks of no rest whatsoever. I dreaded every night, knowing that even if I did sleep, in snatches, the nightmares would make lack of sleep preferable.

Afterwards, for a short while, I did take sleeping pills. We all did, even Molly, who normally won't even touch an aspirin. Everyone urged us to, the doctor, friends, neighbours – you need to sleep, they said, you can't go on without sleep. They were right, we couldn't carry on then without sleep, but waking up after we'd taken sleeping pills and oblivion had descended for a few merciful hours, was almost worse, mouth dry, head heavy, limbs weighing a ton – it wasn't worth it. Natural sleep was what we craved, and it took a long time to return. Even now, I don't often sleep really deeply and well as I used to do, always. I have bad nights, but I have strategies to deal with them, and mostly these are adequate. It is much easier now that I sleep alone, now that I live alone. It is so sad to have to admit that.

*

Christmas is over again, thank God, though in an odd kind of way I quite enjoyed it this year. I didn't have Finn – he went skiing with his cousins – or Molly to worry about. It was Molly who worried about me. I told her I was going to Ruth's, and that satisfied her. She couldn't bear the thought of my being alone, remembering as she did our family Christmases and how I loved them, and how ...

I planned my solitary Christmas quite cleverly. On Christmas Eve I went to Carols by Candlelight at the Royal Albert Hall, at 7 o'clock, an easy time for me to get there. As well as carols, there was other music – Handel, Bach – and I felt perfectly comfortable being on my own among so many strangers. I felt they must all be a certain sort of person, my sort of person in some way, to be there at all. I went home by bus, two buses, and the streets looked so cheerful with all the lights and the glimpses of Christmas trees through uncurtained windows. I was still humming 'O Come all ye Faithful' as I let myself into my flat, and when Judith rang – she'd been most upset that I wouldn't spend Christmas with her – I answered sounding lively and energetic.

I lied to her, too, about Christmas Day itself. She knows Ruth is an old friend, so it was plausible. I had a plan. I'd seen an advert saying 'Celebrate Christmas Day at the Charles Dickens Museum'. Visitors to his Doughty Street home were invited to 'take a step back in time'. Staff, dressed in period costume, would offer mulled wine and mince pies, and there was to be a film adaptation of *A Christmas Carol* running all day. Well, I'd never been to Doughty Street, though I've read most of Dickens's novels, and I thought it would somehow be fitting to visit his old home on Christmas Day – it amused me. I wasn't going to tell anyone where I'd been but all the same it made me smile to think how astonished and puzzled people would be if they'd known. Would it have made me seem pathetic? Maybe, but since it would remain a secret it didn't matter.

I drove through almost deserted streets and parked with ease. My fear that I'd be the only person there was ludicrously misplaced – the house was crowded. But this helped, it meant I wasn't noticed and could move about uninhibited by self-consciousness. People wished each other a Merry Christmas, very politely, and smiled, but otherwise ignored each other, concentrating on what was on show. The banisters were entwined with ivy (fake) and red ribbons, and there was a Christmas tree in the drawing-room, though a caption alongside confessed that Dickens would have been unlikely to have had one. I wandered from room to room without studying the various bits of ephemera too closely, more interested in the feel of the rooms and the pieces of furniture that had been there during Dickens's time. But one notice caught my eye, a quotation from Dickens, pinned up: 'Christmas is a time above all others when want is keenly felt.'

Before I left, I went down to the bottom of the house. There was no one there. I found myself looking through a sort of iron railing at a huge tub, a dolly tub. There were some white rags hanging over the edge of it. The floor was stone. There was virtually no light. It took no imagination at all to visualise a maid on her knees, soaping and scrubbing the clothes while upstairs Dickens and his family sat in comfort. It was how things were. I stood a long time staring into the little cold washroom unable to sort out what I was feeling.

*

Lynne is organising our spring half-term holiday already. She bombards me with brochures, in which she has already marked places she fancies and written comments in the margins. I can't decide whether she is deliberately highlighting coastal resorts, or whether she simply hasn't realised that I don't want to be near the sea. Should I say this to her? Or would it be better to get over my reluctance by facing the sea with Lynne?

The sea she is thinking of is not the sea I am afraid of. The sea in Lynne's brochures is calm and blue and flat. It doesn't rage, there are no huge waves, it doesn't look as if it could ever roar. I might like it. It looks all innocence. There are miles of white sand, or else pretty pink coves sheltered from the winds. There would be no reminders.

Afterwards, Don had insisted that we, he and I, should go at once to where it happened. I didn't even think of objecting. He was so in control, full of fury and energy, and I was limp, able to be programmed as he wished. Judith took care of Molly and Finn. I remember she said to me, 'Louise, are you sure you're up to this?' and I looked at her in bewilderment, as though it was the strangest question. We didn't speak all the way there, not a word between us in the car, in the plane, in the taxi. It was just a marina, a 'yacht haven' they call it in Dutch, crammed with boats. The police met us there, and were polite, but from the first Don was aggressive. I stood dumbly beside him while he asked questions, his voice hoarse and deep, becoming the voice of a stranger. He wanted to see the wreckage of the boat *immediately*. The policemen, two of them, didn't seem to know if he would be allowed to at the moment. Don exploded. He ranted at them, and I closed my eyes, not wanting to see the pity in the policemen's expressions. They took us to a shed, a short drive from the marina. Phone calls were made from their car and when we got to the shed a man in a white boiler suit was waiting for us. I remember he had a clipboard in his hand, and I wondered what it was for. I felt sick, and said I would wait outside, if Don didn't mind, but he did mind. He took me by the arm and led me into the place, insisting that he needed a witness, and I hadn't the energy or strength to shake him off.

It was a huge, barn-like shed with a high ceiling showing open rafters and above them the arc of corrugated iron which formed the roof. There was a wooden walkway round the perimeter and the whole area was split into squares with other, narrower, pathways joining them. Most of these areas had boats in them, resting on platforms of wooden slats, and on these boats there were men poking and prodding and measuring and taking photographs. We were led right to the end, where enclosing one of the squares there was a screen, about four feet high, made of what looked like flimsy white cotton through which we could make out figures moving behind it. The man in the white boiler suit, our guide, who had taken over from the policemen, introduced Don to someone wearing a similar garment, though his was green. I didn't hear a word he said. I was looking at the boat in front of us. It lay on its side. There was a big hole at one end and a lot of broken wood visible through it. I could see that the mast had been snapped off and there were torn remnants of sailcloth heaped round its fractured base. I thought I might faint and sat down quickly on the ground.

Don didn't notice. He was agitating to be allowed to inspect the boat and he was being prevented from doing so. I didn't seem able to focus properly – everything was blurry – and I kept shutting my eyes. There was an echo in the shed, and a great deal of noise, and whatever was being said to dissuade Don was lost. But the next time I made an effort to clear my head, and looked up, he was on the platform, kneeling beside the hole in the side and peering through it. I watched as he crawled inside, his long legs squirming from side to side and one of his shoes coming off with the friction. I don't know how long he was on the boat. Next time I looked he was at the far end, where what I took to be the engine was resting on a small, high table. The boiler-suited men were either side of him, looking anxious and tense. Don took a notebook out of his pocket and a biro and began writing things down.

All this time, I was still in a heap on the pathway, my knees drawn up in front of me, my hands clasped tightly round them. Every now and again I let my head fall forward into my lap, burrowing into the warmth of my woollen coat, stretched over my knees, the buttons pressing into my forehead (when we got to our hotel, I looked in the mirror and there was a red circle bang between my eyes, as though I had been branded). Don, when he was ready to go, seemed not to notice that the bundle of clothes on the path was his wife. 'Where is my wife?' I heard him say, the first distinct words I had heard at all. One of the men pointed. Don came over to me and said, not unkindly, 'Come on, Lou.' He took my hand and helped me up. I said sorry. He said he wanted me to come and look at the boat. He wanted to show me various important things, and for me to check that he had got the numbers and markings on the engine correct. I laughed, a silly, weak little laugh, and said he must be joking, I couldn't possibly go onto that boat, and he asked why not?

I didn't go onto the boat. Nothing Don could say would make me. He pleaded with me, going over and over why it was vital that I should see what he had seen, but I shook my head and said that I couldn't, I wouldn't. He had to give up. He went back on the boat with one of the men and I saw him showing this man what he had written down and, though I couldn't hear what Don said it was obvious enough that he was asking this man to verify his notes. The man seemed reluctant to sign anything. Don stabbed his finger at something he'd written, and I saw the man nod. This went on for some time – more pointings of Don's finger, more nods from the man.

When eventually we left the shed, though Don was reluctant to leave it at all, the taxi, which had brought us there, had gone. 'We'll walk,' Don said, and I was quite glad he'd decided this. But he was told it was too far to the town, a matter of several miles, and then one of the men said he knew someone whose shift had just finished and who was about to drive there and he went to get him. This chap didn't speak any English, but someone explained to him where we wanted to go. He gestured to us to get into the car which he'd brought round to the shed. We got into the back seat. I said to Don, as we did so, 'You haven't thanked them,' meaning the boiler-suited men who'd let him onto the boat. 'I don't feel like thanking anyone,' he said, so I let the window down and called, 'Thank you for your help.' I'm not sure they heard me.

The hotel was the only one Don had been able to find on the Internet. It was in the centre of the small, dreary-looking town, with shops either side, a butcher's and a cheese shop. The smell of cheese was overpowering as we got out of the car. Don did at least thank the driver, and even tried to give him some money, but he wouldn't take it and seemed offended. It was rather dark inside the hotel and there seemed to be nobody about and no reception desk. We stood side by side on the black and white tiled floor and waited, helplessly. Don sighed, and the sigh was repeated and sounded like a groan. 'I can't be bothered,' he muttered, as a woman suddenly appeared from behind a heavy maroon curtain to the right of the stairs ahead. She smiled and asked our name and said she was pleased to have us as her guests, and that she would show us to our room. Her English was excellent. She led us up the stairs to a landing and opened the door of our bedroom, hoping it was satisfactory. There was a question in her voice, but we ignored it. Neither of us took in the room – it was a room, it would do. And then, before she left, she said, very quietly, 'I am so sorry about

51

your daughter. Please, accept my condolences for this terrible accident.'

Don, who had walked over to the window and was staring out of it, spun round as though he had heard a gunshot. 'It was not an accident,' he said. The woman, who had half closed the door by then, opened it again. She looked alarmed, but said nothing. 'Thank you,' I said, quickly, 'you're very kind.' She smiled again, unconvincingly, and this time closed the door fully. 'Don,' I said, 'I wish you wouldn't. There hasn't even been an inquest yet. You shouldn't say things like that.' He went into the bathroom and I heard water running. By the time he came back, I was lying under the cover on the bed, feigning sleep. It was only five o'clock and neither of us had eaten that day, but I hoped he was not going to suggest that we went for a meal somewhere. But no, a meal was not what he suggested. What he wanted to do was walk round the town. I let him do it on his own. He was gone for hours, and I think I did sleep some of the time, because I was startled when he returned. The rain was hitting our window quite hard, driven against it by the wind coming off the North Sea, and it was dark. Don didn't put the light on. There was just enough illumination from a street lamp outside for him to see his way around the room. He'd bought some cheese and bread, and offered me a share. I took it and ate it and felt better for it. There was a coffee machine in the room and he made us coffee. We did not say a word to each other. There we sat, side by side on the bed, munching the bread and cheese, sipping the coffee. 'Can we go home now?' I said finally.

We stayed two days. The next morning, Don hired a car and we drove for about an hour to the place where the boat had been washed ashore. There was nothing to see, absolutely nothing. It was still raining, the wind was still fierce, but he insisted that we should both get out of the car and walk on the beach. It was not really a beach at all. The coast was flat, there were no rocks, no cliffs. It was a drab coastline, dreary but without menace. There were no buildings, no shelter anywhere. If the day had been clearer we would have been able to see for miles. But I stayed beside the car, refusing to walk to the exact spot, near a little inlet, where we knew the wreckage of the boat had been found, but Don walked along to it, the mud coming over his shoes. He stood facing the howling wind, his hair whipped upwards in an almost cartoonish way, his arms crossed in front of him. The waves were crashing against the shore and I could see that the spray must be soaking him, but he didn't move. The sea was hideous that day, spiteful and ugly, a vast expanse of grey and black and white, a heaving monochrome sea. Don appeared mesmerised. I thought, as he stumbled back towards me, that he might be weeping, but he was not. Astonishingly, the frown, which hadn't lifted from his face since the news came, was smoothed out. He looked calm. 'I know what I've got to do,' he said. 'There's nothing you can do,' I said, alarmed. 'Oh yes, there is,' he said, but that was all.

*

It is a week since I wrote those last few pages. I have given up making myself sit at my desk every day for at least half an hour, to see if something will come. Today, entering this room, I didn't feel so reluctant, I didn't feel as if I were forcing myself to concentrate on a task I don't properly understand. The point is, *I am trying*. It doesn't matter what this trying, this straining, is about. I have convinced myself that sitting here, thinking, sorting stuff out mentally, has to be done. And I will do it. In some peculiar way, it makes me almost happy.

*

The phone rang – the landline, not my mobile – just after six this morning. I wasn't asleep but I wasn't completely awake. I was lying there thinking of how to spend the weekend. I got up and answered the phone in a slightly befuddled state, yawning as I said 'Yes, hello?' There was silence, and then the line went dead. A wrong number, probably. But something made me dial 1471.

The number had been withheld. I went to make some coffee, and the phone rang again. I was quick to answer. This time, after I'd asked who was calling, and repeated my number, the line didn't go dead immediately. I could hear breathing. It was not heavy, frightening breathing – more a light sort of sighing, as though the caller was holding the mouthpiece very close and trying to be quiet. 'Hello? Hello? Who is this?' I repeated. And the receiver was put down, gently.

It is a bright, sunny morning. I can hear my neighbour below singing, and in the flat above the couple there have the *Today* programme on. There is no need to be alarmed, but that is how I feel. If the phone rings again, what shall I do? How many times shall I answer it? Will it go on and on? Who rings so early on a Saturday morning, anyway? And then it occurs to me: someone wants to reach me to break bad news about Molly.

The phone rang three more times and then Finn came round, just as I was becoming hysterical, convinced someone in Zambia was trying to reach me. He was on his way to do someone's garden and wanted to borrow some money. I hardly listened to him – I grabbed him by the arm and pulled him into my flat and pointed at the phone as though it were alive, telling him incoherently about the calls and my conviction that something must have happened to Molly.

'For God's sake, Mum,' he said, 'calm down. It won't be anyone ringing from Zambia.'

'How do you know? How *can* you know? You can't !'

'Look,' he said, 'we can settle this easily. All you have to do is ring that emergency number she gave us, the one at the head-quarters out there. Geddit? Come on, you're Mrs Efficiency! Where is it? Find it. Ring them, or I'll do it.'

I had the number in my address book, and also pinned on the notice board in my kitchen, but, though Finn pointing out this obvious solution had calmed me a little, I hesitated. 'I can't call them,' I said. 'If she's OK, if it wasn't them ringing, I'll feel so stupid, I'd be embarrassed, and Molly ...'

'Mum, what do you want to be, embarrassed or reassured? Give me the number, here, give me your address book. Quick. Now, sit down.'

I sat. He rang the number Molly had given us and explained very clearly to whoever answered that his mother had received some phone calls which had not been properly connected and had become convinced someone from Zambia was trying to reach her. Could they check that his sister, Molly Roscoe, working on their aid programme in Nambo, was safe and well? There was a long pause. Finn yawned and looked unconcerned. The waiting went on and on. I began to feel faint, and had to lie down. I kept telling myself to be sensible, *sensible*, but though one part of my brain was telling me that if Molly was dead these people at the HQ would have known immediately, another larger part was sure they were working out how to break the news.

'Thank you. Sorry to have troubled you,' Finn said, and then, 'What? No, no thanks, no need to. Thanks again. Bye.'

I sat up. I tried to smile. Finn looked at me, frowning and biting his lip. 'I'm sorry,' I said. 'It's just that there really were all those calls and ...'

'Mum, they were just nuisance calls. Nearly everyone gets them at some time. It's just someone having a laugh.'

'A laugh? At six in the morning?'

'All right, it was an odd time, and they aren't funny, but it's how sad people amuse themselves. At least they weren't obscene. I mean, a bit of harmless breathing and you panic. Anyway, can I borrow a tenner? Judith's run out of cash, and I haven't time to get to a bank. Dunno if I've got any money, anyway. I think I'm overdrawn again.'

Did he say that bit deliberately, knowing it would distract me, make me start lecturing him on his bad financial habits? Did he hope it would make me pull myself together? I gave him the £10. He hesitated, then gave me a kiss on my cheek and said, 'It's no good getting in such a state. You're always expecting the worst.' I looked at him without saying anything.

'I know, I know,' he said, but gently. 'But just because it's happened once ...'

'It's because it's happened once,' I said.

He sighed and rubbed his face, and closed his eyes, and then seemed to shake himself. 'You shouldn't be on your own,' he said, 'you're not up to it.'

'I'll be fine,' I said.

And, on the whole, I have been. I went out. I made myself go to an art exhibition at the Serpentine, and then I walked round the whole of Hyde Park. I came home tired but feeling much better. Finn called again. He brought me some flowers, some scented stock given to him by the woman whose garden he was doing. I apologised for my behaviour and told him about my day and he was clearly relieved and went off whistling, glad to be able to get on with his own life.

I must not become a burden to my son. He said before he left that I shouldn't be on my own. Did he wish his father were with me, to shoulder the responsibility? I must show him I am fine on my own. I am.

*

Paige had a tube of sweets in her pocket today. She was hiding them, so she was aware she should not be eating them in class. It was the smell which gave her away, a strong fruity smell, which Hussain immediately identified as his favourite sweet and shouted out 'Starburst! Give me one!' I took them off her, saying she could have them at the end of the day but that she mustn't bring them to school again. When she did come to collect them, I gave them to her, but couldn't resist a little gentle lecture on how bad they were for her teeth. 'These are very sticky sweets, Paige,' I said. 'They aren't good for you, you know.' I was gong to go on about her teeth, and what we had learned in our Healthy Eating week, how these sweets would cause decay and instead of pretty, strong white teeth she'd end up with decayed ones, full of fillings. 'But they *are* good

56

for me,' Paige said, 'they make me happy, and it's good to be happy. When you took them away, Miss, I was unhappy.' And she promptly opened the tube and took out another sweet and popped it into her mouth. 'See,' she said, mouth wide open and the bright green sweet in the middle of her pink little tongue. She closed her mouth, closed her eyes, sucked hard, and then said 'Happy.' It was very hard not to laugh. I didn't bother making a fuss with her mother, who would only have flared up at the idea of her child, and therefore herself, being criticised.

*

A postcard came today, forwarded from our old address. It was of Durham Cathedral. The writing was so very neat and small that I felt it had been practised first. The message had an equal care about it.

We were probably unfair to Alexander. Certainly, Don was. None of us, especially Molly, had really cared for him, though I hope we hadn't shown it. But Miranda was quite in awe of him, or that is how it appeared. She thought him very clever and very attractive. His family lived near us, at the top of our hill, but in a side road where there were large detached houses. They are well off, I think. They must be. They have a country cottage in Suffolk, and a boat moored there. Alexander was given a car the day he passed his driving test, on his seventeenth birthday. He said it was 'only' a second-hand Vauxhall, but we all thought this was irrefutable evidence that he was spoiled rotten. He wasn't at our children's comprehensive – he was at the City of London School – though he had been at their primary school. Miranda met him at the tennis club, though she'd also by then seen him at plenty of parties. He was apparently a brilliant tennis player, and even Miranda didn't seem to mind being thrashed by him. He was a year older than she was, and in his gap year he had sailed a lot, I'm not sure where or with whom. Sailing was his passion and he was keen to introduce Miranda to it. He was teaching her to sail during that summer, after she'd finished A levels. They went to Suffolk regularly. And then he invited her on a sailing party, with him and six others from Durham. He would have his parents' boat and the others would hire dinghies. They were all experienced sailors, except for our daughter, the novice.

I knew nothing about boats. Neither did Don, though he knows a great deal now. But he questioned her closely about this boat. It was a Contessa 32, she said. He asked how big it was, since that description was meaningless to him. She said it was small, but not very small. What did that mean? Don asked. She sighed and said, did he want actual measurements, what was his point? He said, yes, in fact, he did want measurements. She rang Alex and we heard her say her Dad was being 'embarrassing'. She clearly felt rather foolish being told and having to report to Don that '32' meant it was 32 feet long. More questions followed. Yes, they would be sleeping on it; yes, it had an engine as well as sails; yes, she would wear a lifejacket at all times. She would only be crewing for Alex, who was very experienced. Do you think, Miranda said, cheekily, his parents would let him sail their boat if he wasn't? It cost thousands, you know – they aren't mad. Don had done his best. Finally, he had to admit that it sounded exciting. Finn was envious, he wished he had friends with rich parents (he always referred to Alex as 'posh boy' to annoy Miranda). Molly wasn't bothered. It wasn't her idea of a holiday, pulling ropes, being shouted at and having to obey Alex.

Don did wonder if he should ring Alex's parents. In fact, he thought it odd that they hadn't rung us. 'You would think,' he said, 'they would have wanted to have some contact with the parents of the girl their son is taking to sail in their boat.' It was in ways like this that Don was – is – so old-fashioned. It made me smile, and feel so fond of him. It was I who discouraged him. I reminded him that Miranda was eighteen. She wasn't a child. She had met Alex's parents and they'd made up their own mind about her. They didn't need to check out her parents.

And so he never did ring them. The only time we ever saw them was at the inquest, across the room.

We did get a letter from them, once it was all over. A letter delivered by hand, at night. I was awake, as I usually was then, and I heard the gate open and heard footsteps on the gravel path and then the sound of the flap of the letterbox dropping back into place. Another person frightened to face us, I thought. Later, much later, when I did read the letter, I remember thinking how devoid of feeling it was and I understood Don's disgust when he opened it and said, 'Three lines – three! – and that's all.' But Alex's father is a barrister and, though there was no blame attached to his son at the inquest, he was doubtless being extremely careful. We did not, after all, know the man or his wife. What else could they have said, except how sorry they were, how tragic the accident, what a beautiful girl our daughter had been, how we had all their sympathy. The restrained, formal tone of those three lines was in keeping with their relationship, or lack of it, to us. Curious, then, that it seemed so offensive.

Alexander tried harder. He came to our house one evening, just appeared at the door. Unfortunately, Don answered. It wasn't late, about half past nine, I think, but it was almost dark and the security light wasn't working, so all Don saw was the figure of a man standing a good way back from the door. He hadn't put the hall light on either, so this whole encounter took place in gloom. I was in the kitchen, clearing up the remains of a meal neither of us had felt like eating. I heard Don say, 'Hello?' and then didn't quite catch the reply. I heard only the low murmur of a man's voice. I thought it was someone collecting for charity. But then I heard Don's raised voice and I realised he had stepped outside the house. The words 'dare' and 'come here' came to me, and I went to the open doorway myself. I was in time to see Don push Alex, though I hadn't yet identified him, and I shouted to Don to stop it and rushed forward to grab his arm. Then I saw who it was he had been pushing. 'Alex!' I said, and he said, 'Mrs Roscoe,' and Don said, 'Just go. I'm sorry I pushed you.' Alex, hands in his jacket pocket and head bent, muttered that it was all right, he understood. Don said he understood nothing, and then he walked back into the house.

I was left with Alex. 'I'm sorry,' he said. 'I just came to say ...' and then he became incoherent, and I only picked up isolated words, 'sorry', 'terrible' and I could hardly bear it and rushed to stop him floundering on. I found myself saying that it wasn't his fault (though of course he hadn't said it was). I actually apologised for my husband's behaviour. I said something to the effect that we were very upset and not really able to talk or think properly. He lifted his head, and his expression was one I knew well, from Finn – a grimace which could be mistaken for a smirk by those who didn't know it was an effort to conceal emotion. 'I'm sorry,' he said, again. His voice was hoarse and barely audible. 'We'll talk later, another time,' I said, and then he did turn and go down our short path to the gate, his hands, either side of him, giving funny flipping movements.

There never was another time. I thought it brave of him to have come at all, but Molly didn't, and neither, of course, did Don. It was one of the few things they agreed on, in those early days. Molly thought that Alexander had taunted Miranda with being a coward, scared to sail on her own. Molly also thought apologising was too easy. Once you've apologised, especially when you know you can't really be blamed, you feel you've done your bit. You've behaved well, there's nothing else you can do. 'He told everyone,' Molly said later. 'He made sure everyone knew he'd come round to our house and apologised, and he told them how angry Dad had been and how he hadn't given him a chance to explain, and how he'd shoved him in the chest.'

But Finn's attitude was different. He once went so far as to say, in Don's hearing, that he felt sorry for Alexander. Don asked him, in a tight, quiet voice (which ought to have warned Finn off) why this was. Finn said what happened wasn't Alex's fault but that we were holding him responsible. 'Think how he feels,' Finn said. Don stared at him for a while and then re-minded him that at the inquest it came out that Alex turned his attention to another girl, which had led to the argument that caused Miranda to take the boat out on her own. She would never have done so if she hadn't been so distressed and not in her right mind. And it was Alex's attitude which had caused her distress. There was no getting away from it, Don said. 'You mean jealousy,' Finn said. 'She was jealous, she couldn't take the thought she might be dumped. You can't blame Alex for that. Think how he feels.' 'No,' Don said, 'I will not think how he feels. I have no interest in how he feels.'

Not long ago, Finn appeared with a newspaper cutting he wanted me to read. It was about a boy who killed his girlfriend in a jet-ski accident. He admitted causing the fatal accident through recklessness. But the point of Finn showing it to me was because he wanted me to read about the girl's griev-ing parents. The father was quoted as saying the death of his beloved, beautiful daughter was a tragic accident and that he didn't want the boy to suffer any more. 'And he actually did kill her,' Finn said. The mother was reported as saying that she absolved the boy of any blame. He had 'succumbed to a momentary lapse in concentration' and had never intended any harm. The idea of him being arrested and imprisoned horrified the mother – 'He will never get over this,' she said, 'and that is enough punishment. Nothing that's done to him can bring our daughter back.' 'Remember how Dad behaved?' Finn asked. 'Couldn't be like that, could he?' No, he couldn't. He can't. But Finn's disgust, if that was what it was, and his desire that Don should have been magnanimous and noble, made me want to defend his father. Yet at the same time I, too, would have been so proud if Don had managed to react as the father in this other case evidently had done. It was a mistake for us not to listen to what Alexander had come to say. We should have asked him in, and been polite, however hard it would have been. We had heard him speak only at the inquest – there was surely a great

61

deal more he could have told us. It had never made sense to us that Miranda chose to take his boat out on her own. It had been interpreted as an act of defiance, but was it? Why hadn't she just left, come home? Had Alex taunted her with being a poor sailor? What exactly had their argument been about? By turning Alex away, Don would never find out.

And now, all this time afterwards, here was a card from him, to me. He must be in his last term. I wonder why he has sent it. The words give no clue. It is addressed only to me, not to me and Don, or to the family in general. Had I really once said, in Alexander's hearing, or to Miranda who'd repeated it to him, that Durham was my favourite cathedral? I didn't know I had a favourite cathedral. But it is a pretty card. I won't tear it up. Why should I? Don would.

*

When I was writing about Alexander, there was an interruption. My doorbell rang, and when I spoke through the intercom and asked who was there, a young woman's voice, light and rather tremulous, said, 'Please, I deliver to you.' She didn't sound like the usual delivery boys who tear around on motorbikes, and I wasn't expecting anything to be delivered, but I thought I'd better go down and see what this was about. It was only five o'clock, on a sunny afternoon, and I could hear that my neighbours below were in, so there was no danger (danger is very much on everyone's mind, locally, after a series of doorstep muggings reported in the local paper). I went down and opened the main door, but even before I did so I could see that this girl – she was only a girl – was harmless. She was cradling what looked like a flat box in her arms and on top of it was a postcard, which she handed to me. It was written in capital letters, and said that she was Polish and that her father was very ill back in Warsaw and that he needed medicines, which she wanted to buy and send to him. She had drawings to sell and asked me to inspect them and perhaps buy one for what I thought it was worth. I handed the card back and she put it in her pocket, and with her eyes fixed on mine she began slowly to open the box and turn over a series of drawings. Her eyes flickered between looking at my face and down at her own drawings. They were all in pencil, heavily shaded, sketches of boats and ships, the last kind of images I wanted to look at. Anxiety was making her hands shake. I felt so sorry for her, sorry enough to buy something. I hadn't brought any money down with me, and so asked her to wait. It's a rule in this block that the outer door must not be left open, so I beckoned her into the lobby and then said I'd just run up and get some money. But as I set off up the stairs to my flat, she followed me. I stopped and said she didn't need to come, but she obviously didn't understand, and the minute I went on climbing the stairs she followed me once more.

She was only a girl, slight, unthreatening, but I didn't want her to come into my flat. I was ashamed of this, but when I got to my own door, which I'd left open, I put up my hand and shook my head and she stopped, looking stricken, her shoulders hunched and tears in her eyes. Quickly, I rushed into my kitchen and snatched £5 from the cash I kept in the dresser drawer, and hurried back to her. She'd gone. I could hear her running down the stairs. I shouted 'wait' and ran after her. She was struggling to open the outer door, which has a very tricky catch, otherwise I could not have stopped her leaving. 'Please,' I said, 'I'm so sorry, I didn't mean ...' But then I halted: what had I 'not meant'? 'Here,' I said, and 'please' again, and I held out the five-pound note. She wouldn't look at me. Mutely, the tears still wetting her pale cheeks, she opened her box of drawings and held them out again. I hardly looked at what I took, I didn't want pictures of boats, of course, but it felt easier just to take something. Then I opened the door for her, and she left.

I watched her from my sitting-room window as she crossed the street and walked off. She trailed along, very slowly, head down, arms holding her box of drawings which she cradled protectively. On that side of the street there are no blocks of flats, only houses. She didn't try any of them, just trudged past. At the corner, she stopped and stood still for several minutes. I couldn't decide whether she was lost, or trying to make her mind up about what she should do. But then a white van drew up and the sliding door in the passenger part was pulled back and she climbed in. The van drove back down our street, passing our flats, and I saw there were other girls in it. Were they all selling drawings? Did they all have postcards written out for them, saying their fathers were ill and needed medicine?

I felt upset, without knowing why. I feel that I let that girl down. Maybe she needed help and was afraid to ask for it. I should have invited her in, and talked to her. But she didn't speak English, so that would have been no good. I tore up the drawing at once. I went on worrying about her, though, worrying about all the young foreign girls like her, possibly at the mercy of unscrupulous people, finding themselves lost in this huge city and unable, perhaps, to get out of the situation they are in and find their way home.

*

There was a news item on television last night about a suicide bomber blowing up a bus in a seaside resort in Israel. I shouldn't have watched it. Don used to be irritated by how I reacted to such scenes. 'Imagine,' I used to say, 'imagine, those children, how can their parents bear ...' and he'd stop me.

'No,' he said, 'I won't imagine, I don't want to imagine anything about it. I'm surprised at you, Lou. You're not, I hope, going to watch all this on television. Don't. It does no good, you'll just make yourself ill. We've had quite enough tragedy in our lives, we don't need other people's.'

I felt angry with Don. He has become so arrogant in his despair and misery, he really thinks he has been marked out for suffering far more than anyone else and that this entitles him to receive, but not give, sympathy. What happened to Miranda doesn't have anything to do with the agonies undergone by the families of those killed in that horrible way in suicide bombings, but it doesn't excuse us from trying to empathise with their distress. But Don somehow thinks that it does. He's separated himself from the rest of the human race.

The children at school see these bombings on television. I remember that in the playground, where I was on duty that week, some of the boys were whooshing around, their arms flapping, wearing their little decorative rucksacks, and shouting 'I'm a suicide bomber, I'm a suicide bomber.' Paige asked me if all the dead people would have gone to heaven. Questions about death and dying pop up often enough in class and can't be ignored, but it's always hard to be both comforting and yet truthful. What I said this time, taking her hand, was that yes, if these poor people believed in heaven, they would have gone there. Unfortunately, Harry heard this. An older child would doubtless have asked me if *I* believed in heaven, which would have led to some evasions, but Harry said, 'What's heaven like?' I said I didn't know, that nobody knew. 'Do you sit around with angels?' he asked. I said maybe. 'I don't like sitting around,' he said.

When Miranda was around four, she talked a lot about heaven. Her best friend (apart from Molly) had a very religious mother, a Roman Catholic, who brought her daughter up, at least when she was small, to believe absolutely in heaven as a delightful garden, full of flowers, where the sun always shone and everyone was good and kind, and nothing nasty ever happened. When someone died she said they went on a journey to this garden. Miranda accepted her story completely. She wanted to go to heaven, even if it meant leaving all of us. I didn't spoil her fantasy, reckoning it would soon enough be challenged by events, as it was. My mother died. Miranda was seven by then, and very eager actually to see someone on their journey to heaven, so after endless discussions, Don and I decided that she should be allowed to see my dead mother, her beloved granny. Mum hadn't had a terrible illness and did not look grotesque, or we would never have let any of the children see her. She looked rather lovely, in fact, her face still plump and hardly lined. (She was only seventy-two, and died of a heart attack, never having been ill – it was unexpected and we were shocked.) The funeral premises where she was taken wasn't a scary place, and the funeral director wasn't a solemn, forbidding man, but a rather pleasant, gentle chap who didn't think his trade prevented him from smiling at a child.

We, Don and I, each held Miranda's hand (Molly refused to come) and we took her into the little room where her granny lay, clad in a simple white gown, her still dark hair beautifully brushed, her hands resting on her stomach. Miranda stared and stared, and Don and I tensed, worrying that she would burst into tears or start screaming. She never said a word. But afterwards, on the way home, she asked how her granny would get to heaven when she was asleep and couldn't move. Don launched into a long rigmarole about how some people thought one thing and some people another and everyone being entitled to their opinion, but long before he had finished Miranda said, 'I don't think Granny can get to heaven.' And then, after more thought, 'I don't think heaven can be a place.' We left it at that.

4

THE WOMAN in the ground-floor flat in my block has just had twins, boys. I must send her a card and something for the babies. When I knew I was expecting twins – I could hardly believe it, since there was no history of twins on either side of our families – I started reading up on them. I didn't know, at the time, whether my twins would be identical (they were not) or the same sex, which, of course, they were, so a great deal of what I learned wasn't strictly applicable. But still, I was well prepared to expect rivalry between them as they grew up, for one twin to be the stronger, or the leader, or more favoured, and I'd absorbed all the advice about how to deal with these various problems. What had cheered me most, though, and hugely outweighed my worries, was that the general consensus of opinion seemed to be how devoted twins usually are to each other. I love that idea. Maybe all only children do.

It felt exciting to me, to be bearing twins. It was Don who was apprehensive – he couldn't see how we could manage two at once when neither of us had any experience of babies. And then there was the cost. We would need two of everything, though both sets of grandparents rushed with generous offers, almost competing over who would buy the cots, the pram, the highchairs, etc. He was anxious, too, about the birth itself, and relieved when the doctor decided I should have a caesarean. But I didn't have a caesarean. The date for it was fixed but I went into labour the week before and against all expectations, and most unusually with first babies, especially twins, dilated so rapidly that by the time we got to the hospital it was too late. Molly was 4 lb 9 oz, and Miranda, arriving twenty minutes later, 3 lb 12 oz. They were both healthy, though Miranda was in an incubator at first. Don sat by the incubator for ages, while I nursed Molly. When they took her out, he held her before I did.

I felt wonderful, elated. It hadn't been a dreadful experience at all. Painful, yes, but I was lucky – it was not long-drawn-out, I didn't suffer as I did, later, with Finn, which has always struck me as odd (though since his weight was greater than the combined weights of the twins, that may have had something to do with it). Don, too, was thrilled. We spent at least the first two days in a haze of relief and happiness, staring at Molly and Miranda as though we had never seen a baby before (we hadn't actually seen many). Bringing them home wasn't quite such a joyous business. Reality struck quickly, and even though my very capable mother came to stay, within days we felt exhausted. Then my father had an accident, not a serious one but my mother had to go home to him, and Don got flu, and ...

How I like remembering that period in our lives. Afterwards, we used to reminisce about it, exaggerating the agony of the night-time feeds, describing to the girls the way they leapfrogged each other so that we never had any rest, and how there was no time to do anything but feed and change and wind and bathe them. Impossible, we used to say, chaos, rolling our eyes. But really we knew they were happy days, everything going right, the future something we looked forward to, and the past of no interest or importance whatsoever. There was nothing in it to hang over us and taint the present or make us apprehensive of what the future held.

*

Dress-up Friday. Every child was supposed to dress up as a

character in their favourite story, in honour of World Book Day, when they will each receive a £1 book token. In the case of my children, the favourite story will have to be one that has been read to them, since only a few of them have begun to read and even they certainly couldn't read a whole book by themselves. And at least half the class don't have parents who read to them at home, so it's what Jeremy and I have read to them that will count. Hard to dress up as the Gruffalo, but *Cinderella* and *Little Red Riding Hood* and several other fairytales should come in useful. Best not to take it too seriously, but Paige, hungry for any sort of competition, will certainly do that. Her mother has been reading *Dr Doolittle* to her, which did surprise me. A book she apparently had herself as a child. Paige wants to be a Pushmi-Pullyu, with two heads. Good luck to her mum. 'It's an animal that can look two ways,' Paige informed the rest of the class, who hadn't the slightest idea what she was talking about. 'Backwards and forwards,' explained Paige. I took up the theme. Who would like to be able to look backwards and forwards at the same time? Would it be useful? Would it be fun? 'It would make you dizzy,' said Sita, 'and sick.' 'You can do it in a car,' Harry suddenly said. Harry never speaks in class. He is worryingly quiet and well-behaved. I asked him how, and he described the mirrors on his dad's car. Paige was impressed in spite of herself. So was Jeremy. He said he'd guessed Harry was clever. 'How do you think he'll turn out?' Jeremy said. I said it was impossible to know. Five-year-olds give few clues to what they will become, whatever the Jesuit view. Wouldn't it be fascinating, Jeremy said, if we could look ahead and see Harry at twenty. No, I said, not really. I'd rather wait. At twenty, I thought, he could be dead.

*

Another meeting with Don. I thought I should be brave – no, not brave, sensible – and suggest that we meet in my flat. He seemed reluctant. I'd thought he might be pleased, but no, he hesitated and said, 'Are you sure? Would it be a good idea?' I said, 'Why wouldn't it be?' and he muttered something about not fitting in with my new life. But he came, yesterday.

It hits me every time we see each other now how awful he looks. No wonder Pat didn't recognise him. I can hardly bear it. It isn't so much his air of self-neglect – his scruffy clothes, his greasy hair – but the pallor of his skin, the way he has aged and looks ill. I wanted immediately to be looking after him, as I always did, and as even at the worst time, I struggled to look after myself. We don't embrace any more when we meet. He doesn't make any attempt, and I don't take the initiative, fearing that if I put my arms round him, or reach up to kiss his cheek, collapse might follow, of either of us, or both of us. We say hello, and he slouches forward, unhappy to be there, uncomfortable on my territory. I am hardly more at ease. 'Coffee?' I ask brightly, and lead him into the kitchen. He leans against the doorframe, hands in pockets, and watches me. 'Small kitchen,' he says, 'not what you were used to.' 'No,' I say, 'but it's big enough for one. I don't do much cooking now.'

That was how it went on. The coffee made – I know exactly how he likes it, of course – we moved into the sitting-room. He made it look much smaller than I had ever realised it was, the way tall men always do. I told him to sit down, he was making me nervous, but he went on standing at the window for a while, looking out into the street as though he couldn't believe it existed. There was a frown on his face, but then there nearly always is now. 'Why did you choose here?' he said. 'It doesn't seem your sort of place. I thought you'd go for something more ...' His voice trailed off. I waited. I wasn't going to help him. But he shook his head, and at last sat down. He asked if I heard from Finn. I said he'd rung last week and that he kept in touch, in an irregular sort of way. 'I'd like to go and see him,' Don said. 'Try to ...' And again, the sentence was left unfinished. 'I think Molly ...' he began, and stopped. 'With Molly ...' he started, and then with a big effort continued, 'Molly has started to e-mail me,' he said. 'I think it's going to be OK. We'll see, when she comes back. But Findlay ...'

Findlay was my maiden name. I thought my father would like the idea, and he did. I was always going to shorten it to Finn, and he was never, except on his birth certificate and on other official documents since, called Findlay. Don wasn't keen, but gave way to my wish and in the end came to like the shortened version. The only name he chose was Miranda's. *I* wasn't keen on that, thinking it too romantic, and that it sat oddly with her twin's name, Molly, my adored grandmother's name, which I'd had in my head waiting for a daughter, for years. To call Finn 'Findlay' all of a sudden was strange, and I laughed.

'You're getting very formal,' I said, and queried, 'Findlay?'

'Finn's a bit babyish,' Don said, 'now he's grown-up.'

'When you grew up,' I reminded him, 'you shortened your name. That wasn't babyish?'

Don's full name was Gordon. He shortened it to Don as soon as he left home, at eighteen, and people always imagined his real name was Donald. When the children found out that he was christened Gordon they called him that whenever he was being particularly pompous, not that he very often was. Except now, suddenly. Finn would not like being given his full name. There is so little of Don in Finn – it's really quite remarkable, how unlike father and son are. They don't look alike, they have very different personalities and talents. But until this happened, till Miranda died, they got on well.

Finn doesn't want to go to university, which upsets Don. Finn can't see there is any point. He says there's no subject he likes enough to study for three years, and he thinks combination degrees a cop-out. Don tried to argue that what you study is not the important part of going to university, and gave him the spiel about having time to work out what you want to do, but it was no good. Finn thinks students are 'dossers'. He wanted to work, straight away. The only concession he made, and that was because of the state we were all in afterwards, was that he

71

would do A levels so that if, as his father hoped, he changed his mind later, then he'd have the qualifications he needed. But he dropped out of sixth form college after one term and started work.

His job baffles Don. It baffles me too, but Finn seems happy enough and that's all that matters. He's not quite eighteen yet, there's plenty of time (well, that may not be true, but it's comforting to think so). As far as we can tell, Finn is a labourer for a landscape gardening firm. He says he's learning the business from the bottom up. The bottom must be very muddy because when I do see him he is always filthy. He lives with his Aunt Judith, Don's sister, because her house is near his work. She doesn't cook for him or wash his clothes or anything – she assures me he is quite self-sufficient – but he has his own room and the use of her kitchen and washing machine. I think she likes having him there, now that her own boys have moved out and David, her husband, died shockingly suddenly five years ago. Finn isn't the only lodger she's taken in – there is another young man, a nephew of David's, who is at the LSE, and a woman, an ex-college friend, who is staying while her divorce goes through and she can get the money to buy another home. Judith likes a full house.

I didn't want to know the answer to the next question I asked, but all the same, looking at Don, seeing his exhaustion and his dejection, I asked it.

'How are things going?' I said. 'Did that lead ...?'

He shrugged. 'Disappointing,' he said. 'The man is a coward. He knows the truth but he won't speak up. I got nothing audible on tape. He played loud music all the time we talked. But he gave me clues he didn't even realise he was giving and I'll follow them up.'

I didn't ask what these clues were. I saw Don was watching me carefully, hoping that I would, and that when he saw my polite, non-committal expression he could hardly bear it. It was he who changed the subject, back to Finn. 'Has he changed his mobile number?' he asked. I said, yes, he had, his original mobile was nicked. 'Can I have the new number?' he asked, producing his own mobile. I sat quite still. 'You don't mean,' he said, 'he doesn't want me to have it?'

'Not as strong as that,' I said. 'But he'd rather you didn't phone him. It wouldn't make any difference, you know what he'll say, why he doesn't want to see you. If … if things change, then the two of you can start again.'

'They'll never change,' Don said, 'if that means what I think it means.'

He left soon after. Wouldn't take any food. Said he had a lot of work to do. I asked how work was going and he said not well. The agency was so good to him afterwards, they let him have masses of time off, but by now they must be fed-up with Don's frequent absences while he makes investigations. When we were still together, I used to be terrified that he would be 'let go'. It's only because he is so good at his job that they keep him, I imagine. It was Don, after all, who only two years ago won a marketing effectiveness award for them. The thought of Don without a job is unbearable – unemployed, he would go to pieces, if he hasn't, in so many ways, done so already.

*

Book group tonight. Afterwards, the first month afterwards, when the evening for the meeting came round, and I saw the words written on the kitchen calendar, it never occurred to me to go, or even to ring Alice and say I wasn't coming. But Alice rang me. 'Come,' she said. 'No one will ask you anything. We'll just talk about the book, nothing else.' I said I simply didn't have the energy either to come to her house, or if I did, to say a word. She said she would come and get me and as for talking, I didn't need to, I could just listen. But I did say something.

Alice came at seven o'clock, drove me back the short distance to her house and all she said herself was that she thought this month's book was 'unconvincing', that she couldn't wait to see what everyone else had made of it. It was almost a month since I'd read it myself – I read it immediately after the last meeting – and as Alice made this comment I was astonished to be aware of a protest stirring in my numb brain when we got to her house, where the other five were waiting. The discussion began with Alice repeating her remark and all except Shirley seemed to agree with her. I found myself looking encouragingly at Shirley – she is very shy and finds it hard to argue – but she just mumbled that she'd liked it. 'But did you *understand* it?' Alice demanded, and that was when I spoke. My voice croaked, as though I hadn't used it for a long time. The book was Carol Shield's *Unless*. I said I couldn't believe the novel had seemed unconvincing to Alice, or that it was difficult to understand. It was about a mother's anguish for a daughter who had separated herself from her family in search of what she thought of as 'goodness'. What was there to understand about that? I said if my daughters – and then I stopped. I corrected myself. I said if my daughter ... but then I couldn't continue. Alice jumped in with some platitude but I found I wanted to continue. I blurted out, 'the pain' and stopped again, and then gathered my courage and said I thought the mother's pain was so well described. I quoted a bit I remembered about her head being a ringing vessel of pain, and another bit about how she tried to dodge sadness with deliberate manoeuvres, and how she had endless dialogues with herself in her head. I said this had impressed me when I read it, but later, when it was over – that's all I said, 'when it was over' (they might have thought I meant the book) – I'd remembered all this and felt a kind of relief that the way I felt, in different but similar circumstances, had been so accurately expressed.

There was silence when I finished, and a lot of uncomfortable shifting about on chairs, then someone, Anita, I think, said she had liked the part about cleaning, about what a comfort it was to clean the house thoroughly when one was distraught, and a discussion on this followed, but I wasn't listening. I was recalling another bit in the novel, about the narrator and her husband still having sex in the midst of their grief, about how they cried afterwards, but how they still fitted (I think that was the word) and lived in each other's shelter. Don and I didn't.

*

Lola was still there. Turning round as the last parent left with their child, at the end of school today, I realised Lola was still in the classroom, standing quite still beside the model of a castle Jeremy's been making with them. She didn't seem alarmed, not yet, and I was careful not to seem alarmed myself, though I was. Lola's mother is almost always the first parent waiting outside the door. I see her face peering in as early as the beginning of story time. She has never been late. It was already quarter to four, a full fifteen minutes after end of school, and even the playground outside had almost emptied. Well, Lola, I said, I expect Mummy has got held up. You can help me sharpen the pencils till she gets here. All the children love sharpening pencils in the little machine we have, most of them turning the handle so hard they break the points off, but I knew Lola was careful and would concentrate beautifully. I sent Jeremy off to the office to check if there had been a message and I busied myself sorting out books, chatting to Lola as I did so, praising how well she was doing. There had been no message. The school secretary had rung Ms Adams and there was no reply. She'd also rung the neighbour, down as stand-by in emergencies. No reply from her either.

  I let Jeremy go and when she'd finished the pencils asked Lola which book she'd like me to read to her while we waited. She picked an illustrated copy of *The Wind in the Willows* but I could tell from almost the beginning that she wasn't really listening. 'Where's my mummy?' she asked, and the first signs of anxiety appeared in her trembling voice. I sat her on my knee and said I was sure her mummy would be here soon, but by 4.30 the pretence wasn't fooling her. She began to cry, softly. I tried,

75

gently, to ask her some obvious questions, but this agitated her further. She had no idea where her mother might be. No, she hadn't said anything that morning about going anywhere. No, she hadn't seemed ill. So now there was a real problem. The usual system in these cases was to give it an hour and during that time try to contact all available numbers, which had been done, and then ring the social workers, which had also been done. They would place the child in a foster home for the night if necessary. I was not having Lola subjected to that. I knew perfectly well that in no circumstances is a teacher allowed to take a child home but in this case I was prepared to flout regulations and take the consequences.

I knew that Margot was not in school that day, and that the secretary would not challenge me. I told her to give my address and phone number to Lola's mother when she turned up, and said I'd ring the social worker back myself in a couple of hours if she didn't. I took full responsibility.

I tried to turn going home with me into an adventure but by then Lola was frightened, and the hurried conversation between the secretary and me hadn't helped reassure her. I held her hand tightly as we left the school and talked to her about the jacket she was wearing and how much I liked it and asked where her mother had bought it and was pink her favourite colour, and she trotted along beside me, giving little hiccups occasionally as she tried, I guessed, to stop crying. Once in my flat I poured her some juice and found some biscuits, and she accepted both but wouldn't take her jacket off. I sat with her, holding her close, and we watched the end of *Blue Peter*. I was already wondering if the social worker would let me keep her for the night. She could sleep in my spare room. I knew they wouldn't approve of her sleeping with me, in my bed, though it would have been comforting for her to be with someone. She was a distressed five-year-old little girl who had never, I was sure, been apart from her devoted mother for a single night in her life. When it grew dark, she was bound to get more frightened.

I asked her what she liked best for supper. She said she and her mum had tea. They had beans on toast or boiled egg or sometimes chicken or ham sandwiches. I made chicken sandwiches but she wouldn't touch them, just fingered them suspiciously and left them, shooting worried looks at me. I suggested toast, and she nodded, and when I brought it, she ate it all. Her jacket was still firmly buttoned up to the neck, though my flat was warm, but she seemed to regard taking it off as some kind of defeat – she had at all costs to believe her mother was about to come. Putting her to bed was never going to work, and so I settled her down on the sofa, her head on a cushion over my lap, and as I read to her she gradually nodded off. I didn't dare move. I sat there, stroking Lola's hair, listening to her breathing. It was so quiet and I felt as though something had loosened inside me. I was content. This would not last, but for the moment I was doing what I liked best, watching over a sleeping child, even though soon she would be taken away from me, and there might be upsetting reasons for it and unhappy consequences for her.

It was such a short time, after all. At half past seven, Lola's mother came for her in a curious state of both agitation and resentment – there was just the faintest suggestion that I might have been trying to kidnap her daughter. Certainly, there was no gratitude, no fulsome thanks. She maintained that she had been assured that someone had phoned the school, when she woke up in casualty to find she'd been knocked down by a moped on a crossing. It was her first waking thought, she said, Lola, collecting her, and a nurse had calmed her and asked for the name of the school and said she would call and would also call the neighbour who could keep her for a few hours. They wouldn't let Ms Adams leave the hospital until she had been checked out, and then it had taken her an age to get home, because by then it was rush hour. And when she got to her neighbour's and found no Lola she had practically had a heart attack.

On and on the saga went and, though I sympathised with what Lola's mother had gone through, I wanted her to be relieved rather than still so hysterical and full of blame for the nurse, the hospital, everyone. Lola, during all this, slept on. 'Oh,' her mother said, 'she's still got her jacket on, she'll be boiling,' and it sounded like a criticism. She managed to pick up Lola without waking her. She did then say thanks for looking after her, and I said it had been no trouble. I wanted to say it had been a real pleasure but thought that might be misconstrued. In the end, she accepted my offer to drive her home. Lola woke up just as we got to their flats, and the tears and kisses between her and her mother made me ashamed to feel envious. Envious of what, exactly? But I think I know.

*

Plans are made. I am going on holiday. I'm to meet Lynne at Gatwick on Sunday morning next week, at the BA check-in desk.

*

We were on holiday. Don and I. We were on holiday. Molly was in France. Camping, with friends. Finn was with his cousin, Judith's youngest son, in Devon. We were on holiday, Don and I. Lindisfarne. Lovely day. We came back to our hotel, pretty place, and there was a message. She'd tried our mobiles, Judith said later, but we hadn't taken them. I'd left our itinerary with Judith. I'd given it to Molly and Miranda, and Finn too, but they'd laughed and said they didn't need to know our every movement. 'In case,' I'd said, just in case. I made sure they had our mobile numbers. And I'd made them tell me where they would be. They had mobile phones of course, but Molly's did not work abroad. Molly said she couldn't give me an itinerary, anyway, she didn't know where they would stop *en route* for Nice. But she had promised to call when they got there. How will I reach you if I need to? I asked. Mum, she said. *Please.* But in case anything happens, I pleaded. Mum, please. Miranda gave me Alex's mobile number, with instructions not to *dare* to

78

call except in a dire emergency. There were no difficulties with Finn.

They say I am arrangement-mad. That I love organising, and that I over-organise, and try to over-organise them. Probably true. But if so, is there anything really wrong with this? Anything wrong with trying to cover all eventualities? For two whole days we couldn't contact Molly. We were home in four hours. Finn was home that night, but Molly – we had to wait. One of the other parents ... I rang all the other parents. One of the group had a mobile which did work. I called her and asked to speak to Molly. Molly wasn't with her at that moment. Molly. Molly had to be told to ring back. Molly got the news on a terrible crackly line, two days later. She flew home. We met her at Luton. That's as much as I can bear to write.

Does it make any difference? Did it matter that we were all scattered, that no one was at home? Would it have been any less agonising if there had been an accident outside on our busy road and the rest of us had been together, eating supper? No. Of course not. The end result would have been the identical – shock, grief, misery. All the same. And yet, and yet. Somehow, us all being on holiday, already parted from each other, did make those first days afterwards harder. Our home life was usually reliably structured, our movements clicking into place more or less effortlessly every day. But because we were on holiday, different holidays, we had no stability. Emotionally we were in turmoil but on a practical level, too, we were in chaos. And we were not used to it. Those four hours travelling back were cruel, time was not so much suspended as crushed, the minutes, the seconds forced into a sickeningly tight framework. There was the time before, a loose wavy sort of time through which we were pleasantly ambling, and there was the time after Judith told us, and soon we were in the car holding our breath until our chests hurt. Our being on holiday made a difference. We coped less well. We did not cope well at all, but we coped less well than we would have done.

79

*

Another instance of feeling shaky, after I finished writing that. It upsets me so much going over any of the details and yet there is something pushing me to insisting that I should, even though I am reluctant. I don't want to write about what happened, or talk about it. It is *over*. It's been over for two years. It is *afterwards* that matters: *now*. I've told Don this repeatedly. He is keeping all the agony alive by refusing to stop dwelling on the tragedy itself. But now I am being as foolish as he is, torturing myself by recreating that July day. It has to stop.

*

Not many of the children are going away for this half-term holiday. Some, but not many. Most of them will spend it at home, lucky to be taken to the park. Quite a few are going to holiday school at the local community centre. The mothers who work and have no other childcare pay a small amount to book them in there. Lola goes, so do several others. I've seen them in the park, groups of a dozen, herded round by two youth leaders who do a lot of shouting. The children always look so different from how they look in my classroom – less confident, more vulnerable. When they see me they wave and call my name, but slightly fearfully, as though they don't want me to stop. And I don't, afraid of the urge to take them home with me.

The mothers, most of them, find this half-term week a strain. They resent it. It upsets their arrangements. But a couple – Emily's mother and Harry's mother – make a great thing of it being more than welcome. 'What fun we'll have next week, won't we?' Emily's mother declared, rather loudly, but then Emily's mother doesn't work. She devotes herself to Emily and her younger sister. I'm sure that she annoys the other mothers with her virtue. I do wonder if I was a little like her – though not, I hope, so stridently pleased with myself – during the decade when I wasn't teaching. I think there was some pretence

80

in my delight at half-terms, if so. I *felt* I should be thrilled to have my children at home, and I made great efforts to see they had the fun Emily's mother talks about, but I think I was always relieved to get them back to school and felt guilty about this.

'Miss, what will you do next week?' Lola asked. 'Will you be lonely here?' I said no, I was going away, to another country. Alarm filled her little face, and I had to explain.

*

I have to let Judith know that I will be away. Finn will mention it, but I owe it to her to tell her myself. It's odd how I dread – no, 'dread' is much too strong – how I am always reluctant to contact my very kind sister-in-law. I put it off again and again – it is so silly. She has helped me out so many times, willingly, and lets Finn live in her house, and has always been eager to be friends. It's to do with her being the bearer of the news, that Greek thing of wanting to shoot the messenger. Judith became tainted. That is such a horrible label to hang round her neck, but it fits. It's unfair, outrageous, but the mere sound of Judith's voice —

Don blamed her for the way she broke the news. He said she blurted it out, just the two words, no preamble, no 'I've something terrible to tell you', no 'Are you alone?' or 'Sit down, Don'. She didn't work up to it with 'I've had a phone call from the police/hospital'. She just said – shouted – those two words, Miranda's dead, in a hysterical voice. Don said he didn't take it in, the information was too absurd, too gross, and he had to ask her what on earth she was talking about, and then she burst into noisy sobs and hiccups and he could get no sense out of her. Why, he raged afterwards, could she not have been calm? Why could she not have taken a deep breath and spoken quietly? She had, he said, increased his suffering and he couldn't forgive her for it. He still hasn't.

I didn't speak to her on the telephone that day. I thought afterwards of pointing out to Don that he himself had not passed this shocking news on to me with any degree of calm. He stood there, the phone in his hand, staring straight ahead, his jaw clenched, his body rigid, and I had to beg him to enlighten me. Again and again I asked what had happened and he appeared not to hear me. I had to grab his arm and shake it and say his name over and over, and then, finally, he managed to say, 'It's Miranda, she's been killed.' Like that. He didn't take me in his arms first, he didn't present this appalling news any better than his sister had done. From the very minute he heard he separated himself. We were never together.

When we got home, Judith was there, waiting. He treated her disdainfully, almost with contempt. She held her arms out to him and said his name, and mine, and Don brushed past, going straight to the telephone. She embraced me instead and I leaned against her large, soft body and felt her wet cheek against my dry one. She was shuddering, vibrating with emotion, and I found myself patting her on the back. I still hadn't shed a tear myself. My throat had seized up, my head throbbed, and I felt unsteady on my feet but I hadn't yet wept. Judith took me into the kitchen and sat me on the basket chair there. I flopped into it obediently, very glad to be taken charge of. She had a bottle of whisky on the table, which she opened, and she poured out a large measure for me. I shook my head. I'd be sick. She swallowed it herself.

It was awful for poor Judith. Afterwards, I put myself in her position and suspected I would have done no better. It was bad luck that she was in our house, feeding the cat, as I'd asked her to do on the day my neighbour couldn't manage it. She'd driven over and was putting the cat food out when the phone rang and she automatically answered it. What else could she have done but ring us straight away, before she had got a grip on herself? Suppose she'd waited – I could imagine what Don would have thought of that. And then how could she work up to such shattering news? She loved Miranda, she loved both my girls, especially as she had no daughters herself. No wonder she let it just spill out, no wonder she was almost incoherent. But Don resented my attempts to feel sorry for Judith. He absolutely would not feel any sympathy for her situation.

They used to be close, Don and Judith. They liked each other, teased each other. When I first met his sister and saw how fond the two of them were of each other I felt wistful – that kind of sibling affection was something I knew nothing about and envied. Don took his duties as a brother seriously, always concerned about his sister's welfare. Her husband David's death was so devastating, so cruel – he was only forty-two – and Don took over all her financial affairs, dealing with their accountant and straightening things out for her. He was her rock, she said, and meant it. But when her turn came to support him, he felt she was useless. It was not her fault. She tried so hard afterwards to help but he simply wouldn't let her get anywhere near him – it was as though, in that initial phone call, she had done some kind of irreparable emotional damage.

Don said, at one point, 'I don't want Judith in the house. I can't stand the sight of her any more.' She was afraid of him by then. She'd arrive, bringing food, and try to smile at him, diffidently, not sure if smiling was offensive, and he'd simply walk away. 'What have I done?' she'd whisper to me. 'Lou, what have I done?' She hadn't done anything. She'd just been the one to tell him his daughter was dead. All I could say to her was that her brother was being unreasonable and that he was half-mad with grief and there was nothing any of us could do. But Judith was, if not a rock, then a useful support to me. Even before he actually went to live in her house, Finn practically lived with her, for weeks on end. He was the first to tire of the poisonous atmosphere in our house and at every opportunity he would accept his aunt's invitation to go back with her. Her house was normal. His cousins didn't have to creep around as though they were in a church. And as Finn pointed out, when his Uncle David died it was just as tragic, but when the funeral was over, what his aunt concentrated on was trying to be happy again. 'It's not as if they don't know what it's like,' he said, 'but they got over it.'

He did attempt to use this argument with Don, who was furious. He said there was no comparison, and that in any case making comparisons was repugnant. He reminded Finn that his uncle died of a heart attack, which nobody could have done anything about. It was a natural death, involving no one else. No one was to blame. Nobody caused his death. No one had to be brought to account. But, Don said, his sister was killed through some unknown person's negligence. She was in effect murdered. That couldn't be accepted and 'got over' until the culprit was found and brought to justice. He told Finn that we had no right to try to return to 'normal' until that day arrived.

That was more or less what he said. Finn didn't have the power to come back at him. I remember how red he became as he stood in front of Don, how frustrated he was. He didn't recognise this aggressive, arrogant man as his father. But then none of us did.

*

We have been considering senses today, though only in a general sort of way. We did sight first. How do we see? Yes, with our eyes. What did we see on our way to school? Cars, dogs, buses, people, and Paige saw half an apple in the gutter but her mum wouldn't let her pick it up. What happens when we close our eyes? Yes, it is dark. We can't see anything. 'Like we're dead,' Paige said, knowingly. 'The dead can't see, can they, Miss?' I said no, they couldn't, thank you, Paige. We moved on to hearing and tasting and touching and smelling. Predictably, Yusuf said he could smell Hussain's fart. Loud laughter. Paige began to say something but the laughter went on. I knew she would be going to say that the dead can't fart, or something similar. Her obsession with death is perfectly normal, at her age, but still not usual. Has a relative died recently? I should find out. Then, as the cackling stopped, one of the quietest children in

84

the class, Emily, suddenly said what was feeling funny called. Feeling funny? When you feel funny, Miss, she said. Funny? She couldn't explain. She's only five. 'It means you're going to vomit,' Paige shouted, filling the gap. Emily shook her head, and blushed. I felt I was failing her. Well, I was. She must mean, surely, a sixth sense exists. But she can't, she's too young. I wanted to ask her when she had 'felt funny' but it was not the right time to press her. Does she mean that even at her age she has felt as I have so often felt in the last two years? As though I didn't exist? As though a stranger inhabited my body and made it function?

We said goodbye as though we were going to be apart for months not just for a week – the classroom rang with the word. I was laughing at how exaggerated these farewells were becoming, but I was enjoying the children's exuberance too. There were hugs between us, affectionate little nuzzlings, arms thrown round my knees so that I was hobbled and could hardly walk. Then they were all gone, and Jeremy and I left to do the last tidying up.

'Going anywhere?' Jeremy asked. I said yes, I was going abroad, with a friend. He didn't ask where, but instead said, 'That sounds romantic.' Romantic. I was about to put him right, and tell him I was going with Lynne, but for some reason I didn't. I just smiled, and said no, I didn't think so, and then I pointed out someone had left a denim jacket behind and he should put it in lost property. 'Romantic', I thought, looking at myself in the cloakroom mirror, bending down to see myself. There has been no romance in my life for a very long time nor do I expect there to be ever again. Romance belongs to years ago. I have had romance, I thought. I don't need any more.

I walked back to my flat, wondering about this, not in a self-pitying or gloomy way, but just checking the statement out. But nudging behind that question – are all thoughts of romance over? – was another, not so easily answered: did I expect to live alone from now on and never have another man in my life? It was complicated, answering myself on this one, because Don is not really out of it. We are separated but not truly apart. We don't live together but neither of us lives with anyone else. So what does that make us? Where would the space be for anyone else? But it has never occurred to me that there ever will be anyone else. I am forty-five years old. But even as I remind myself of that fact, I see how silly it is to imagine my age alone is sufficient explanation for why I expect to be on my own. The real question is do I *want* to remain alone?

At the moment, yes. Definitely. Is that because I entertain hopes of Don coming to his senses and of us being together again?

*

Finn came last night, to wish me a happy holiday. He looks terrific, all tanned and healthy, and he was wearing a new shirt because he was off to meet a girl. He asked me if I liked it. There wasn't much to like – it was an ordinary blue cotton shirt, a bit crumpled – but I said it made a nice change from his usual T-shirts. Finn is so cheerful, that's what I like best. He takes life lightly, or so it seems, quite content to live in the present, never worrying about the future or dwelling on the past – a trick I've never learned though I've tried hard enough.

Don used to reckon Finn was superficial, or as he expressed it 'seriously trivial'. He said it was impossible to have a real conversation with him – he was too flippant. Well, if that is true, it is very engaging. He seems happy and I've no desire to press him on whether he really is or not. I have never burdened Finn with my troubles, never wept in front of him or clung to him in desperation except when I was in a panic about those phone calls. I didn't do it then, afterwards. Whenever Finn came into the room, I managed to stop crying. It was for his sake I so often sent him to Judith's for a while, wanting to protect him from the raw grief that drenched the atmosphere in our home. Keeping Finn as happy as it was possible for him to be in the circumstances became a prime concern of mine. It helped me, trying to protect Finn, especially from his father. And later, when he came back home, I kept up the effort.

Don got tired of it. 'He isn't a baby,' he said. 'He's fifteen now, nearly sixteen, old enough to appreciate what we're going through.' Another time he asked if I'd seen Finn cry – this was one evening, when Finn was on the phone to a friend and laughing hysterically – and I said that, yes, I had, and I didn't want to see it again. I wanted him to laugh. I wanted him to be noisy, and crash around. I wanted him to ignore our misery. It was vital to me that he should be his usual self. 'Well,' said Don, 'it gets on my nerves.' That was obvious. Every time Finn tore through the house, taking the stairs two at a time, whistling as he went, banging the doors of every room he went in or out of, Don winced. He'd always winced, but indulgently. Now he did it with real resentment and pain. 'How *can* he?' he kept saying. I said how could he not? Why should he creep around, whispering, all this time afterwards? This was his home, he had his own life to lead. I asked why it didn't make him glad to see Finn so normal, because it made me very glad and relieved indeed.

'Heard from Dad?' Finn asked, before he left. He said it casually, as he said most things. I told him about Don's visit, and that he'd asked for his new mobile number. 'He wants to call you, and to see you,' I said. Finn smiled, but it wasn't his usual open smile – more a rueful expression, half-apologetic. 'Has he finished his investigations?' he asked, stressing the last word satirically. I said I didn't think so, but I hadn't inquired. 'I just don't want to get into any more arguments,' Finn said. 'He's only got one topic, banging on and on, and it's over two years now, it does my head in.' I said it did mine in too. 'You're not like that, Mum,' Finn said. 'You've got over it, why can't he?'

I just shook my head. We had a little more chat, and then he was off, with a kiss and a hug. It amused me to smell the aftershave lotion. I must e-mail Molly and tell her. But when he'd clattered off down the stairs and I'd gone back into my flat, I felt I'd somehow betrayed Don. I should have corrected Finn. I should have pointed out that I had not 'got *over* it' any more than his father had. I simply hide my feelings better. Maybe, it occurred to me, I was offended that Finn thought I'd 'got over it', whereas Don hadn't. Did he tell his friends that 'Mum's fine, she's happy, she's got over it ages ago'? I didn't want to think that he did. Don and I are not in a competition to see who suffers most, who cares most, who is scarred most but, nevertheless, I don't want to be outranked.

5

AFTERWARDS, so many people told us that what we needed to do was 'get right away'. But we didn't take their advice. Apart from that trip Don and I made to Holland, to the place where the accident happened, we all stayed at home. It seemed safer. We hid. We holed up, until Christmas. I wonder every day whether getting 'right away' almost immediately afterwards might indeed have helped. If we had had the energy, the courage, to try it.

But now was the right time to come here, when I'm not afraid to take pleasure. I can sit on this balcony, a wooden affair on the top half of a little house in the grounds of our hotel, and look out to sea and I am not overwhelmed by the memory of another sea. The vast expanse of blue water looks entirely benign. Soon, I will go and swim in it and then I will walk the white sand and pick shells. Everything tragic and ugly is a million miles away. I don't even feel guilty about enjoying myself. But it's true that I am bothered, all the same, by fleeting images of Don. I would rather that Don, the old Don, were with me, and not Lynne. Then, if that Don were here, everything really would be as happy as it is ever again going to be.

Lynne is an irritant. That is an unkind, ungrateful thing to say, but I am only saying it here, to myself. It is years and years since I was with Lynne for more than a day or two and I'd forgotten how annoying she can be. She is so bossy. The moment we arrived, she had our time mapped out without consulting me. I just go along with her decisions. For example, Lynne says it is much too hot to be outside between noon and three o'clock, and so she makes me retire with her to rest, if not sleep, in our room. 'Be sensible, Lou,' she says, and I obediently am.

But I don't sleep. I think of Don. I think of the times we left the children with Judith and indulged ourselves. Four times in twenty-odd years, and each of those holidays was memorable. We would have a siesta after lunch. I can see those hotel rooms now, the shutters closed, the blazing sun struggling to pierce them, coming in through the slits and making patterns on the tiled floors. I can see the bed, festooned with mosquito nets hanging from a hook. I can see Don slipping out of his shorts and coming towards me as I lie on the bed, half drunk, arms behind my head. I can especially remember afterwards, Don instantly asleep, myself drifting in and out of consciousness, hearing the faint lap of the waves outside. Siestas were like that, it was what they were for.

That's a long time ago. I lie on my bed, with Lynne snoring gently on hers, and think how very long ago. Eight years since the last time we went away like that and enjoyed siestas. Since Miranda's death, nothing. No lovemaking. No sex. It was unthinkable, afterwards. It is different for others, I'm told. Extreme grief brings couples closer together. They find relief in sex, it comforts them as it did in that novel, *Unless*. Through it, they can express what can't be expressed in any other way. But we couldn't. Often, I wanted Don to hold me, cuddle me, wrap me in his arms, but he couldn't seem to manage to do it. I would go towards him, my own arms half lifted, my expression, I expect, pleading, and he would do his best. He would hold me, but awkwardly, with distaste, it seemed to me. He would even murmur an apology before breaking away. And I understood, or thought I did. He was afraid of breaking down completely and he felt he could not afford to do so. But maybe that wasn't it at all.

90

I waited. Time passed. A veneer of normality returned, but not in the bedroom. I thought perhaps it was up to me to approach him, and I did, trying to act as I used to, trying to be loving, but he flinched every time I touched him. 'I can't,' he said. 'I just can't, not yet.' And then the next bit – 'I don't know how you ...' and then he'd stop. I'd finish his sentence for him. 'You don't know how I can want to make love, that's it, isn't it? You think it's somehow indecent, because of ...' and he'd stop me. He'd say no, that of course he didn't, but that it was about being too unhappy, too wretched, to take any kind of pleasure. Once his investigations were finished, once the culprit had been brought to justice, then his body wouldn't feel so dead.

I told no one about this. Who could I tell? Not Molly or Finn. Not Judith. Not any of my women friends, though once I almost confided in Ruth. I thought that I must just be patient. I didn't see how Don's normal nature could not in the end reassert itself. I never for one moment thought of urging him to see a therapist – he would be appalled at the idea, anyway – and I thought only briefly of consulting one myself. Embarrassment stopped me, and also a slight feeling of shame, which I couldn't understand – why should *I* feel ashamed? I couldn't bring myself to go to our GP and request help and see the pity in her eyes. Or maybe something else.

I didn't need sex. I told myself that very firmly. It was not important. I needed love. I needed Don to love me, and I felt he still did but that the feeling was dammed up inside him and I didn't know what it would take to release it. When he was ready I'd be there. But it didn't work out like that. After a little over a year, he said he thought we'd both sleep better in separate bedrooms. So he moved out. He moved into the tiny box-room next to his study, and there he stayed until the house was sold.

I didn't need sex. I don't need it. But I'm reminded of it here, and the loss is there. It is painful.

*

Lynne sunbathes seriously. She is on the beach by ten o'clock, flat on her back on a comfortable lounger facing the sun, a book at the ready, together with a cold drink. She is blissfully content. At midday, she suggests that we go for a rum punch to the hotel's beach bar, and I agree. It's an attractive spot, circular, with rattan chairs all round. There are usually a few other guests there, to whom Lynne likes to chat, very graciously. She likes being asked, as she invariably is, where she lives and what she does. I don't say anything. There comes a point when she does the talking for me – 'This is my friend Louise, she's a teacher too.' I see people looking at our wedding rings, and wondering. Lynne deals with that. 'We're on a girls' holiday,' she tells them, 'getting away from everyone.' Inevitably, someone asks about children. It's when Lynne says that I have two, both grown up, that the test arrives.

I can keep quiet, which is what I've usually been doing anyway, or I can contradict her. The contradiction would not be accurate, of course, because Lynne is correct, I do 'have' two children. There is no need to volunteer the information that I once had three. If I do that, I have to say one is now dead. And that will lead to more questions which I don't want to answer. So why provoke a situation I dread? Molly has learned how to do it swiftly. She told me that when she's asked if she has any siblings she always says immediately that she is a twin and that Miranda was killed in an accident when she was eighteen. She is ready for the 'how awful, what happened?' and she gets it over in two or three sentences. Finn doesn't do that. I've heard him being asked the same question and he just says he has a sister. Finished.

But my heart beats wildly, even now. I don't want to name Miranda or say she is dead and yet I feel that if I don't I am denying her. Talking about her, and her death, is too intimate. Why should I share this still excruciatingly painful knowledge with strangers? I don't want to see their curiosity or their concern, or embarrassment. I don't want to hear their eagerness for details.

What do I want, then, if I bring Miranda into conversation? Not sympathy, surely not. I've had plenty of that. Yet there is always this need to give my dead daughter recognition and I struggle with it. I've tried out the sort of response Molly gives but I can't manage, as she can, to be brisk and matter-of-fact. I blurt out that my other daughter was killed and then I can't go on, and whoever I am telling this to is embarrassed for me.

At the beach bar today there was an elderly woman, on her own, newly arrived. She smiled, we smiled back, ordered drinks, Lynne introduced us. She is called Florence, this woman, Florence Hart, and she told us straightaway that she has just been widowed and that this is her first holiday on her own and that it had been very hard, making the decision to come. 'I don't like the idea of dining on my own,' she said. And, of course, Lynne then invited her to join us, without consulting me. She was right to do so. It was kind. But I'd already realised that Florence was garrulous and I didn't know if I wanted to have to listen to her every evening. When she returned home to Yorkshire she was going to go and live with her daughter but wasn't sure that she'd be happy there. 'I don't get on with Lorraine the way I did with Karen, but Karen died. She was killed in a car accident when she was twenty ...'

I left them. I didn't want to hear about Karen or her fatal accident. I am beginning to agree with Don. I don't want to hear about other people's tragedies. I don't want to empathise, to say *I know how they feel*. Even if I think that I do.

*

Lynne is as tired of Florence as I am. Two dinners have been enough. On and on Florence drones, about Herbert, her husband, about Lorraine and her family, and most of all about the dead Karen. I have absolutely forbidden Lynne to mention Miranda, and she has promised me she will not. When Florence said to us that I had no idea what it was like to lose a child, I said nothing. Lynne looked anxiously at me, and changed the subject adroitly. But it is a subject to which Florence likes to return again and again. She is obsessed with the dead Karen. She told us that she has kept her room exactly as it was when Karen died. She goes into it once a week and dusts everything.

Lynne and I have agreed. This can't go on. We will have to think of an excuse not to dine with Florence for the rest of our precious week. Being kind has its limits. I did not do this to people. I didn't burden them with my misery. I didn't – well. I was going to write that I didn't spoil other people's happy times by pushing my own unhappiness onto them. But is this true? My face may have been enough of a dampener, for the first year afterwards at least. I didn't have to say anything. My expression, I suspect, was sufficient. But I couldn't help that.

But I will not share a table again with Florence and if she is at the beach bar I will not go.

*

We wrote and posted postcards today – we'll be back home before they arrive, but Lynne insisted. All part of the holiday, she said – and so we sat and diligently scribbled messages.

I still have Miranda's last card. Posted the day before the accident. It arrived three days after she died. It was a joke. Once, when she was young and on a school trip she sent a card saying, 'I am in Scotland.' That was all. We teased her ever after for only telling us the one thing we knew anyway. Her last card said, 'I am not going to tell you where I am but I am having a brill time, weather fab, company ditto.' She sent Molly one too, *poste restante* to Nice, and Finn, and Judith. Finn wouldn't read his. I tried to hand it to him but he saw the writing and shook his head. 'Morbid,' he said, 'tear it up.' But, of course, I didn't. One of Molly's friends collected her mail in Nice and sent Miranda's card on. It was in a code they'd invented and Molly wouldn't tell me what it said. She said it was just cheeky stuff about Alex. I think she's kept it, though.

*

94

We sat on our balcony late last night, drinking white wine The tree frogs were croaking lustily and we could just faintly hear the sea hissing over the sand. We'd eaten and drunk well, without Florence (who providentially has a new victim, an elderly man). I was half asleep when Lynne spoke, very quietly. It was a question. 'Happy?' she asked. I didn't reply, but I knew that Lynne would just keep on and on until I did, so I said that at this moment I did feel happy. 'And you,' I said, in a mocking tone, 'are you happy, Lynne?' She shocked me by saying that no, she was not.

To hear Lynne state that she was not happy made me uncomfortable. Stupidly, insultingly, I tried to lighten the atmosphere, which had suddenly become tense and jumpy. 'Oh, come on,' I said, 'who could not be happy after all this wine we've drunk – have some more.' She was silent and I felt ashamed. 'Sorry,' I said. Silence again. I couldn't see her clearly – the candlelight was meagre and we had put the lights out in our room behind us – but I leaned forward and peered at her in the gloom and was alarmed to see what might be a tear running down her cheek. Even as I saw it, she had brushed it away.

'Lynne,' I said, 'tell me.' She sniffed, and then gave a little laugh, a characteristic Lynne laugh, self-deprecating, and said, 'Oh, I don't know. It just keeps coming over me that I'm not happy. Something's wrong. I don't know what. Nothing serious. It's probably hormones.' Her voice was stronger, she wasn't almost whispering any more. 'Do you think,' she asked, 'it's because I couldn't have children? Do you think all the pretending that I didn't mind is catching up with me? Or is that fanciful?' I said I thought it was fanciful.

We sat there until after midnight. One by one the other lights went off and a deep darkness obliterated the outlines of the cottages on the far side of the garden. Every other night, the stars had been a sharp, glittering mass above us, but last night clouds hid them and there was no moon. The atmosphere suddenly felt a little sinister though we were perfectly safe. It was still very warm, but I found myself shivering slightly. I was sure that Lynne wanted to tell me more but that she couldn't express whatever it was that she was feeling, and I wasn't helping her.

As a friend, I failed. She was the first to move. 'Bed,' she said, in her usual brisk tone of voice. I followed her inside. We shut the shutters. I was so glad to sleep.

*

Our last day. A nice little scene to start it. Florence emerged for breakfast, accompanied by her new friend. She gave us a regal wave, and then sat with her back to us. She was wearing a pair of vivid orange Capri pants, revealing what are still very elegant ankles, and a white top zipped up to her neck, hiding her wrinkled chest. From behind, she could have been our age and not, as we knew she was, in her seventies. Her friend seemed in awe of her. She talked and talked and he listened and said not a word. He was rather distinguished himself – tall and lean and though his hair was white he had plenty of it.

'Maybe a romance is on the cards,' I murmured to Lynne. 'Lucky Florence,' she said. She looked wistful. 'Lynne!' I said, and then she did laugh. But was this what that late-night confession was about? Did Lynne yearn for a romance?

Lying on our loungers that last morning, I took up what Lynne had said – it was odd, the way the bright sunlight made it easier than the dark night had done to become personal. I asked why she had seemed to envy the aged Florence a possible romance. At first, she was evasive but then, from behind the shelter of sunglasses and hat, she said, 'I just want some excitement, that's all. I never seem to have had any real excitement in my whole life.' 'But you haven't had the wrong sort of excitement either,' I said. She took her sunglasses off and looked at me. 'You know I didn't mean that, Lou,' she said. 'I just meant that everything in my life has been humdrum, predictable, no surprises, everything chugging along satisfactorily. If I'd had children ...' I didn't take this up. 'Well,' she went on, 'children bring excitement all the time, don't they? Life is never dull, watching them grow up, being involved in whatever they are doing.' 'I thought it was romance you wanted,' I said, 'that kind of excitement.' She laughed and put her sunglasses on and lay down again.

She's right, children do provide a certain sort of excitement, there's a natural drama to having them. But then there is so much fear too, and this can sometimes seem to outweigh the excitement of the pleasant variety. I don't think I've ever controlled it properly. The awful worry about safety has often overwhelmed me, right from when my children were born, and as for fretting about their happiness – that has been never-ending. It was one of the more bewildering things that people said afterwards about Miranda's death, that she had had a short but *happy* life, as though that would comfort me. It was no comfort. Her life, I reckoned, had in fact been too short to know real happiness. I looked at my own life and saw that my true happiness lay in meeting and marrying Don and in giving birth to my three children. Miranda never experienced any of that. Her happiness, at eighteen, was a restricted happiness.

And there was Lynne, feeling unhappy, craving what she called excitement, confusing it with happiness.

*

I went, on my own, for a longer walk than the beach offered. I went along the road to a track leading up the hill to a little church I'd noticed. It was evening, before dinner, and cooler, but I wore a straw hat to shade me from the still strong sun. I wanted to watch the sunset in half an hour's time, and planned to be on top of the hill by then. I walked slowly not because the path was steep but to avoid churning up the dust. I was so self-absorbed that it wasn't until I was almost at the church that I saw the procession. It came from the other direction. I stopped just in time not to be noticed and lingered behind a bush. It was a funeral procession. A white coffin was being carried by six men in black suits and behind them were thirty or forty people, the men in black, the women mostly in white. They were singing, but I couldn't make out the words, and as they sang they walked in a curious swaying motion, their heads moving from side to side in time with the song. I could see a preacher standing at the church door and beside him a boy carrying a cross. I turned and hurried back down the hill.

We had dreadful arguments about a funeral. There was no body, we had nothing to bury or cremate. How could we have a funeral, in any understood sense? But Don wanted something. Not a church service, but some sort of memorial service at which we would all talk about Miranda. I accused him of wanting to use such an occasion for publicity purposes, so that he could set forth his theories about negligence being the cause of her death and try to precipitate the inquiry he wanted. He said I was perfectly right and that there was nothing wrong with wanting to do this. But I couldn't bear the prospect of hearing him rant about murder and killers and justice not being done, and all when we were mourning Miranda. Molly, as ever, was the peacemaker. She said it was too soon. We should wait. And we did. We waited so long that there never was a memorial service, and I was relieved.

A proper funeral, such as the one I had just glimpsed, might have been different. Afterwards, I felt the lack of a coffin and of some formal service. I suppose I wanted the comfort of the ritual, the dressing in black, the open tears, the laying to rest, however it was done. I would have liked a gravestone or some such symbol. I would like to have stood in front of it and seen Miranda's name and her dates and the words 'beloved daughter of Louise and Gordon'. But there was nothing. Her body was never, as expected, washed ashore, giving rise to unspeakable suspicions of what had happened to it. We gave her school some money to give a prize every year in her memory. That is her memorial. It isn't enough.

*

98

Strange, thinking this morning about going home as I packed. 'Home' is not really home as I had known it for twenty years. My flat hasn't had time to become home. After every holiday we had, I always liked reaching home, however enjoyable it had been.

Going home today will be a test. I'm not sure I will pass it. I might feel dismayed as I go up the stairs and open the door onto ... what? Four small neat rooms with no history. Miranda had never been within their walls. There is nothing at all to remind me of her, not even photographs. This is my home, and no one else's.

*

Our seats were not together on the plane. Lynne made a great fuss but it did no good. I wasn't worried. It was a night flight and I wanted to sleep, so it seemed immaterial to me where we sat. Lynne was behind me in any case, should I wish to talk to her (and as we'd been talking for a week there was nothing left to talk about). I had an aisle seat beside a young couple. The man was next to me, the woman next to the window. I decided they were returning from their honeymoon – they held hands, and both wore very bright gold wedding rings. We smiled at each other, and settled ourselves, and I closed my eyes, preparing to try to sleep, and put an eyeshade on. Then I heard him say. 'Miranda, do you want your book? Because it's in the bag I've put in the overhead locker. Shall I get it?' She said no, she was too sleepy to read.

My heart thudded, hearing her name, the way it so stupidly does, as though my Miranda was the only one. I turned my head very slightly and peeped from under my eyeshade. She was about the age my Miranda would have been. She had blonde hair, like my Miranda, and was tanned and healthy-looking, and slim and pretty – all like my Miranda. But her face was very different, much narrower, the nose longer, the forehead higher. I calmed down.

When we landed at Gatwick this morning, I saw her stand up and realised this Miranda was much too small to have been my Miranda. She didn't look like a Miranda at all. I felt she wasn't really entitled to the name. The silliness of this thought meant I was smiling as we came into the arrivals area. 'You look happy, Mum,' Finn said.

*

I should have known that Finn would not be meeting me at Gatwick just to please me, to give me a lovely surprise, which it did. That sounds bitter, but it is not. I would never want anyone to drag all that way when it's perfectly easy to get the train to Victoria and a taxi from there. Meetings at airports are only for special occasions, in our family, for those returning after long absences. When Molly comes back, I will certainly meet her whatever time she lands.

But Finn was there, and there was a moment of pure pleasure at the sight of him. He even looked presentable, wearing a very clean white T-shirt and smart-looking black chinos (which should have been another clue). It wasn't until he said he had a minicab waiting that I realised something was wrong. 'Minicab?' I queried, and then 'Finn, tell me. Whatever it is, just tell me.' So he told me, standing there in the middle of the arrivals hall, scores of travellers rushing past and a loudspeaker booming some incomprehensible information. Lynne had taken hold of my arm and was squeezing it, thinking, I suppose, to reassure me that support was there for whatever I was going to have to bear. 'Everything's fine, honest,' Finn said, at first, and then, 'It's Dad. He's OK, but he had a slight accident. He's in hospital, the Middlesex.'

Lynne was going in the opposite direction, so didn't come in the minicab with us. We said goodbye, hurriedly. I didn't even thank her properly for arranging our holiday, which I must do. Once we were settled in the back of the car, I asked Finn to tell me exactly what had happened, but he didn't seem to know. He said he'd had a phone call at work from Judith, asking him if he could go to the Middlesex hospital where his dad had been admitted after an accident. She was in bed with a bad back and couldn't go herself. So he'd gone there, and found Don in bed, in a room of his own. He wasn't attached to any tubes or anything and he looked just as if he was asleep. There was a plaster, a transparent plaster, not very big, on his forehead covering what looked like a couple of stitches. No blood. Finn spoke to him, but he didn't open his eyes. After a few minutes, he spoke again. Still no response. There was a chart hanging on the end of the bed but Finn couldn't understand it. Eventually, he went to find a nurse to tell him what was wrong with his father. It took ages – they were all very busy, rushing about in the ward next to Don's room. He stood at the desk and waited, and finally a nurse asked him whom he was visiting and he told her and she said the staff nurse would come and explain, and he should go back to his father's bed and wait, which he did. Don still appeared asleep or unconscious. When the staff nurse did come, she asked first where his mother was and said she should be contacted. Finn hadn't liked to say his parents were separated, so he just said I was on holiday, back the next day. He asked what had happened, and was told his father had collapsed in Tottenham Court Road, hitting his head on a traffic bollard. It was thought that he was concussed, but he had not come round from his faint, if it had been a faint. He was going to be given a brain scan, to check for any other reason for his collapse.

'I hate hospitals,' Finn said, at the end of this account. 'I just wanted to get out.' I said, of course, he did, we all do. We've been a healthy family, with little experience of hospitals, thank God. And it was one thing we were spared, or so I tried to tell myself, when Miranda was killed. We didn't have to sit beside a bed in a hospital ward, seeing her with tubes stuck into her, watching her die. We didn't have to go through the horror of identifying her in a hospital morgue. A pathetic attempt to catch sight of an entirely elusive silver lining, but I tried.

I said that Finn should carry on in the cab, taking my case, and that I would go to see Don on my own. He was very easily persuaded. I said I'd go to Judith's after I'd found out what was happening, and meet him there. Judith would be alarmed and want to know anyway. So I was dropped off, feeling shaky and tired, and not at all as though I'd just come back from a wonderful week in the sun, and I made my way into the Middlesex, a hospital I'd never had reason to visit before. It was bewildering, with more corridors and staircases than seemed possible, but after getting lost several times I found the ward. There was a toilet next to it and I went into it first and washed my face and brushed my hair. My face looked odd in the mirror, calm but strained, as though it were a mask. I saw a nerve twitching to the right of my right eye, and put up a hand to stop it. I'd seen this face before. It used to stare back at me, afterwards. I hated it.

Then I was ready. I was ready to see Don, whatever state he was in. All the way from Gatwick, listening to Finn, I'd been saying over and over in my head 'it isn't Molly, it isn't Molly' – the relief! I could tolerate something dreadful happening to Don, but not to Molly or Finn – that was the shameful truth. I'd felt no surge of terror when Finn told me Don was in hospital. Slowly, on the long drive to the hospital, I had begun to feel anxious and troubled about Don and what might have happened, but there was a certain luxury about my concern. I could afford it. This was awful to admit, but I didn't have to admit it to anyone but myself. It showed me that my love for Don had been altered, maybe damaged, more than I had thought. He'd done most of the damage himself.

The nurse, who took me in to see him, said he was about to be moved into the general ward but I could have half an hour with him in the side-room. She told me that a brain scan had shown no abnormalities, no sign of a haemorrhage. He hadn't had a stroke, or a seizure. It seemed that it had been a simple faint, probably due to lack of food. He was malnourished and dehydrated and his blood pressure was very low and, of course, he had been concussed. They were going to keep him in another night and then I could take him home. I nodded.

Don had his eyes closed. He was lying very still in the bed, the covers up to his neck, his arms underneath them. He was very pale, and gaunt, his cheekbones standing out alarmingly. I said his name, and his eyelids flickered, but he didn't open them. I sat down at the bedside and waited. I didn't kiss him. If his hand had been above the covers, I might have held it, but it wasn't. I just waited. I was there. I had come straight to him. It was enough, surely.

6

IT FELT good, after all, coming back here. Not exactly like coming 'home', but definitely a relief and a pleasure – it was reassuring to find the flat quite familiar and not as soulless as I'd feared. Maybe it felt welcoming because I'd come to it straight from the hospital, before I went to Judith's. I felt I had to check myself in first, and change my clothes, and then I could face my sister-in-law, who I knew would have lots of questions. It was the second time that she'd had to take our family's bad news and pass it on (and all because hers was the only phone number listed on Don's mobile that answered when the hospital called).

Finn was there, of course, watching football on Judith's television, a plate of sandwiches at his side and a can of lager in his hand. No reason why he shouldn't have been. He did put the sound down to ask in what I recognised as a deliberately casual tone of voice, how Don was, and I replied in the same style, saying he was fine, no real damage done, it had just been a faint, probably due to lack of food. 'He doesn't look after himself,' Finn said, biting into a sandwich. I agreed. 'What'll they do?' he asked. 'What'll they do with him?' I said there wasn't much they could do. They'd feed him, and tell him to eat sensibly, and send him home. 'Home?' queried Finn. 'Home,' I repeated. 'Where's that, these days?' Finn asked. 'Wherever he's living,' I said, too abruptly, so that for a moment he took his eyes off the screen and we stared at each other, each knowing how worried the other really felt.

I didn't stay long. I was exhausted, and it was school today. Judith had heroically got out of bed to prepare a simple supper for me, but I couldn't eat it. She, too, started on what was going to happen to Don. 'He needs looking after,' she said. 'You've seen him, he's just a skeleton, it's dreadful.' I nodded, not trusting myself to reply to this with the unkind words that he is a grown man and it is his own fault, because that was what I was thinking. 'You know he's lost his job? He's been fired.' Judith said. That did shock me, and yet it shouldn't have done. I'd known Don's agency must at some point get tired of his absences on 'investigations'. They'd been tolerant, they'd put up with a lot. I'd always assumed that Don's flashes of inspiration, even if rare now, had been worth his neglect of his work for long stretches of time, but maybe these days inspiration wasn't flashing at all, and the advertising world had decided it could do without him. 'Didn't he tell you?' Judith said, seeing my face. He hadn't. We hadn't spoken for a while and when we had it had been about Finn. 'Oh, he came here,' Judith said, 'wanting to talk to Finn, but he was out, I didn't know where. He wouldn't stay. But he left his mobile number and his address. Look, that's where he is living.' She dug a scrap of paper out of the kitchen table drawer and handed it to me. It was an address in Green Lanes, Tottenham. Not the kind of road I'd have imagined Don, who likes peace and quiet, choosing. Cheap, though. What kind of flat could he have rented in a place like that? Maybe it really was only a bedsitter. It was distressing to imagine it.

'He can't go back there,' Judith was saying. 'He's sick, he needs looking after.' I reminded her she'd already said that. 'Well,' she said, 'you don't seem to care – no, no, sorry Lou, I didn't mean that, what I meant was you don't seem worried at the thought, that's all.' I told her that what worried me was what she seemed to be hinting at: that I should look after Don in my flat. 'Am I right,' I said, 'is that what you've got in mind? Do you see it as my duty?' She shook her head vehemently and denied it, but of course I was right, it was exactly what she had been thinking. 'Judith,' I said, trying hard to speak quietly and calmly, 'I'm as upset as you at the state Don has got himself into, but it isn't going to force me into becoming responsible for him again. I've tried. You know I've tried, but I can't cope with him while he goes on being obsessed. He was making me ill too. I can't try again, just when I'm beginning to recover and have my own life back. I can't.' Judith reached across the table and patted my hand. There were tears in her eyes. 'I know,' she said, 'I know. You've been wonderful, you've ...' I stopped her. 'I'm going home now, Judith,' I said. 'I need to sleep, and it's school tomorrow. But I'll call you, after I've seen Don again. I can't think straight now.' We kissed – Judith's cheek so warm and soft and scented with vanilla soap – and I went and said goodnight to Finn, and kissed him, lightly, on the side of his head (and smelled smoke ... is he smoking now?).

*

That was yesterday. Today was busy, too busy until four o'clock even to think about Don. First day back after a holiday is always chaos. Every child seemed to have forgotten the routines we follow and to need constant individual attention. The vocal ones – Paige, Sophie, Haroun – clamoured for it, wanting me to listen to where they had been and what they had done. The quieter ones plucked at my jacket and whispered and then cried when I didn't hear them, and they felt ignored. Jeremy and I struggled to restore order and make them feel secure and attempt some semblance of teaching, but it was only towards the end of the day that anything like normality was achieved. At story time, there was silence. When I'd finished reading, I told them all that tomorrow I want them to remember what we do in class. What do we do first? That's right. And then? That's right. And what do we do now, after story time? Yes! Then let's do it. And they did. They got their coats and sat on the mat until their names were called as their parents arrived.

The classroom was messy. I told Jeremy to put it to rights, because I had to dash off. I didn't tell him why, or where to, just said I'd do my share another day when he wanted to go promptly himself. It's the good thing about having Jeremy – he's very biddable and not normally very curious about me, a convenient combination. I was at the Middlesex by four-thirty, which was good going. I could have been even earlier if I hadn't stopped to buy something for Don. Not grapes. It's the only fruit he doesn't care for. I bought peaches, his favourite, and some bananas because he clearly needs carbohydrates. I needn't have bothered. When I got to his room, he'd gone. I thought at first he'd simply been moved into the general ward, which I'd been told would happen, but then he wasn't there either. 'He discharged himself,' the sister I finally found told me. 'About an hour ago.'

She said he would have been discharged by the doctor tomorrow anyway, so it didn't really make much difference. I asked if he was well enough to go, and she said yes, but of course he needed to be sensible and eat and drink properly or he'd faint again. He'd been advised to go and see his GP and keep having his blood pressure monitored, and he'd been given a prescription for iron tablets and vitamins to take to the hospital pharmacy. 'You'll probably find him at home when you get back,' the sister said. 'He'll have passed you on the way without realising. He should have phoned, shouldn't he?' I said yes, he should have, and left, clutching the fruit.

And now here I am wondering what to do. Writing this down should have cleared my mind, but it doesn't seem to have done.

*

Three days have passed, and no one has heard from Don. We ring him, but his mobile is switched off. We tried to discover

107

his landline number at the address he'd given Finn, but there was none registered. I rang all the North London hospitals, just to check he hadn't collapsed again and been admitted. There was nothing for it but to go to Green Lanes and find the house or flat or room where he lives, something I didn't want to do but, as time went on, felt I couldn't avoid. Finn went with me. I didn't ask, or expect him to do so, but without making a fuss about it, he volunteered and, since I dreaded what I might find, I let him come.

The house was at the busiest end of that long, ugly road. To the left of the battered-looking front door – by the look of the bottom panels, which were splintered, it had been kicked repeatedly – there was a row of bell pushes, eight of them, each with a name alongside it. Don's was not one of them. But three of the names had been crossed out, so I assumed he hadn't bothered to put his name on whichever was his bell. He wouldn't have anticipated visitors, or wanted them – it would have suited him to be unnamed. Finn and I wondered what to do, which bell to ring first in the hope that we would hit lucky and it would be Don's, but as we were deliberating the front door opened and a tall, bearded, wild-looking man came out. He was as startled as we were. We stood back as he hesitated, pulling the door behind him. 'Excuse me,' I said, 'but do you know if Don Roscoe lives here? Which is his bell?' He shook his head and said, 'No, no,' repeatedly, then made a run for it, his long coat flapping in the wind.

It was such a lost opportunity. We cursed ourselves for not being quick enough actually to get into the house when the door had opened. It was no good just standing there, so I pressed the first of the bells which had a crossed-out name beside it. We couldn't hear if it was ringing or not – maybe none of these bells worked. I rang again, hard, then after what I thought a long enough wait I rang the next one. Immediately, a window opened on the top floor and a woman stuck her head out and yelled, 'What? What?' 'I've come to visit Don Roscoe,' I shouted back. 'Do you know which is his bell?' 'Never heard of him, and I was *asleep*, get it? Asleep!' I apologised and began to describe Don, but she had slammed the window shut again and, presumably, gone back to bed, though it was four in the afternoon.

The last crossed-out name was at the very bottom. Finn pointed out that this probably meant it belonged to a ground-floor room and that we might be able to peer through the window and maybe we'd spot some sign that it was Don's. I rang the bell just in case. There was no response. Both ground-floor windows had dirty-looking net curtains across them, and one had heavy curtains, almost closed, over them. These windows were quite high up, for ground-floor windows, and Finn looked around for something to stand on. He was just carrying over an empty dustbin when a postman arrived, a young man dragging a trolley on wheels full of post. 'Breaking and entering, eh?' he said, very cheerfully, and then 'Forgotten your key?' I nodded, not sure what to say. He was sorting out letters. They all looked like bills, except for one, which I could see had a foreign stamp. Finn nudged me – he'd seen what I'd seen – and I said quickly, 'That's my husband's.' He gave it to me without a second thought – looking such a respectable middle-aged woman has its advantages. He shouldn't have given me Don's letter of course. I imagined it might get him into serious trouble, but no one need find out. The address of the sender was on the back. I recognised it. It was from Holland, where else. I put it in my pocket. It would keep.

Meanwhile, Finn was standing on the upturned dustbin and peering into the window to the left of the door. He reported that the room was empty. We'd definitely heard the sound of the bell coming from there so if it *was* Don's room, and if it was empty … well, that was good.

'Good,' I said aloud.

'Why?' asked Finn.

'Means he hasn't collapsed again on the floor,' I said, quickly.

'He might have collapsed somewhere else. That would be worse,' Finn said, getting down.

'If he has, someone will call an ambulance and he'll turn up in some hospital again. But he hasn't so far, or we'd know. I've rung the North London hospitals already.'

'What are we going to do now, then?'

'Go home.'

And here I am, still endlessly trying Don's mobile, still waiting for him to contact one of us, still with the letter in my pocket.

*

I should tell Molly. It isn't right to keep her in the dark, but I so hate worrying her. What can I tell her? That her father fell – fainted – in the street, spent a night in hospital, discharged himself and then disappeared? What would be the good, when she is so far away? And she sounds so happy and busy, her e-mails and text messages full of detail about what she's doing. 'Don't tell her,' Finn said, 'it's pointless.' I think he's right.

*

The class has quietened down, thank God. We had a good day today. It was Parveen's birthday and her father has come from Iran, where she was born. He looks emaciated, with long hair and beard, a hollow-eyed, suffering appearance. Naomi, Parveen's mother, carefully following what she's seen is the custom among the mothers in our class, brought in a cake, definitely home-made, which I cut up and we all had a piece. It was an odd-tasting cake – 'Yuk!' said Paige, and spat it out – made, I guessed, with some kind of strongly scented honey. Parveen is proud of her father having come. 'I have a father,' she told me, 'see?' and she pointed at him as he waited at the door. 'He don't live with you,' Paige said, accusingly. 'My dad lives with me, all the time. That's what dads do.' 'Not all dads, Paige,' I said. 'Every family is different.' He was quite a striking man, a powerful presence, even though so frighteningly thin. I

110

could see Parveen was shy with him. He stood at the open door and held out a hand, but didn't smile, or bend down to her level. His eyes met mine over her head. 'She has been good?' he asked. 'No trouble?' I laughed, and said Parveen was never any trouble, her behaviour was impeccable, she was a pleasure to have in the class. 'And me,' Paige said, still at my side, but I ignored her. 'I am Zahid,' he said, 'her father.' I said I was pleased to have met him, and off they went, Parveen holding his hand. I watched them from the window as they crossed the playground. He did not speak to her, or look at her, just held her hand and walked with his head in the air like a kind of God.

It worried me. I wonder if anything will emerge in Parveen's behaviour to indicate how important her father is to her, or what his visit has meant to her. It's always easy to see how important mothers are to my pupils, but often harder to calculate the influence of their fathers.

*

Judith thinks that we should inform the police of Don's disappearance. Four days without any of us hearing from him, and with no reply from his mobile, is too long. Is it? I don't know. I pointed out to her that more than four days have often passed without any of us being in touch with Don. These long breaks in communication are part of a fairly regular pattern lately. But it's true, as Judith pointed out, that he hasn't been ill before. We haven't in the past been worried about him collapsing. I said I thought we should wait a little longer before going to the police. Don could be abroad, on 'investigations'.

I'd thought, just briefly, that when Finn and I went to Green Lanes we might find that Don had ... well, I don't like writing down my morbid fear. Afterwards, it had seemed something that he might end up doing, so extreme was his grief, but rage and his quest for justice (as he thought of it) kept him from doing anything silly. Silly? It wouldn't have been silly. It would

111

have been tragic, compounding the tragedy we were already suffering. He did, though, about six months afterwards, say one night that he couldn't go on, there was no point. I thought he meant go on with his investigations and it was a relief to hear him say this. But that wasn't at all what he meant, though it took me a while to register this. When I did – he said he just wanted to 'have done' with everything – I was appalled.

There has always been this streak in Don, this melancholic undertone to his apparently gentle, cheerful nature. Very few people glimpse it. I'm quite sure that no one at work ever suspected it existed. It would overwhelm him sometimes, what he called the hopelessness of life, and he had to struggle to control his gloom. If he had been a woman, I'm sure hormones would have been blamed, but as it was it seemed a mystery. They didn't last long, these moods, though they were more than mere moods – a couple of days, and then he'd be back to normal. I learned how to deal with them. Oddly enough, distraction was not the key, that was my mistake in the early years of our marriage, believing that he needed to be jollied out of his depression. He didn't. He needed the opposite, the seclusion I'd thought the worst possible thing. Sometimes it meant letting him stay in bed. I'd phone the office and say he had a stomach bug, or flu, or something, and I'd tell the children the same. Everyone accepted this. He always looked convincingly pale and shaken when he emerged, seemingly confirming the truthfulness of my explanation.

Judith told me he had had what her mother had called these 'turns' as a boy. They started when he was twelve. He wouldn't go to school, wouldn't eat, wouldn't speak, but because he was back to his usual cheerful self so quickly, within a day or two, no doctor was ever consulted. Their mother thought he was just being a sulky teenager and that he'd grow out of it which, since he learned how to conceal his 'turns' from her, she always believed he had done. Judith herself thought that marrying me had 'cured' him, but she was quick to see through my protective lies when I had to tell them. She challenged me once when I said we couldn't come to supper after all because Don had a chest infection and had to stay in bed. 'What does the doctor say?' she asked me, and when I hesitated, she said, 'It's one of his old turns, isn't it?' There wasn't much point in saying no.

Don always worried that one of our children would inherit his depressive tendency but none of them have done so, though for a year or two it did look as if Miranda might. She was very moody and easily upset around puberty, but then lots of girls are, and I reassured Don her behaviour was quite normal. He watched her anxiously, though, whereas Molly never came under such close scrutiny. I did sometimes wonder if Don's reaction to Miranda's death was stronger than it would have been to Molly's or Finn's. It was unfair, but I couldn't help this suspicion that it was because it was Miranda, his favourite, who had died that he wanted to die too. Parents are not supposed to have favourites among their children, or at least not to acknowledge that they have, but Don admitted it, though only to me. He put it rather well. He said he *loved* them all equally, but that he identified most with Miranda because she seemed like him. I'm not sure that this was really true, but Don believed it was. Life without Miranda became simply less precious to Don.

But, of course, part of the reason why I was so shocked by what Don had said was because I had been tempted myself. Not seriously – I assured myself I had never seriously allowed myself to have this appalling thought – but it had floated before me in the middle of many a miserable night. Just to have done with this anguish, that was all. To stop the pain, the endless suffering and distress. I never imagined actually doing it, killing myself. I never contemplated how I might do it. It was more that I imagined sleep, a real, deep, everlasting sleep, then a blankness – how beautiful it would be. I never thought of this as a way of joining Miranda – nothing like that. But then always I saw Molly's and Finn's faces and was ashamed and angry with myself. All that guilty anger went into attacking Don when he spoke of what I had kept silent about.

I remember trembling as I sat up in bed and put the bedside light on. I couldn't go on lying beside him. I got out of bed and went round to his side and looked down at him lying there, his eyes closed, his arms behind his head. 'Look at me,' I ordered him. 'Look at me, Don, *look* at me!' He didn't open his eyes and I reached out and struck his shoulder and repeated my words. He sighed and turned his head away but opened his eyes. I forced his head back towards me and held his face in my hands. I was weeping by then, but his eyes had no tears in them. They were tired eyes, red-rimmed, frighteningly without expression. 'Never,' I said, 'never, never do this to us, never!' He closed his eyes again and sighed, and I let go. I stood for a while, shivering, half with cold, half with fear, and then I tamely got back into bed and curled up on my side and tried to sleep.

This was at the most dangerous time, six months afterwards. Everything was black to him, no glimmer of light anywhere. I don't flatter myself that I prevented him from doing anything dramatic. No, it was shame did that. The next morning, I could see he was ashamed. It happened to be a frosty, sparkling January morning. I got up, aching all over after my sleepless night, most of which I'd spent weeping in a particularly weak way, the tears just endlessly, silently flowing, and as I opened the curtains the sun lit the frosted garden and I said out loud, 'Oh, look! How lovely!' Don came up behind me, and put his hands on my shoulders, and looked. The leafless trees were glittering with a fine powdering of snow which had set hard and was now caught by the sun, and all the shrubs were wrapped in thick white canopies making them bow to the ground. The bird house had icicles hanging from its roof and on the frozen water in the bird bath a leaf lay caught at the edge by the ice, half-submerged, half free. The holly tree was heavy with berries still and the red stood out, clusters of colour contrasting with the purity of all the white. But most beautiful of all was the lawn, an unbroken, unmarked white, sweeping its way between the brick walls to end in a great bank of snow on the little hill at the bottom where the gate leads into the tennis courts. Everything was serene, innocent. Or so it seemed.

We didn't speak of what he had told me. I was determined not to speak to him at all until he gave me some sign that he realised how unforgivable his confession had been. I think I was frightened that morning, of what he might really do. I wanted to break down myself and say *I* couldn't go on, but there was Finn to think of, wanting to know if I knew where his bus pass was, and my own things to get ready for school, and the humdrum nature of the morning rituals carried me along. But before he left for work, Don paused at the door and said, 'I wasn't feeling so well, I'll be fine now.' 'Stomach bug?' I said. His smile was feeble, but at least it was attempted. 'Stomach bug,' he said.

*

I told Ruth about Don disappearing, the first person I have told. She rang to see how I enjoyed my holiday with Lynne, and I told her. 'Poor man,' she said. That slightly annoyed me, but I managed to agree, if a bit half-heartedly. I told her Don had lost his job too. 'Oh,' she said, 'that's very bad news.' It was at least easy genuinely to agree with that. 'So,' said Ruth, 'he's wandering round somewhere with no job and in a weakened state and not answering phone calls … It's serious, Lou. You'll have to do something. His sister's right.' I said I knew that, but going to the police seems so drastic. 'You just report him as a missing person, that's all,' said Ruth. 'You never know, he may just have lost his memory.'

I wanted to say that Don had been a missing person for a long time now, 'missing' even when with me. And as for loss of memory, he suffered from the opposite. His memory was acute. It tormented him. He thought only of Miranda and her death and his investigations. There was no room for anything else in his memory.

*

I opened the letter to Don. It was wrong of me, but I excused myself on the grounds that it might tell me where he had got to. I didn't try to open it so that it could be sealed up again – no, I ripped it open. It was a very short letter, merely thanking him for his latest letter and saying that it was being dealt with and had been put on file with the others. He would, as ever, be informed of the outcome of their enquiries into the particular matter in due course.

He has scores of such letters from a wide variety of people. Each time a letter with that foreign postmark arrived his face would first light up with hope and then darken, after he'd read it, with disappointment. I grew to hate the post arriving and learned to absent myself after it had. His silence always told me everything.

*

I stopped reading newspapers, afterwards. We still had them delivered but I never even turned the pages. But somebody must have done. They got lifted up from the mat behind the front door and later I'd find them in the recycling box. For a long time, I didn't watch the news on television either but sometimes I heard it on the radio, which I listened to a lot – radio seemed so much less demanding than television. I'd catch items which, at one time, would have shocked me, and had me aching with sympathy for the people involved. Boys swept out to sea, I heard once, while fishing from rocks, and not seen since; a British teenager drowned trying to cross a stream, swollen by flash floods, somewhere on the Aegean coast; a young sportsman, at the beginning of a great football career, smashed to pieces in a horrific car accident. I felt nothing that first year afterwards. Nothing.

But I felt something when I heard good news about young people. Anger, mostly, that they were alive to celebrate. I couldn't help catching sight of the usual beaming, lovely girls, captured on the front pages of newspapers as they opened their A level results. The twins' results came soon after Miranda was killed. Molly went to their school and brought Miranda's home as well as her own. They were good. Not brilliant, but good enough for her to have been able to take up her place at Loughborough. Molly's were excellent, exceeding requirements. How they would have celebrated, and us with them. Miranda had had to work so hard, really slog, especially over biology. To get a C was a triumph. A completely pointless triumph, as it turned out. I hated those pictures in the newspapers.

So it wasn't surprising that I didn't know about Emma, a girl who had been in the twins' class. It was Finn who told me. He turned up wearing a suit yesterday. The only suit he's ever owned and it is too small for him. He had a tie, too, a tie I've never seen before and which I didn't know he possessed (he'd borrowed it, of course). 'Heavens,' I said, and, 'You're not going for an interview somewhere, are you?' 'Been to a funeral,' he said. I didn't want to ask whose. He was irritated. 'You must know,' he said. 'It was in the papers.' I reminded him that I didn't read newspapers, not even the local one. 'Well, you should,' he snapped. There was no point getting into arguments. As quietly as possible, I asked whose funeral. It must be somebody I knew, however vaguely, if he knew them well enough to go to their funeral. 'Emma Carter's,' he said. I was shocked, and, in fact, it was a relief to feel shocked instead of indifferent.

I sat down, and Finn pottered about, looking in my fridge, taking an apple from the bowl on the table. He wasn't going to tell me anything unless I begged for the information – his silence was a punishment, and I knew it. 'I'm sorry,' I said, eventually, and 'how awful.' He nodded. Did I want to know how the poor girl died? No. But because I didn't ask, and instead wondered how his work was going, Finn chose to tell me after all. 'Suicide,' he said. 'An overdose. Left a note and everything. "No point in life ..." etc.' He sounded laconic to the point of callousness, but his act didn't fool me. We stared at each other, Finn frowning heavily. 'She was nice,' he said. 'She was popular too. It doesn't make any kind of sense. It wasn't as if there was anything wrong in her life. Her father said that at the funeral. He said it was "inexplicable". The vicar said that as well, but he said her family shouldn't feel guilty, it wasn't their fault. But they think it was. You could tell. Just the look of them.'

Guilt? It wasn't something we had had to suffer from, but maybe we should have done. I thought of what we might have been guilty of. Not knowing our daughter well enough? Not knowing how she really felt about Alex? Or perhaps more mundane things, of not at least ringing his parents as Don had wanted to, and asking about their boat and inquiring how competent Alex was to teach her sailing. But she was eighteen, she wanted to manage her own life. We would have looked fussy, as I'd told him, interfering. But we never talked about guilt. Strange.

Finn left me silent and somehow ashamed. I hadn't known Emma's parents well. The slight contact we had had through our daughters had long since ended. They wrote, I remember, after Miranda died. But I don't recall what they said. The usual platitudes, I expect. I didn't keep their letter. Should I write? No, it would be insulting, writing now, so long after the event (though I hadn't asked Finn when that was). There wasn't anything I could do to show my … my what? How I shared their distress and misery? But do I? I can't, just as no one could share mine. They wouldn't be interested in how shocked I was, in how I felt for them. They have enough to bear, without the weight of an acquaintance's pity.

Yet there's something wrong with that reasoning. I, of all people, know that. I should have been at the funeral. I should have read the newspaper. Finn should have told me.

*

Sports Day. Not a proper Sports Day – we don't have those any more, goodness me, no – but I can't help calling it that. We took the entire school to the running track and there were races, but with prizes for all, last as well as first. The children loved it, even the completely uncoordinated ones. Paige, surprisingly, was one of these. She's tall and big and strong, but she can't run for toffee, whereas skinny little Haroun runs like the wind. But as usual Paige didn't recognise failure or defeat. I heard her telling Haroun the track was too short. If it had been the *right* length, in the end she would have caught and passed him. Haroun accepted this without question. They all got rosettes. Haroun's was the only red one but Paige turned that into something to pity him for. 'We all won, didn't we, Miss?' she added. 'Not exactly, Paige,' I said, 'not exactly.'

*

The week is over. I didn't need Judith to ring and leave that message on my answer phone. I was going to report Don's absence anyway. Judith refers to it as his 'suspicious disappearance', but that is too melodramatic. It would sound as if we thought he had been murdered.

I tried to be brisk and matter-of-fact. I rang the police station nearest to Don's address in the Green Lanes house and, of course, got the duty sergeant. I said I was concerned that my husband, who had been admitted to hospital last week after collapsing in the street, and then discharged himself two days later, had not returned to his current address and had not responded to phone calls. I simply wanted to register his lack of contact in case he'd had an accident or had collapsed again somewhere. The policeman could hardly be bothered to take down Don's name, and then mine. He asked no questions, didn't query my status as wife – I mean, didn't ask if we lived together. He said a week was a very short time, and had I heard of the missing person's bureau? I said, yes, I had. He suggested that I wait another two weeks and then think about contacting them. I thanked him.

Judith isn't satisfied. She thinks we should be 'doing

something'. I asked what she had in mind, reminding her we'd had this conversation. 'Look, Judith,' I said, 'I'm sure he is abroad. He'll have gone off to follow up some so-called lead. His mobile may not work abroad. He'll turn up soon, or phone one of us.' She asked if I'd told Molly. I haven't. But on that one she may be right. Molly still doesn't even know about his collapse, and she would want to, I suppose. Would she? Being so far away? It's hard to know. What could she do? Nothing. Worry, that's all. It was difficult enough telling her that Don and I were separating, and that we were selling the house, but there was no choice about that, she had to be told. I dreaded her response, but she surprised me by taking the news, which I'd imagined she might find devastating, calmly. She said she could understand why this was happening, but she didn't then go on to say what exactly she thought *was* happening. I'd like to have asked her, but I didn't. She wanted to know if we were going to be divorced. I said no. We just needed to be apart. That was fudging the truth – I was the one who needed to be apart from Don – but she accepted it.

I didn't e-mail her. I wrote a proper letter instead. It seemed more appropriate, sending such news privately, secure in its envelope. It will take a week to reach her and maybe by the time it does Don will have turned up (as I said at the end of the letter). She'll phone me, if she can, when she gets it. I can't calculate how upset she will be – her feelings towards her father have become so complicated. She's far closer to me, or do I flatter myself? I don't think so. If I had gone missing ...

*

I met an old neighbour of ours in the street today, Miss Jackson. We never knew her well, but she lived two doors down from us and was part of the scenery. She had two rooms on the first floor and, when we arrived, was a sitting tenant, paying some ludicrously small rent. She used to stop me in the street and harangue me about her landlord who was forever trying to get

120

her out. I'd sympathise, without knowing much about the situation, and desperately try to move on. Usually I'd be pushing the twins in their buggy when she accosted me, and she'd bend down and peer at them and say, 'What's the pretty one called?' I'd say I didn't know what she meant, my girls were both pretty, and then I'd tell her their names again. Next time she stopped me, we would go through exactly the same irritating performance. I really didn't like Miss Jackson.

Today, she blocked my path as I came out of the greengrocer's. 'You've moved!' she said. 'You've left the hill!' I said yes, we had, and some time ago. 'Well, it's no wonder, I suppose, with what happened to your daughter, best to get away, start again, leave the memories. It was the pretty one, wasn't it?' It's like some sort of test, this kind of thing: how does one deal with the Miss Jacksons of this world? I've always thought it best just to smile and say nothing and move on, but suddenly today I'd had enough. Her offence was slight and she is now an old woman of at least eighty, and she knows no better, and so on and so on, but I couldn't help telling her that I'd always resented her description of Miranda as the 'pretty one' and that I'd had no intention of trying to leave the memories but that I'd taken them with me and loved them dearly and would never want to be parted from them. Then I turned, and almost ran home.

Doubtless, Miss Jackson will hear in due course that Don and I have separated, and the next time we meet she'll have some gem of a remark to make about that. She loved Don. She was always telling me 'You've done well there, he's a gentleman.' It became a family joke – if Don broke something in the kitchen, or let milk boil over, the children would chorus 'You've done well there, Mum.' He helped her with her shopping when he saw her struggling up the hill, carrying it right into her flat, and she took to coming to ask for his assistance on a wide variety of trivial problems from filling out forms to how to get a bus pass. He was her 'pin-up boy', she simpered. 'You couldn't have a kinder man,' she would say, when he'd done whatever she needed.

121

I wish Miss Jackson could have seen how Don behaved during those months afterwards. He hardly spoke to me or the children. He would get up in silence, his face tightly closed, his eyes narrowed as though focusing on something no one else could see, and if we said anything to him there was not only no response but no acknowledgement that he'd heard us speak. He left for work, on the days when he went to his office at all, without any farewell, and he returned in the same mood. The only time we heard his voice was on the telephone, talking to other people about his investigations. I would rather have had furious arguments but these were rare and only took place when I cornered him and demanded some communication. He was a zombie, moving through the house in a sinister fashion. Was *that* kind?

Is he still kind? Has the kindness that Miss Jackson saw disappeared, together with so many other attributes? I can't believe it has, but I can detect no trace of it now. But then Don isn't really in his right mind. Wherever he is, whatever he is doing, whoever he is with, he isn't the same. It's the part of the tragedy nobody sees, except me.

7

MOLLY WAS sitting on the doorstep, leaning against the glass doors, her legs stretched out and her feet resting on her bag. Her eyes were closed, but she wasn't asleep – I could see her eyelids fluttering. Four in the afternoon. She'd known what time I would be coming home. I saw her from yards away, and I knew, there was no mistaking her. But I didn't call out. I approached her softly. I wanted just to look at her before she looked at me. It would have been awful to cry.

It had all been planned. She knew she was coming back but didn't tell any of us, wanting to avoid the emotion of being met at Heathrow. She said it was worth the aggro of making her own way into London to my flat just to adjust as she went along, in her own time. So much to adjust to, and all after travelling virtually twenty-four hours without a break. It pleased her that it was raining, that endless drizzle which never either completely stops, or turns into proper rain, on days like this. She saw everything through its haze, and it helped, she said. All the way in the bus she was staring through the misted-over window and seeing nothing.

She isn't back for good. She's been sent to make a report in person to the charity's headquarters, telling them how things really are 'in the field', and she has lots of other tasks to carry out involving visiting various people and places. She'll be busy, she says. It isn't a holiday, though she can have some time off.

Can I stay here? she asked. I was hurt that she thought she had to ask. Of course, of course, I said, it's your home now. She looked at me oddly. It is, I repeated, of course it is.

*

She's gone to see Finn and Judith. I've told her about Don (she left for London before my letter arrived). She didn't seem shocked or upset. He'll be all right, she said, don't worry. I tried to say that I wasn't worried, that it was Judith who was fussing, but she smiled and shook her head and said, 'Mum, your middle name is worry.' I watched her walk off down the street. She knew I would be watching, and turned and waved when she got to the corner. That's what the twins did when first they started walking to school on their own, aged seven – they turned and waved when they got to the zebra crossing at the bottom of the hill, and then I watched them safely over the road. In time, of course, it irritated them, this watching-from-the-upstairs-window, but still they stopped obediently, turned and waved. I went on watching all the same, until they finished primary school and no longer took that route.

She's lost even more weight. Not surprising, of course, with all that heat and the physical hard work. She's really thin for the first time in her life, but not alarmingly so – it suits her. And she looks well, much better than when she left. Then, she still had those dreadful dark shadows under her eyes, and she was so pale it was frightening. Her clothes are the same as they always were, jeans and loose shirts. Unlike Miranda, she's never had any interest in clothes. But she's wearing an old jacket of Miranda's. The sleeves are much too long for her. I didn't comment on it but I was surprised she had it. When did she start wearing it? I'm sure I would have noticed if she'd worn it before she went to Africa, even in the state I was in. She saw me taking it in, of course, but she didn't say anything either. When she zipped it up we smiled at each other.

She's put her stuff in the spare room. She asked what had

happened to the furniture which was in her old room: 'Not that I care,' she added. But I felt that maybe she did care, and would like to have seen the old pine chest of drawers, with most of the knobs missing, instead of this new white piece. Too late. It felt faintly embarrassing to watch her glancing at all the new stuff, though up to now I've been so pleased with it. 'I hope I don't muck the place up too much,' she said, looking down at the spotless pale-blue carpet. 'Must remember to take my shoes off.' 'Don't be silly,' I said. She sat on the bed and fingered the coverlet, and I wished I'd never bought it. She was still fussing with it, and looking down at it, when she said, 'Mum, did you actually tell Dad to go? To get out?' I was shocked. I said that, of course, I hadn't, I'd written and told her at the time what had been agreed and that it was all perfectly amicable. 'You didn't tell me exactly how it happened,' Molly said. 'There were no details in that letter.' 'I didn't think you would want details,' I said. 'The important thing was ...' But she interrupted. 'Of course I wanted details,' she said, quite angrily. 'I couldn't imagine it, could I? I couldn't think what must have been said. I thought of you and Dad, and the words I had to put in your mouths didn't fit. Who said what, and where, where in the house, and what time of day, and what you were doing? ... all that. What *did* you say?'

'I can't remember.' I said that to Molly, and she raised her eyebrows and clenched her hands on the bedcover and shook her head. 'Fine,' she said, and sprang up and left the room. I trailed after her, repeating that I really could not recall the sequence of events leading to Don going and the house being sold. And I can't. There was no point at which I asked him to leave. At least, I don't think there was. It didn't happen that way. *I* was the one who said I wanted to live alone, somewhere else. Surely I'd written that to Molly? But apparently not. Or she misinterpreted what I wrote. I just got to the point when I couldn't stand Don, or the house, any more, but I did not ask him to leave. I did not turn him out. It all happened quite easily, smoothly. I'm sure it did. I must make Molly understand that.

*

Leaving Molly to go to school this morning felt strange. I peeped into her room, but she was sound asleep, a huddle under the duvet, motionless. She didn't come in until after midnight, and all the travelling and change of climate is catching up on her. She was out with old school friends, at the pub, and then to a flat one of them has got. Tilly's flat. Tilly was Miranda's friend more than Molly's. I'm longing to hear how she's getting on, but when I came home Molly had gone out. There was a note on the kitchen table saying she'd be back about six, so I'm waiting for her. I've made her favourite dish – stir-fry prawns with coriander – or what used to be her favourite dish. It was such a pleasure shopping for the ingredients, making sure the coriander was fresh, then preparing it, and now I am looking forward to us eating together.

*

Molly walked to school with me this morning. Neither of us used the word 'remember'. We went early, before any of the children would be making their way there. I'm nearer now, living in my flat, than I was in our house on the hill – it only takes five instead of fifteen minutes to get there. She's the same height as me, our stride is the same length. There was no need to talk but I wanted to. 'It's changed, the school,' I said, 'it's more mixed than it was in your day. 'Mixed!' she mocked. 'What a word, Mum, what do you mean?' I said mixed wasn't the right word. What I meant was that it seemed noisier, rougher, more crowded, and that having a lot of children now who couldn't speak much English gave it a different feel. She shot me a look. I told her I was just stating a fact. 'That's what everyone says,' she said, 'but they mean more than that.'

Jeremy was already in the classroom, surprisingly (for a

Monday morning). I introduced Molly to him. She was a bit curt, I thought, a little abrupt. He asked her fairly obvious but harmless questions and she hardly bothered to reply. She turned her back on him and went to look at what he had been putting up on the walls. We are going to be doing transformations this week – tadpoles into frogs, caterpillars into butterflies – and so he'd been putting up appropriate illustrations. She studied them intently. There was an uncomfortable atmosphere and I was glad when Molly said she'd go, she had to get to Islington, somewhere near the Angel, by ten o'clock. When she'd gone, Jeremy asked if he'd 'said' something. I asked why on earth he thought that, and he shrugged and said Molly had seemed either offended or upset.

I don't know if she was either. It is a very long time since she was ever in this classroom, but I can't imagine that she was affected by memories of when she and Miranda were last in it. She doesn't do those sentimental memory-lane trips. When I indulge myself, I exasperate her. But if she was not overcome by some sort of memory I don't know how to account for her attitude.

*

Time to tackle the Foundation Stage profiles demanded by the government. Nothing like the old school reports, either. Children, our guidelines tell us, should not be aware that they are being assessed. But what about the parents? Doesn't fool them. They know their children are being well and truly assessed, and immediately they begin to compare and to worry.

I try so hard to phrase my observations tactfully, and I always point out that in Reception there are no formal tests to pass or fail, but parents are acutely sensitive to what they interpret as criticism. The children at this stage are supposed to be able to talk clearly and confidently. Some hardly talk at all and have virtually no confidence, but it is difficult to write that without causing consternation. It is equally hard to describe overconfidence in an acceptable way. I struggle on, thinking what a waste of time this is. I want to tell parents to take no notice of these assessments – far too much emphasis is put upon them, and it will get worse. Next year, reading and writing and arithmetic will all be rated – below average, average, above average – oh, the dismay this will cause! The point of life is made to seem this kind of success: 'above average', or all is lost.

My little ones have no idea what is in store for them.

*

Molly insisted on going to the Green Lanes address, the last we had for Don. I told her that Finn and I had already been, but she wanted to go herself and somehow gain entry. She said I didn't have to go with her, but of course I did.

It was the same performance again, ringing bells and either getting no answer or being yelled at. This time there was no friendly postman. 'Well,' said Molly, 'we'll break in.' I said, to take her seriously, that we couldn't be absolutely sure that the ground-floor room on the right really was Don's, but she peered through, as Finn had done, and identified Don's jacket hanging on the back of the door and a canvas bag he'd had for years. 'This is wrong,' I kept saying, but she ignored me. I was so nervous, looking round all the time for policemen to appear, or even just a neighbour who would phone them, but no one gave Molly a second look as she tried to lever the bottom window open. She stood on the upturned dustbin, as Finn had done, but she isn't as tall and couldn't really reach high enough. She got down, began looking for something else to stand on. Then the front door opened and she was in immediately, brushing past the woman who was coming out as though she was in a great hurry. I was left standing outside. The woman, leaving, didn't say a word, just set off down the road.

I hovered anxiously, wondering what on earth Molly thought

she was going to do, and then all of a sudden there was her face at the window, giving the thumbs-up sign. She pointed to the front door, then came and opened it and I followed her in. The hallway was dark – the minute the front door closed I could barely make out anything. There was a corridor going off down the side of the staircase and Molly led me a short way down it to the door she'd forced open. It hadn't, she whispered, been difficult – 'It's only a Yale,' she said, as though that explained everything. Where on earth had she learned to spring a Yale lock? I didn't bother asking. I didn't like being in Don's room. It emphasised more than anything else could have done how he had changed. For Don, who loved space and colour and light, to live here ... Everything about that room was ugly. The dreary, torn wallpaper, the brown paint, the worn hair-cord carpet, the single divan bed sagging in the middle, the huge wardrobe, the Formica table with its spindly legs – everything. It was untouched by Don. His jacket and bag might be there, and as Molly opened the wardrobe I glimpsed some of his clothes, but *he* was not even faintly there. There was no impression of him at all. I hated to think of him reduced to this, a faceless, name-less man in a squalid room. It was perverse, there was no need for it.

To be truthful, it was not really squalid. It was clean enough, and tidy, there was no mess, no horrible smells. I couldn't see any cooking facilities, though there was an electric kettle plugged in on the floor, but maybe he had the use of a kitchen. I saw a small sink in one corner, but he seemed to have no bathroom of his own. All this time, as I stood there taking this in, Molly was searching. She had opened the drawer at the bottom of the wardrobe and was going through its contents. I recognised the folders Don used for his investigations. I doubted if she would learn much from them, but I said nothing. Then she turned to the table, where there were several neat piles of papers. She was looking, I could see, at the postmarks. I'd given her the letter I'd taken from the postman and she'd already rung the person who'd written it (no, he hadn't seen Mr Roscoe, or spoken to him). But she was convinced there would be some clue as to where her father had gone.

I still hadn't moved from the doorway. I felt that if I strayed further into this sad room I might be contaminated by it. Molly had no such fear. The room was nothing to her. She dismissed it as an irrelevance in her father's life. His time there was an aberration. She talked out loud as she searched, commenting on Don's efficiency, his organised mind. 'He ticks everything he's answered,' she said, 'and puts the date on.' That was no surprise to me. Don has always been efficient and careful. He isn't a man who ever mislays anything – he always knows where everything is, unlike his children who seem to him to live in chaos, constantly shouting that they'd lost something vital. That unappealing motto, 'A place for everything and everything in its place' was – is – Don's.

'Durham,' Molly suddenly said, holding up a letter. 'He might be in Durham. When did he disappear?' Well, of course, I didn't know that. I only knew when he had last been seen, and that was when he was in the Middlesex, twelve days ago. 'Look,' said Molly, and handed me the envelope, pointing to the postmark. 'If he came here from the hospital this would just have arrived. Maybe he turned round and went straight off.' I didn't ask why he would do that. I could guess.

*

An interruption there – Finn came. Molly was excited, longing to tell him about what she'd discovered. Finn was more interested in how she'd got into the house, and Don's room, and how she'd left it. She was impatient with his curiosity, and even more impatient when he chose to discredit her theory that Don had gone to Durham by wondering why in that case he had switched his mobile off, why would he not want to be contacted when he had nothing to hide. 'He isn't well, remember?' Molly said. 'He just doesn't want to be bothered, or to speak to anyone.

And he doesn't want Mum telling him that what he's doing is stupid or ridiculous.'

Yes, I am upset. Did I tell Don he was stupid? Did I call him ridiculous? I didn't think I ever had done, but Molly must think so. She must have heard me say such things. When? Not for a very long time, and not often. We never shouted at each other in front of the children. The few arguments afterwards were behind firmly closed doors, I'm sure. When I did start to become angry, and knew I was about to risk losing control, I remember I always rushed to close the door of whichever room we were in. It was a favourite position of mine, my back to a closed door. But perhaps the closed doors did not keep in all sound. Did Molly hear shouting, and come to the door, and listen? She would have been unlikely to hear Don shout. When he was angry, his voice became hoarse and gruff, not loud at all. I was the shouter, shrill and almost hysterical. And evidently I called him stupid and ridiculous. If so, they were the wrong words. I didn't mean stupid – how could I, when Don is so clever? I meant stubborn, misguided, blind – different words entirely. And he was never ridiculous so much as deluded. That was what I'd meant: he was stubborn and deluded, refusing to face up to facts.

Does Molly imagine I drove him away? I hope not. It isn't true. Don moved himself, in every respect, away from all of us, long before we actually separated. She's forgetting that. Ought I to remind her? Maybe Finn will do this for me. I noticed how concerned he looked when Molly said that. He's been here all the time and he hasn't forgotten what Don was like, which Molly may have done. She seems to have returned as her father's champion, though she left for Africa appearing to be dissociating herself from him.

*

That's better. Ruth rang and, hearing how upset I sounded, asked what was wrong. She listened patiently while I told her

131

and then said she thought I was looking at Molly's behaviour in the wrong way. Think about it, she said. The girl has been away a long time. She left with no inkling that you and Don were going to split up, and that you'd sell the home she'd lived in all her life. She left after a fairly painful scene with her father with whom she's had virtually no contact since. Then when she comes home, she's told he has vanished after collapsing and being hospitalised. She's shocked. You don't seem unduly concerned. You're angry with him. You no longer seem to her the caring person you used to be. To her, it is all the most awful mess, don't you think? So she wants to try to sort it out. She feels concern and compassion for her father, and is puzzled by you ...

'Don't Ruth,' I said, '*Don't.*'

*

Molly's spoken to Alex. Don did go to see him, it turns out, but that was last week and he isn't in Durham now, she's fairly sure of that. Alex said he was perfectly civil, there was no ugly confrontation. He just asked questions, the same questions about the boat that Alex had already been asked a dozen times, and the crucial other question: how did Miranda come to be sailing on her own? This had, of course, been gone into at the inquest. It was the part I'd listened to most intently, my eyes never leaving Alex's face for a second. Details about the condition of the boat might have passed over my head, because I didn't understand the terminology, but when it came to understanding the relationship between Alex and Miranda I felt capable of understanding anything. And yet I was unable to do so. Something remained inexplicable. I listened to Alex say that he and my daughter had 'not been getting on too well' the day before, ten days into the holiday. The coroner pressed him: had there been an argument? Alex, visibly upset, shook his head and looked down. The coroner repeated his question. Alex said no, not until the following morning. He had told Miranda he

fancied going cycling for a change. He'd hurt his finger pulling ropes the day before and wanted to rest it. Miranda said
how could he hold the handlebars of a bike if his finger was so
sore and had accused him of pretending it was painful. She'd
said he just wanted to get away from her, didn't he, because
he'd gone off her and preferred Trisha. He'd told her she was
paranoid. She'd told him just to go off with Trisha, then, she'd
sail on her own. He had laughed. (It was hard to hear this – the
coroner had to ask him to speak up.) He'd laughed, said she
wasn't capable. 'Anything else?' the coroner asked. 'Did you
say anything else?' Alex was silent. His hands gripped the rail
in front of him very tightly. I knew instinctively that he *had* said
something else. Some insult. The coroner almost certainly knew
it too. Alex was allowed just to shake his head.

None of the rest of the party had much to add, except Trisha.
She was older than Alex, a second-year student with him at
Durham. I felt she'd dressed carefully for the inquest, and that
a plain white shirt, buttoned up to the neck, and a calf-length
black skirt were not her usual clothes. Even clad in these prim
garments she looked voluptuous and sexy. She was at great pains
to insist that there had been 'nothing between' her and Alex.
The coroner only wanted to know if Alex had said anything to
her about Miranda and whether she had seen Miranda take his
boat out. Her voice trembled slightly when she repeated what
Alex had said when he came to find her. She began 'He said'
– and stopped. She started again, and stopped. The tension in
the courtroom was high. We all waited. 'He said he was sick of
Miranda, she was a wimp.'

It wasn't so terrible. A wimp. Hardly devastating as an insult.
The coroner passed straight on to the next question, whether
Trisha had seen Miranda take the boat out. No. She and Alex
had gone straight off to hire bicycles. No one had noticed
Miranda leave the marina. It was busy that morning. The others
were either still asleep in their boats or else were in the café.
The coroner remarked that in spite of hearing that Miranda was

not a competent sailor she must have had more expertise than suspected to manoeuvre such a boat out of the marina without mishap and without attracting attention. Quite. I was pleased he said that. He went on to say that the boat had been judged seaworthy – there was no evidence that the engine or any other part was at fault. It had been well maintained by the owner (Alex's father) who had had it regularly checked. The cause of the fatal accident was freak weather conditions combined with the inexperience of the sailor.

Still, there was something missing. Why did Miranda have such a violent response to Alex's wish to go cycling with Trisha? Why did she not just cry, or sulk? Why did she not simply pack up, and leave, tell him their affair was over and she was going home? Why did she not turn to us, or Molly? But maybe she was in a rage and merely wanted to prove she could sail the wretched boat and had meant simply to get it out to sea and then return it to its mooring. But she couldn't manage it. She got it out into the open sea OK, and calmed down, but she'd gone too far and the storm came ... who knows? We don't. We have to accept the unacceptable, that Miranda acted dangerously, and died.

But Don had to go on not accepting this. He asked the same old question again and Alex gave the same answer. He told Molly there was only one new question, about the weather. Did he listen to the weather report that morning? He said he didn't. The weather was good. The sky was blue, just a few small clouds, and there was a light wind. And, anyway, he wasn't going to be sailing. At the inquest (everything was translated for our benefit), there was a lot said about the weather and how dramatically and unexpectedly it had changed, with winds sweeping in which gusted up to 30 knots. These winds had not been forecast until an hour before Miranda set sail. An unusually strong high-pressure system had driven the barometer up rapidly, causing these conditions, and producing steep seas.

Was Don becoming *so* deluded that he was seeking to blame

the boy for not listening to the weather forecast that morning? And to go on from that to deciding he was culpable for Miranda's death? I couldn't think why else he would be asking. I'm trying now to imagine how Don would think but it is almost impossible. Does he know that a weather warning was given and that someone knew that a violent storm was about to sweep into the area? And that Miranda was allowed to take the boat out by this someone, who was, or was not, aware that she wasn't an experienced sailor? This would fit his peculiar understanding of the word 'negligence'. Maybe he'd got nowhere with his investigations into dodgy parts – masts, engines, it made little difference – and now he was chasing the human element.

How can he bear to, all this time afterwards? Suppose he finds that someone at the marina did hear the storm warning and failed to stop Miranda – why should they, anyway? – what does he want to do about it? It is up to sailors to listen to weather reports. It was no longer the responsibility of the marina. Or was Don now switching from finding a culprit to emphasis on the other part of his mission – establishing the truth. So, if the truth turns out to be that someone official at the marina listened to a weather report, but that nobody thought to stop a young woman taking a boat out, how does that help? How does 'the truth' help?

He won't be able to prove anything anyway, just as he couldn't prove that the zip on Miranda's lifejacket was faulty – the lifejacket was eventually washed ashore, so either she had never worn it or it had been torn off her body – or that the metal tank of the engine was corroded. He tried hardest of all to prove that, but the Swedish manufacturers said they used the best grade stainless steel and none of their engines had ever corroded. There was no proof, either, that the engine had malfunctioned or that the fuel had been dirty, causing it to be inoperable. Everything, absolutely everything, as the coroner said, pointed to Miranda's inexperience, her inability to handle the boat in the freak weather conditions, that arose. He cannot accept that his daughter took out a boat she was not fit to sail.

*

Glad, as ever, to be back to school. Other people groan at the thought of Monday mornings, but I love them. My mind stops swirling around in frantic, pointless patterns and once more I know what I am doing and how to do it. 'Don't you like weekends?' Jeremy once asked as I bounced into the classroom one Monday morning when he'd crawled in barely able to face the day. 'Of course I do.' That is what I told him, very briskly, but it isn't the truth, or it is no longer the whole truth. I used to love weekends in the old days when I wasn't teaching, because they meant Don was at home and we did things with the children – ordinary things, like swimming and going to the zoo, and so on. But now the weekends find me at a loss, consciously trying to organise my time so that I won't simply loll around and panic at the emptiness. I can't tell Jeremy any of that, so I stick to saying I like weekends but I like Mondays too. I can't tell him that only work keeps me sane. I ought to get to know Jeremy better, show more interest. I would have done at one time, but these days I don't make the effort. It takes too much energy. I do occasionally, when we're tidying up, ask him about himself but maybe he senses that I'm only being polite because his replies are as brief as my enquiries. I know he has a girlfriend and they share a flat with another couple. I know he plays the guitar. I know he went to university but dropped out after a term, hated it. And he suffers from asthma. That's about it. I've been too wrapped up in myself to develop any but a working relationship with Jeremy. I wonder if he minds?

*

We have two new children in the class. It's unusual to admit new pupils at this stage of the term, and not a good idea from their, or my, or the class's point of view, but I gather there are extenuating circumstances. They are twins. Girls. Shalima and Sima. They come from Iraq but speak a fair amount of English, which is a relief. They are small for their age, and slight, with enormous dark eyes dominating their thin faces. I don't think they are identical – already I can spot clear differences – but they are very alike. They were brought into my classroom by a woman I recognised as a foster mother, accompanied by a social worker I know well. They didn't seem frightened exactly, just blank and stiff, their faces void of all expression and their little bodies held rigid. They were holding hands. I held out a hand to each of them, watching their reaction closely. When anyone did that to my twins, they used to grasp the offered hands with their spare hands forming a circle. They never dropped their own tightly gripped hands to allow anyone to come between them. But Shalima and Sima did let go of each other. They did so, it seemed to me, as an act of obedience. I took hold of their freed hands, squeezing each one very gently, and led them into the classroom.

All day they stayed close to me. They wouldn't hold Jeremy's hand and were clearly alarmed by his presence, though he is the least alarming of men. They wouldn't let any of the children touch them either, shrinking away at any approach. It was lucky that I was wearing a skirt today – it gave them something to cling on to when I needed my hands free. I liked the feel of them, the pull on my skirt. Tomorrow I will have to encourage them to move around the classroom and playground without me. They will still have each other, of course, the biggest comfort of all. Whatever has happened to them, which I will doubtless soon be told, they are together.

*

There was a case, last year, maybe the year before, when a man was found on a beach, just standing there, apparently lost. He didn't speak, and the police took him to hospital where it was discovered that all the labels had been cut out of his clothes.

He was looked after, and came to be known as the Piano Man, because he made gestures of playing a piano and when he was taken to one he was said to have played beautifully. Weeks went by, and still he had not spoken a word. It was assumed he'd lost his memory. Great efforts were made to establish his identity with his photograph – he was quite handsome – widely circulated. Eventually, he spoke. It turned out that he was German. The whole thing had been a deliberate hoax, though why it was carried out was never revealed. No one could understand what the point had been.

I dreamed of the Piano Man last night, only he was not a man, he was Miranda, and she played a flute, not a piano. This dream was like one of the fantasies which I had constructed to keep me going: I imagined Miranda had miraculously been washed ashore somewhere and had lost her memory. I could see her quite clearly, staggering out of the water, and I could see, though less clearly, another figure, another woman rushing towards her and wrapping her in a coat and leading her to a cottage at the end of the beach. This woman lived on her own and was a recluse. Miranda couldn't speak, she'd lost her voice, as well as her memory, from the shock, but the recluse hardly noticed because she rarely spoke herself. The two of them got on well. Miranda recovered her strength and began helping her guardian angel gather driftwood and do other simple tasks. In my imagination she looked so well and happy. Sometimes I made her wave at me, and I made her mouth the word 'soon'. I nodded. I made it clear that I was content to wait. I wouldn't hurry her. I knew that one day she would speak and regain her memory and she would leave her kind rescuer and walk to a telephone and call me. I loved that fantasy, re-enacting it again and again, but I never told Don about it.

Then last night I had this dream, which began like my fantasy. I was enjoying it until I realised the figure approaching Miranda was not a woman but a man. I cried out, to warn her, but she was smiling and her arms were open wide as he went towards her. My anxiety was intense – would he be kind, or was he dangerous? He reached her, and hugged her, and they swayed together on the sand, and suddenly I knew that of course it was Don. He'd found her. I woke up drenched in perspiration. The dream had spoiled my fantasy, but why? I ought to have been happy, comforted by this new vision, but I wasn't. I had a feeling of alarm: Don had found her, Don would keep her. She wouldn't find a telephone and ring me.

It was a hope we had both clung to for ages – that Miranda was not drowned, that she'd survived and been swept ashore somewhere miles and miles away from the marina and was wandering on a beach until found by some fisherman, who would have taken her home and would be ringing the police any minute. At first, during the first hours after the boat was found smashed, and then the lifejacket was washed ashore, such a scenario was a possibility. Miranda was a strong swimmer. She could have clung to a piece of wreckage and survived. But then, after helicopters had taken over from lifeboats and scoured the entire area, it was no longer sensible to think like this. But we were not sensible, we were not thinking logically, and so we allowed ourselves to go on imagining she was still alive. When no body was washed ashore, we didn't acknowledge that this meant she had drowned and been washed far out to sea instead of to the shore, but we saw it instead as evidence that she must be alive. Other possibilities didn't enter our heads. Not then. Later, when it was all over, but not then.

There was a report of a girl being eaten by a crocodile, somewhere in Africa. The horror of it almost made me scream – the teeth, the hideous teeth, sinking into her flesh … How could her parents bear it, knowing the pain their daughter experienced, the terror she died in. And then I thought of what was in the sea where Miranda disappeared. No crocodiles, certainly, no killer sharks, but what about whales? Were there whales around? Or some man-eating fish I knew nothing about? Don said there were no fish like that in those cold northern waters. He said that was one thing I needn't torture myself with. She drowned, instantly, he said. But I could see in his eyes that he didn't believe this. He didn't know if she had been injured and died in great pain, her limbs perhaps broken, her head perhaps cut open and bleeding – he didn't know. And the drowning might not have been instant. I thought about it: drowning cannot be instant. Surely it must be long-drawn-out? She would fight it, she would struggle to swim through the huge waves, it wouldn't be instant at all.

It is the hardest thing, to tell myself that, since she is dead, it is now irrelevant what the process of her dying was like. How does it help to try to imagine it? It doesn't. It is pure masochism to think about it. But it happens, the endless re-rolling of the story. The screen comes up, Miranda sets sail – she looks so athletic and healthy, adjusting the sails, tanned and fit, lithe and supple – and then the storm comes and my eyes widen at the height of the waves and I see the little boat lurch to one side and I hear the roar as the sea crashes down upon it, and then Miranda is swept away and … the screen is blank. I can't leave it blank. I insist it must continue with the story. I fill it with alternative images: Miranda with her eyes shut, slowly sinking, dead before she sank, unconscious, knocked out by the blow from the mast splitting and catching her on the head. But then I see her clutching a rope, desperately trying to haul herself onto the deck, her eyes wild, her mouth open in a scream no one can hear, and …

Nobody knows. Nobody will ever know. It isn't like the girl and the crocodile. So is it better, I wonder? Not to know? To be spared the detail? It's something I've heard people say, when describing a death from a disease kept concealed by the sufferer – 'Thank God I knew nothing about it.' Ignorance is a comfort, then. But I've never found it comforting. Not knowing added to my distress for a very long time. Don said he didn't allow himself to imagine exactly what happened – he just closed his mind to that. I couldn't do that. Only by imagining my Piano Man scenario could I stop tormenting myself. I learned to switch on that image – Miranda on the beach, the woman finding her – to eliminate the others.

*

'You're the bride,' Paige was saying to Lola today in the playground. I lurked, and listened, trying to catch their words above all the general shrieking and shouting. 'Do I have a white dress and a veil and flowers in my hair?' Lola asked. 'No,' said Paige, 'you're a corpse, your dress is black and your veil grey and you have no face.' 'What's a corpse?' asked Lola. 'A dead body,' said Paige. 'Listen, I'll tell you what happens and then we do it, yeah? Right. Victor is going to marry this beautiful girl but he's worried he won't put the ring on properly, yeah, and he goes into the wood and he practises putting it on the branch of a tree, but it isn't a tree, it's a hand, and it comes alive and drags him down to the underworld, and you run after him ...' The rest was lost because a fight broke out between a couple of boys and I had to intervene. But once back in my classroom, I asked Paige about this game. It turned out she'd been recounting the plot of this year's Best Animated Feature Film, *The Corpse Bride*, Certificate PG. Her dad took her to see it on Saturday. He, her dad, laughed a lot but Paige thought it quite scary – so scary she hasn't stopped trying to act out the story ever since. An example of an imagination successfully stimulated? Over-stimulated? But her dad laughed, after all. An animated-cartoon-death can surely be safely laughed at. Maybe I should watch it. Laugh at death.

*

Walking to Judith's takes me nearly an hour, but I like to walk, not just because the route is interesting and pleasant but because it makes me feel better, more up to facing Judith. Going from my block of flats to her house means crossing two main roads, going through the park, and then negotiating a compli-

141

cated pattern of minor, quite countrified, roads, before I arrive. What fascinates me is how I go from our street, full of small shops, most of them Greek- or Italian-owned, and cafés, usually crowded with people, and then to the thundering main road until I come to the park where all this frantic activity drops away. The expanse of green, and the background of trees, is miraculous.

After that, the other side of the park has a suburban feel to it. The roads – crescents and groves – are achingly quiet. Most of the houses are detached and have front as well as back gardens. I can hear my footsteps on the pavement, click-clack in the strange silence. I rarely meet anyone. The occasional person, usually a woman, rushes out of a front door but always straight to a car. There never seems to be a postman or a delivery van, and certainly no vagrants. And yet, although I appreciate the gardens, and enjoy the hushed peace, I'm never entirely at ease on this stretch. It feels to me as though there is something hidden behind this composed face, a hint of menace of a different kind from the danger that might lurk in the park or in my own crowded street. I keep thinking there might be an explosion. But what could explode? And why on earth would I think like this?

As you come out of this suburban labyrinth there is a long incline up to Judith's house. It isn't a steep hill such as the one we used to live on, but it is a long, slow climb. There are houses on one side only. Then, just before I reach Judith's house, there is a gate and through it a perfectly framed view of the canal, and across it a church and a factory, and behind and around these buildings are more houses. I feel I've travelled through several cities, not just a section of one. Driving there, I never feel that. Driving, it is all of a piece, just a muddle. Like life.

*

At least Judith was not distraught today. Molly's discovery that Don has been to Durham to visit Alex, and that Alex had said he seemed well, had calmed her. She managed to smile as she opened the door and there were no tears trembling in her eyes. We ate in the garden, in the shade, under the chestnut tree. She had a little table set there and two white wrought-iron chairs, comfortably padded with soft, bright pink cushions.

It was her birthday. Not a special one, but we agreed that at our age every birthday starts to become special. She isn't having a party this evening but her sons and Finn are taking her out for dinner. I was invited too, but declined, inventing another engagement. It didn't matter, somehow, that Judith would not believe I was busy – she was probably glad of the lie. It meant she would have the boys to herself. They are all very fond of her. I gave her some earrings and she put them on and seemed pleased. We ate the salad she had prepared and had a glass of chilled white wine and chatted, mostly about Molly. And now we come to it.

Molly, said Judith, had become 'odd'. Didn't I think so? 'She's changed,' Judith said. I said that of course she had, how could she not have done, coming back from Africa and what she had been doing there. No, said Judith, it is more than that, she isn't herself any more, she's lost something. It is always the way with Judith – she can't explain what she means, yet she has this instinctive knowledge which is usually right. I've spent hours in the past trying to drag out of her what she has sensed, and often I never succeed. Her conviction that something is odd or strange or weird or just plain wrong hangs in the air until something happens to make her say 'Remember, I *knew*, I had this feeling.' It can be maddening.

I tried today to be patient. I pressed Judith gently on what she might mean. She didn't know, but she was disturbed. She asked if Molly and I had had a 'heart to heart'. I lied and said of course we had, we had had long talks about what she was doing, and she'd described to me what Zambia was like and – 'No,' said

143

Judith, 'I don't mean all that. I mean, how she's managing without her twin, how she's coping.' I know I frowned and sounded cross when I said we didn't need to talk about that, we'd done it, ages ago, afterwards. Judith said that didn't count. She said everything had changed since then. Molly would be feeling different. 'Think of yourself, Lou,' she urged. 'You've changed in how you feel. You've changed for the better, but has Molly? Don hasn't. I think that girl's in trouble, as well as her father. She doesn't feel right to me. She was too brave, too stoical, straight afterwards. It wasn't natural. Then she ran away. Have you thought about that? About what she left and what she's come back to?'

It was Judith's birthday. Only that fact stopped me becoming angry with her. She talked such nonsense, and all with that special 'caring' look on her face. But of course, as ever, her words carry a sting. I can feel it, pricking me. It hurts. Has Molly become 'odd'? I tried to think about what Judith might mean. It was true that there was a new abruptness about Molly, which I don't remember being present before. She breaks off conversations suddenly with a rather sharp 'whatever' and a dismissive gesture of her hand. She doesn't seem to want to discuss anything. There's a distance between us, which she is placing there, that didn't exist before. Or am I imagining it? Is Judith imagining it? And even if it is true, can it all be explained by a natural growing away due to her new life in Africa, even if Judith thinks not?

But she's right about Molly having been too brave, too stoical afterwards. She was so quiet, so calm, and yet not catatonic, as Finn was, briefly. She kept herself together admirably. I never saw her distraught. We depended on her, during those first dreadful weeks. She was the sensible one. Don never took into account what it might be like to lose a twin, the significance of it. I think he may even have thought that he had been closer to Miranda than anyone was. Wrong. He didn't recognise Molly's particular brand of suffering. When she insisted on going to

Africa, he took it as a sign that she had severed all connection with her dead twin – as if she ever could.

I must watch Molly, look for signs of this 'oddness' Judith senses. Is she in trouble? And if she is, what on earth can I do about it?

8

FINN HAS a girlfriend. I can't quite believe it. It makes me laugh.
Well, that's one good thing.

Even more surprising, Finn brought her to meet me. It seemed
formal and quaint, the way he asked if he could drop in 'with
my girl'. He wasn't embarrassed about this either, but quite
nonchalant and pleased with himself. It can't, I suppose, be his
first girlfriend, but with Molly abroad and Miranda not here
– *dead*, I should write dead and not be afraid of the word. With
Molly abroad, and Miranda dead, I've had no one to tell me.
They'd have teased him rotten, passing on names of whoever
he had been with. I'd have known all about it, and would have
been protecting my little boy from their mockery.

So, he brought her here today, Sunday, not for anything as
old-fashioned as tea, though I did offer it. He said they were
just passing. Her name is Shivaun, but she isn't Irish and
doesn't spell it the Irish way. It gave us something easy to talk
about. I said I liked the sound of her name. She said she didn't
like the way it got shortened to Shivi, which made her think of
'shiver'. I said I had the same trouble, with Louise shortened to
Lou. She seems shy, blushes easily. And she's small and quite
plump. I hadn't thought Finn would be attracted to a shy, small,
plump girl – how unkind that sounds, how 'lookist' as the twins
would say. I ought to have learned by now. I did the same with
Alex. I said at the time that I hadn't thought Miranda would be

attracted by 'that type', and got a terrific telling-off from Molly (even though she was surprised herself that Miranda found Alex attractive). I think Molly had been expecting someone like Alex to come along, though. She herself never seemed interested in boys, or if she was she hid it well. The phone rang often for Miranda from about the age of fourteen – boys asking her out, boys wanting just to chat to her. But until Alex she had never seemed interested in any of them, though she went to plenty of parties, and to the cinema, and pop concerts, with boys, though always in a gang, with other girls. Molly was never one of them. Slowly, Miranda was separating herself, and Molly knew it, but until Alex I don't think she felt any real sense of loss. Miranda wasn't being particularly influenced by any of the boys she socialised with – it was still Molly's opinion that mattered to her, still Molly to whom she turned for advice and support. It gave her such confidence to have Molly always in the background, someone utterly dependable to return to, someone who always put her first. And then along came Alex, and suddenly it was what *he* thought and wanted that mattered.

Shivaun is friendly, though, and she smiles a lot. Finn is very pleased with her. I remembered not to ask what her father did. It's OK to ask her where she lives, but not anything to do with her parents' occupations. It turns out she lives not far from Judith, in one of those side roads I pass through. Unlike Finn, she wants to go to university and has a provisional place at Warwick, if she gets the grades. So, she's bright. I asked if she had any idea what sort of job she'd like to do after university, not expecting that she would have. She said she wanted to be a psychotherapist who specialised in grief counselling. I said, 'Good God!' before I could stop myself, and Finn said, 'Mum,' in a warning voice. I tried to excuse myself. I said it was just that it seemed an odd ambition for a young woman, that I couldn't see what attracted her. She said, 'Grief. It's everywhere, but it gets so little attention.'

What? Should I laugh? I stared at her. Was I frowning, scowling?

Probably. I wanted to tell her – oh, all kinds of things. Not to be so insufferably virtuous, so absurdly prim. Not to refer to grief as though it were a sickness. And I wanted to ask her what on earth she could know about grief. But I didn't. I got up and fussed about and cleared my throat repeatedly. My discomfort was obvious and she clearly thought she had to acknowledge it. 'I'm sorry, Mrs Roscoe,' she said, her friendly, pretty face suddenly anxious. 'I didn't mean to upset you. I know you've had a lot of grief, you know all about it, and so does Finn, and you've dealt with it on your own, and it must have been very hard, but ...' I stopped her. I couldn't bear her to go stumbling on. I smiled and said I was sorry too, and that I was sure that in time she would make a very good grief counsellor, and that it was a very worthy ambition. Oh, and a whole lot more lies. I can't remember, I was just prattling, trying to lighten the now awkward atmosphere.

Finn was no help. During this little interchange he said nothing. In fact, he went into the kitchen and boiled the kettle again, quite unnecessarily. But when he came back, he had an expression on his face which reminded me of his father. It is a look Don lost, afterwards, a mixture of pride and admiration. I'd never seen it on Finn's face before, and it made me think I didn't understand my son at all. He told Shivaun that they should go, they were going to be late, though he didn't say for what. Shivaun said it had been a pleasure to meet me. I said it had been a pleasure to meet her. Out they went. I felt – I feel – so depressed. The fond amusement has all gone. I don't want Finn involved with a girl like that.

*

'Oh, her!' Molly said, when I told her. 'I knew her sister, she was in our class once. The whole family are do-gooders. Her mum is a psychotherapist and the dad is religious, I forget what, no, not a vicar. Can't imagine what Finn sees in her. It won't last.' I said he'd seemed very taken with her. 'She's

148

pretty, in an obvious way,' Molly said. 'A bit sort of sugary-pink, but he's only starting, he's young, she'll do for a while till he wants a serious shag.' They all talk like that, my children and their friends, it's no good objecting. I said that it hadn't seemed shagging possibilities were what attracted him so much as her noble aspirations.

What does Molly know about shagging, anyway? Have things changed? Has she got a lover? I wouldn't dare ask her. I didn't dare ask Miranda, when Alex appeared on the scene. Don wanted me to. He thought I should 'talk to her'. About what? 'Taking care of herself,' he said. As if I hadn't done that years before, as if she wasn't living in the twenty-first century. But he was very agitated when Alex became serious, and Miranda was always either in his company or waiting to be. He was convinced that the boy was not making her happy. And it's true that there were plenty of tears when Alex failed to pick her up when he'd said he would, or rang, cancelling some date at the last minute. 'He doesn't appreciate her,' Don fumed. 'He doesn't deserve her.' Even though he'd given up trying to stop her, Don didn't want her to go on that sailing trip. 'Look at her,' he said, the night before. 'She's all tense.' I said she was just excited. 'Excited?' Don said. 'It doesn't look like excitement to me. It's as though he has some sort of hold over her and she has to please him – a beautiful girl like that, wanting to please *him*.' I pointed out that she was probably in love with him and that love could sometimes be painful. Don snorted with disgust.

Don thought we failed her. He thought that I, especially, failed her. Going back and back, rewinding all the time, it was one of the madder conclusions he came to. But he did not exonerate himself either. He went on torturing himself with the fact that he had let her go sailing with Alex when he should have prevented her. I asked how he could have done that. We had the same conversation again. I repeated that she was eighteen, she had earned the money she needed with her Saturday job, how could he have stopped her? That was when he changed tack and said *I* could have stopped her, or Molly could have. He alleged that we both knew she had 'set her cap' – that was the quaint expression he used – at Alex and that he took her for granted. She was making a fool of herself over him. We, Molly and I, should have pointed this out, for her own good. It was as though he hadn't known his own daughter. He thought she was like him, and yet couldn't see that she had just his stubbornness, and that all argument would have been futile. We were to blame, all of us. That was all he could think of. The only blameless one in his opinion was Miranda.

*

I didn't look at the clock so I don't know exactly what time it was when I was wakened, but it was somewhere around two or three in the morning. I was deeply asleep anyway, because it took me a long time to realise that the bell wasn't being rung in a dream. It's a shrill doorbell, which I've meant to have changed but never got round to it. I want a soft buzzing tone, not this harsh, insistent sound. It frightened me. Who rings a doorbell in the middle of the night? I waited. I remembered that Molly was here, I was not on my own. I listened, wondering if she too had heard the bell and had got up, but there was no sound of her moving about. The bell was rung again, someone's finger jammed hard on it. Whoever it was was not going to go away.

I got up, wrapped a robe round me, switched on a lamp, then quietly tip-toed along to the door where the intercom is fixed. Should I answer at all? Was it wise? Was it sensible? I told myself that I was perfectly safe here on the second floor, surrounded by other people and with my own daughter sleeping nearby. Whoever was ringing my doorbell couldn't possibly threaten me – and so I decided it was foolish not to find out who they were and what they wanted. I lifted the handset and pressed the button and said, 'Hello? Who is it?' 'Me,' he said.

*

I held the door open and waited for him. He came up the stairs stealthily, his shadow moving ahead of him, huge on the left-hand wall, and then, when the timed light switched off and the shadow had gone he was just a blur until he arrived. I couldn't see his face properly – I hadn't put the light on in the little hall – and I seemed to hesitate, as though I still wasn't sure it was him, and he said, 'Lou.' I put my finger to my lips and whispered, 'Molly's back, she's here, asleep,' and then led the way into my bedroom, where I'd put the lamp on, and closed the door. He sank down onto the bed immediately, dropped his bag on the carpet, and then swung his legs up and lay back, his arms covering his face. I should have taken him into the sitting-room or the kitchen, but I'd returned without thinking to where the light was on.

I felt helpless. There was nothing for me to fuss over in my bedroom. I couldn't make him some coffee, or find him a drink or offer him food. Should I go and put the kettle on, ask him if I could get him anything? But I didn't. I stood looking at him, waiting, noticing everything about him. His shoes were dirty. I vaguely worried about them, lying on my white duvet. His trousers were wrinkled and there was a small tear in one knee, as though they had caught on a nail. The jacket I recognised. It was an old, very old, reefer thing, much too heavy for the summer, but he had it buttoned up to the neck. The arms had always been a little too short, and now, with the way in which he was shielding his face, they rode up and showed his thin wrists. I took in that he wasn't wearing a wristwatch.

I couldn't stand there for the rest of the night. He was clearly exhausted. I should leave him to sleep, but where would I go? 'Don?' I said, but there was no reply. I touched his foot. He didn't move. I could hear that his breathing was deeper. I undid his shoelaces and gently slipped off his shoes. One of his socks had a hole in it. I wouldn't touch the socks. He was lying on the side of the bed where I had been lying, and as I'd got up I'd thrown the duvet aside so that it was now bunched up alongside

151

him. Gently, I pulled it over him up to where his jacket began, just covering his feet and his legs in their thin trousers. Then I put out the lamp, and left the room, closing the door.

Still Molly hadn't stirred. I opened her door and peeped in, almost wanting her to hear me and ask what was going on, but she didn't, she was sound asleep. I padded quietly into the sitting-room and, without putting on the light, lay down on the sofa. It was too short to be comfortable for sleeping on but I propped my legs up on a cushion so that they hung over the end and tried to settle myself. But I felt cold, and had to get up again and go and find a coat to drape over me. I thought: I can get into my own bed, with Don. Why not? He was asleep, fully clothed. We could have been side by side, for the first time in many months. The idea of this made me want to weep, but I forced myself not to. I needed instead to be alert, to face whatever was going to happen when Don woke up. There must not be a scene, I told myself. We must not get upset. We must be calm, *I* must be calm. And he must go.

Then I suppose I drifted off into a sort of sleep. Not a deep sleep because I heard the traffic noises beginning outside and a door banging in another flat. And then, later, I heard Molly. I heard her get up and go into the bathroom and then I heard the shower. Hurriedly, I got up and straightened the cushions on the sofa and went to hang up my coat. There was a hair-brush on the chair beside the hook where I hung my coat and I picked it up and brushed my hair vigorously. Then I began to make myself some coffee. That was how Molly found me. 'You're up early,' she said. 'It's only 6.30. I was hoping not to wake you.' I muttered something about not sleeping well and asked her if she wanted some coffee and she nodded and went back to her room while it was being made. Why didn't I say, straight out, that her father was here? I don't know. I thought Don would come out and I'd have no need to say anything. But it was crazy. I should have said that Don was asleep in my bedroom, that he had turned up in the middle of the night and hadn't said a word to explain why. It would have been natural.

I knew Molly had a very early appointment on the other side of London and needed to leave soon. She came for her coffee with her things all ready, looking very fresh and organised and eager to go. She's always been good in the mornings, like me. 'You look rough,' she said, 'what's up?' I repeated that I hadn't slept well. When she asked if there was any particular reason I let another opportunity go. I just shrugged, and yawned. It was as though I were trying to hide a lover. The thought made me smile, cynically, but Molly didn't know it was a cynical smile. 'Well,' she said, 'at least you can smile about it.' And then she was off.

*

I drank my coffee, wandering aimlessly round the room, pausing again and again to look out of the window as if expecting to see something helpful there. Then I opened my bedroom door, needing to get my clothes and get dressed, ready for school. 'Don?' I said. Still no reply. Was he faking sleep? I hesitated, wondering if I should go over to the bed and shake him awake, but then I thought why do that, why not just leave him asleep and go off to school and maybe he'll be gone when I get back. It gave me such a feeling of relief to think of that. So I took my clothes and closed the door again and went into the bathroom and showered and dressed. It was still too soon to set off for school, but I wanted to go. I decided I'd walk a long way round and when I got there I'd plenty I could get on with till the children arrived. It would be better than staying in the flat, knowing that Don might emerge at any moment.

The thought panicked me. I wasn't ready for whatever Don was going to tell me, if there was something, if it wasn't just a case of being desperate and having nowhere else to go. But what I dreaded even more was a distraught Don at the end of his investigations because he'd finally realised they were pointless. I was suddenly in a rush to leave, but as I put my coat on – I'd seen it was raining outside – and looked for my umbrella, I thought that I couldn't just abandon him. I would have to leave a note. I sat at the kitchen table, biro in hand, paper in front of me, not knowing what to write. All I needed to tell him was that I was off to work and wouldn't be back until after four, and that Molly was out too and didn't expect to be back until six. I wrote this, and then stared at what I'd written. Such a cold little note. I added that he should help himself to food and make himself comfortable, and then I crossed out making himself comfortable. Once crossed out, it looked bad, as though I'd written something I regretted, which of course I had, but not anything significant. I screwed up the paper and started again. Best just to be matter-of-fact, even at the risk of sounding cold. I thought about leaving him a key, in case he wanted to come and go, but decided not to. Leaving a key was the opposite of sounding cold and it was just as unwise.

Then I left. All the unnecessarily long way to school that I'd chosen, I fretted about leaving him asleep. Suppose he was ill? Suppose he wasn't in a normal sleep? And then, if he was just worn out, what about when he woke – there was no one to look after him, he might not have the energy to make himself something to eat. I should have left a snack beside the bed. My steps slowed as I thought that and I almost turned and went back, but pulled myself together just in time and walked on. It was absurd to be fussing like that, and a big mistake to want to go back to cosseting Don. I mustn't. I would get sucked in again.

It was a hard day at school. I was distracted the entire day and it is impossible to be distracted in charge of a Reception class. The children sensed it at once and responded by being extra demanding and growing noisier and noisier. Jeremy asked if I had a headache, and I said yes, because it gave me a simple justification for my vagueness. He tried his best to help by telling the children this and appealing for their sympathy – disastrous. Children of that age don't respond to pleas for compassion.

154

They don't know what it is. 'Poor Miss' lasts a second, and then they expect complete attention. I had to resort to an audio-tape – we had three stories, one after the other, before I could do anything interesting with them and even then I was watching the clock.

At lunchtime, I almost rang my flat. Don might not answer of course, I knew that, or he might already have left, but I thought I should try to reach him. It would show my concern, and I wanted to show it. I honestly did. But then I thought of having the afternoon to get through and that if he did pick up the phone and talk he might upset me and I'd be even more useless as a teacher than I'd been in the morning. So I didn't ring. I didn't go to the staff room or have anything to eat either. I told Jeremy I'd just take some paracetamol and sit quietly in the classroom. He kindly brought me a cup of tea, but unfortunately Margot Fletcher saw him bringing it and came to enquire if I was ill, did I need to go home? No, no, I said, my headache was lifting. I'd be fine. She said she'd take my word for it but that I shouldn't struggle on if I was not up to it. 'It won't do the children any good,' she said. As if I didn't know that.

I managed better in the afternoon and the noise died down. By home time, I was exhausted with the effort but in no hurry to leave. I invented all kinds of reasons why Jeremy should go at once and why I needed to stay. And go he did. I pottered about, taking things off the walls, pinning other things up, and then, as the cleaners started to appear, I couldn't put off going home any longer. Again, I took a circuitous route, and once in my street, thought of several things I needed to buy in the shops. If Don were still there, he would need feeding. Molly wasn't eating with me that night, and I'd only been going to have an omelette. I bought steak and mushrooms and some potatoes and green beans. At least I could cook a proper dinner for him. It would give me something to do. I wanted my hands to be busy.

I stood outside my block of flats for a while and stared up at my sitting-room window, wondering if I could see anything different. Had the curtains been as far apart as that? Or had Don pushed them further along their track? But why would he? He wouldn't. He wouldn't touch the curtains. And during the day they were always pulled as far apart as possible to let in the most sun, if there was any. I groaned at my own absurdity. Best to march confidently, briskly, into the building and up to my flat. I must not creep in apologetically, or look anxious or fearful – no, I would be calm, calm. So I almost ran up the stairs, swinging my bag of food, and when I'd opened my door I shouted, in what I hoped was a cheerful fashion, 'Hello? Don?' There was no reply, but somehow I sensed he was still there. I hummed deliberately as I took off my coat and hung it up, and then I went into the kitchen and began emptying my bag. I wasn't going to go looking for him. He would have to come and find me. Which he did, eventually. I heard his slow footsteps coming along the little passageway from my bedroom and I heard him coughing, and then he was there, in the doorway.

*

There seemed, at the start of this, too little to write, or not enough that I could manage to write, but now there seems too much. Too much has happened suddenly, too much has changed, and all in one week. I don't know how to set it down, or even if it will help, to set it down.

*

Yes, it will. I want to try to trace how we got here, and I want to try to decide where exactly it is that we all are. How awkwardly I've put that, but then awkward is just how I feel. Days now since Don arrived and I haven't got used to it. I don't know if I want to get used to it, but what can I do? He seems so content. He seems so much more like his old self. That should be good news, and it is, but it's also, somehow, dangerous. I think he imagines we can put the clock back. Maybe we could, but do

156

I want to? The trouble is, it can't be rewound far enough back. But does Don realise this?

He looks better. That was the first thing to happen, the change in his appearance. When he appeared, all haggard and unshaven, in the kitchen doorway that afternoon he caught sight of himself in the mirror hanging opposite it, behind the main door, and said, 'God, I look awful.' He seemed shocked, as though he hadn't looked at himself for months, and maybe he hadn't, or maybe he'd looked without seeing, his eyes dead. 'Can I use your bathroom?' he asked, and I nodded, registering how normal he sounded. The shower ran for ages, and when he re-emerged he'd shaved. His razor can't have been strong enough to give him the close shave he needed, but the worst of the stubble was gone. He'd washed his hair too, and brushed it straight back, the way I liked it. But he had no clean clothes, and was still in the creased trousers and a shirt with a grimy collar. 'Sorry,' he said, gesturing at his clothes. Then he went to the kettle, as easy as anything, and asked could he make some tea, and maybe some toast, and I nodded again, bewildered, wondering when he would say something to explain himself. I was the one who was tense. And awkward. That was when the awkwardness began and it still hasn't lifted. He seemed not so much to take over my kitchen – I had to remind myself it was *my* kitchen – as to inhabit it naturally. He located the tea without needing to ask where I kept it and he reached up to take a mug from its hook as though he didn't need to look, he knew where it would be. Then he sat, smiling, at my table. Smiling.

My voice sounded hoarse when I said I'd bought food to make a proper meal, he didn't need to have toast. He said that was thoughtful of me and he'd appreciate it, he hadn't had a real meal for so long he'd forgotten when that was. I began peeling the potatoes, my back to him as he sat there. 'Can I help?' he asked. I shook my head. Slowly, mixed with the feeling of awkwardness, which I resented but couldn't get rid of, there was another feeling growing, of anger. He'd disappeared, had all of us worried, and then had the gall to turn up in the middle of the night and sleep in my bed without offering a word of explanation. And now he was being very much at home, still without apologising for his behaviour. He appeared so pleased with himself and seemed to want me to respond and welcome him with open arms. Well, I was not going to. I was suspicious.

But he knew all that. We had been married twenty-two years. He knew me, he knew how to interpret my silence and my turned back. 'Lou,' he said, 'there's so much to tell you.' His voice was soft, but I just waited, busy now with trimming the beans. 'I've finally got somewhere,' he said, 'I've proved that ...' And I stopped him. I said that if he had come to tell me about his investigations I did not want to hear. I said I couldn't bear it, and that I'd told him this again and again and again. Didn't he understand? I didn't care any more what he'd proved. To me, it would be irrelevant. My voice was shaking then, and he heard, and started to get up from the table to come to me, but I moved away. He tried again to talk, managing a few words – I think along the lines of 'it changes everything' – before I said no, and put my hands over my ears, dropping the knife I was holding. He picked it up for me, and retreated to his chair at the table.

I cooked. For a whole twenty minutes neither of us said a word. I set the table. The vegetables bubbled in their pans, the salad was tossed in its bowl, the steak spat on the grill. When it was all ready, I sat down at the table with him. I thought about opening a bottle of wine – I had two or three bottles in the rack – but decided it would be too much like a celebration, so I just filled a jug with water and offered it to him. He ate carefully, slowly, as he always does. I kept my eyes on my plate. 'Delicious,' he said, when he'd finished. 'You've no idea how delicious that was, Lou. Thank you.' I had struggled to clear my own plate and hadn't quite managed. None of it tasted delicious to me. I couldn't go on not looking at him, once I'd stacked the plates and pans in the dishwasher, but when finally

I turned towards him, his expression infuriated me – he looked so *sorry* for me, there was pity in his eyes. And that decided me. 'You can't stay here, Don,' I said. 'It's my flat, there isn't room. Molly's in the spare room.'

He nodded. He said, of course, he understood, he'd go. It was just, he said, that he'd arrived back so late and he'd lost the key to his bedsitter and he hadn't known where to go except to Judith's and he hadn't wanted to face her, and besides he had so much to tell me. 'I didn't mean to fall straight asleep,' he said, 'not without telling you what you won't let me tell you. It's good news, Lou. You needn't be afraid, you ...' But I stopped him again. I knew I was behaving childishly, but I couldn't help it. I was so afraid he would come out, as he always did, with some crazy theory; that his 'proof' and his 'good news' would turn out, as before, to be delusional nonsense. Yet at the same time I knew perfectly well that he no longer *seemed* demented. He sounded rational. His face had relaxed, it wasn't taut with strain. Something had happened to cause this transformation and I knew I was being silly, perverse even, not to let him tell me what it was.

We went into the sitting-room and I put the television on. It was still early, only just after six o'clock. 'Coffee?' I asked, and went to make it without waiting for a reply. When I took it back in, I didn't sit beside him on the sofa. I sat at right angles, on the easy chair. He seemed to be listening and watching with rapt attention but that was always how he treated television – if it was on, even if he hadn't turned it on himself, he had to concentrate. It drove him mad when the children had it on as mere background and talked over it or even went out of the room leaving the television still on. When the news is over, I thought, I will ask him to go. If he can't get into his bedsitter, he will have to go to Judith's. I don't have to feel responsible for him, I'm not turning him out into the cold.

But as the news ended, as I opened my mouth to say what I had practised, I heard the door of my flat open. It was Molly.

That was it, the point at which everything changed – it's suddenly so obvious. If Molly hadn't come in then, Don would have left, I'm sure. Maybe he would have had one last attempt to tell me what he'd found out but if I'd stopped him again, and I would have done, he would have gone.

Molly was, of course, astonished. She stood in the doorway, stock-still, gaping. Don got up and smiled at her and said, 'Molly!' and held out his arms, but still she didn't move. For a moment, he looked uncertain, his arms falling to his side, but still he smiled and at last she moved towards him, half-stumbling, saying, 'Dad?' with almost a question in her voice. Then they did embrace, but tentatively. Don, I'm sure, reminding himself that, unlike Miranda, Molly was not a great hugger – in that one respect she was like him, and not like me. She looked so small beside him, her head only up to his chest. She's the same height as I am, and as he gave her this hug I felt the strangest sensation of pressure on my own chest, as though *I* was being enfolded in his arms.

So, Molly took over. She asked all the questions I hadn't asked, and I had a choice then: either I stayed and listened to the answers or I went into another room and deliberately ignored them. I stayed. I heard Don tell Molly where he had been, and why, and what the result had been. I don't think I took half of this information in, probably because I didn't want to.

Then I heard Molly ask, 'So are you satisfied? Can you stop now? Are your investigations over?' I saw Don was looking straight at me, and that he was addressing what he said next to me, not to Molly. 'I'll never be satisfied,' he said, 'but yes, I can stop. I needn't carry on. There's a lot more could come out, *should* come out, but the crucial thing is ...' I hardly understood the rest. Whatever this crucial thing is, it is also complicated and I didn't understand what Don was talking about – nothing new there, then. Molly seemed to, though. It was all to do with weather reports and how from now on no one would be able to take a boat out from that marina without being made aware, automatically, of the latest update. Don explained how this would be done and Molly nodded. There was a strange expression on her face. She was looking at her father as though she was struggling to hold something back because it might upset him – her lips kept constantly folding in, disappearing, and then she'd relax them and almost pouted before she did the same again. Words, I thought, were being swallowed. Her eyes were not so much narrowed as intently focused on Don, weighing him up, deciding something. And then it began to occur to me, in the most peculiar way, that Molly knew her father was a fraud. She knew he was making no sense at all with this rigmarole about inventing a new system of weather reports being passed on to boat owners in the marina. He was improvising, finding a way out of the mess he'd got himself into. He'd decided to find an escape route, unable simply to admit he had been deluded all along. I was suddenly sure of this, and sure that Molly had realised it and was deciding whether to expose his fantasy.

How had it happened, this coming-to-his-senses? When? After the blow to his head, when he'd collapsed and ended up in the Middlesex? Had he brought himself to the point of complete breakdown and then negotiated this strategy with himself to make a climb-down acceptable? It was so elaborate – why couldn't he just have admitted Miranda's death was an accident? – but it would appeal to Don's mind. Nothing was ever simple with him, he liked concocting scenarios. I thought about how he'd turned up that night, exhausted, of how he'd fallen onto my bed and slept so deeply and then, when he'd woken up, been transformed. He'd gone to Durham, seen Alex, asked his absurd question about the weather, and then probably returned once more to Holland and persuaded the authorities that it was their duty to issue storm warnings to every boat. They must have thought he was mad.

But maybe not. Maybe I am the deluded one. Maybe I was reading into Molly's expression more than was there. Perhaps Don really had thought of a way of the people at the marina becoming responsible for storm warnings. Just because it was unlikely, and seemed fanciful, didn't mean it was not feasible. What did I know? Nothing. I tried to listen more carefully. Molly was talking now. But she was not, I noticed, asking him how this new system he claimed to have invented would work – she wasn't being suspicious, she wasn't cross-questioning him. Instead, she was concentrating on getting him to state, unequivocally, that the investigations which had dominated his life for three years were definitely, *definitely*, over – that was all that mattered. I knew she was right. What would be the point in deliberately humiliating Don, forcing him to admit what I believed to be the truth? Why shame him into confessing that after bringing himself to the point of complete breakdown he'd had to acknowledge he'd been misguided? The cost of my being right was far too high. Molly instinctively knew that. I should keep quiet.

Yet Molly had apparently decided not to let him off the hook so completely, after all. She returned to questioning him about the state of the boat. She said, 'So the mast wasn't faulty? The engine was OK?' She was still watching him closely, as though this was a test he had to pass. Don hesitated. Here we go, I thought, he can't keep it up. I was waiting for the tirade that would follow, but it never came. 'Maybe not,' he said, 'it's impossible to prove either way. I tried. I don't know.' He then launched into a little lecture about masts and engine parts and I could tell that this time Molly understood no more than I did. She repeated – 'Can you stop now?' Don said, yes, he could. He hesitated. Did he look shifty, or was I imagining it? He went on that Miranda should never, in view of the storm warning, have been allowed out and now no one ever would be again. Molly didn't ask him how this could possibly work, though she did frown. In addition, the makers of the mast and of the engine were checking the finished products even more rigorously just in case there had been a fault.

I should never have spoken. I should have gone on keeping silent. I should never have said, 'So, no one was to blame, really. There isn't any justice to be done. Miranda took a boat out without knowing a storm was coming and she wasn't experienced enough to cope. That's it. Human error. Hers. The inquest said so. You just couldn't accept it, and now you do. Well, I'm glad something has brought you to your senses.'

*

Molly was angry with me. She defended her father, saying he'd only been trying to establish the truth. 'Was it worth it?' I asked. 'Worth putting himself, and us, through the last three years? I don't think so, Molly.' Molly started to say something, but Don stopped her. The smile had certainly been wiped from his face by my nasty, sarcastic words and tone, but he was still calm and looked almost relaxed. 'I had to do it, Lou,' he said, 'you know that. However mad, I couldn't rest, I couldn't …' I interrupted. 'Oh, you don't need to tell *me* that. Nothing else mattered to you. No one's suffering was as great as your own. You couldn't stop your investigations for *our* sake, seeing what they did to us, you couldn't admit they were pointless.' Don spread his hands out. 'I'm sorry,' he said. 'I'm so sorry.'

What was wrong with me? My God, what was wrong? Why wasn't I thrilled that at last my husband had seen sense and accepted the truth we'd all known? It didn't matter, surely, that he was deluding himself in a different way, convincing himself with all this nonsense about weather reports, that he'd done some good so that others wouldn't die as Miranda had done, that all his investigations had been worthwhile. As he said, he had to do it. It was a process, which for some stubborn reason he had had to go through, and now he *was* through it, and all was well. But that was precisely the trouble – all was not well, and it still is not. He is still too proud to admit there was no need for his investigations, that they were quite unnecessary.

*

Molly gave him her bed. When Don said he was leaving, she was startled and asked why. He said, without looking in my direction, that I wanted him to leave. She turned to me and asked, 'It's not true, is it, Mum? You don't want him to leave, do you? He's got it wrong.' 'No,' I said, 'he's got it right. There's nowhere for him to sleep.' I hated my own defensive tone. 'He can have my room,' she said, 'the spare room. I can stay with Judith. I promised I would, anyway, before I go back. That's settled, I'll ring her now and tell her Dad's here and he's fine.' Out came her mobile and she rang Judith. And then, to make things even worse, Judith said she would come and pick her up and see Don with her own eyes.

There was nothing I could do, short of creating the kind of ugly scene I detest. I felt beaten. It wasn't Don who had beaten me but Molly. She didn't want me to throw her father out. As far as she was concerned, he was the old Don, restored to life, as it were, she didn't care how or why, and she now thought I would rejoice and we would all be a happy family again. Except that Miranda is dead. Except that everything that has happened has changed me, not just Don. He is 'back'. I am not.

9

DON SAID he could do the cooking, do the shopping, do anything to make himself useful, but I refused his offer, said there was no need. I've no intention of slipping into a chummy set-up. I don't want him to imagine that we are going to become a unit again. We are not. If he doesn't want to return to his bedsitter, and he doesn't – who would? – he will have to find himself somewhere else. He may have spent a lot of money on his investigations and, of course, he's now lost his job, but he can't surely have spent everything he got from his share of the sale of our house.

He isn't embarrassed about being here, in my flat. I expected him to be, I even thought it right that he should be. I would have been, if the situation had been the other way around. I'd have felt an intruder, an interloper, but Don seems alarmingly at ease. Well, he alarms me. I don't want him to be comfortable here. When I come back from school he is sitting in my kitchen drinking coffee and reading the newspaper and he looks up and smiles and says, hello, had a good day, as though we are an old married couple. What have I written? Of course that is what we are, it is exactly what we are: married, still.

Nothing has been said about our marital status, by either of us. I'm not even sure if we are officially separated. How official does it have to be? When the house was sold, and the money divided, I signed some sort of agreement, but I don't think it amounted to a declaration that Don and I are officially separated. Neither of us cared about that. I wanted to be free of Don but I wasn't looking far into the future – I just wanted a new life, afterwards, when it was over. And I've got it. I've made a new life, by myself, in this flat, and I want to keep it as it is.

Molly and Finn and Judith are all here often. We have what they all seem to think are enjoyable family meals. Judith brings the food and Molly helps her prepare it, in my kitchen. There's that very air of celebration I don't want. Suddenly, against my nature, I am the quiet one. I can't stand being round my own table with them all for very long and keep making excuses to go into my bedroom or sitting room. It is crowded in the kitchen, anyway – the table there was never meant to cater for five people. It isn't like our old kitchen, which was spacious and had such a big pine table that it could, and did, accommodate a dozen people easily. But they don't seem to mind the crush. They like it, or at least there are no complaints. The very fact that Judith is here, and sitting next to Don, seems remarkable. He hasn't snapped at her once, he hasn't winced when she's gone off into one of her long-drawn-out, completely boring anecdotes. I even saw him put his arm round her at one point as though he'd forgotten that she irritated him. And Judith knows Don must have forgiven her even if he will never say so – she senses the change.

They try, in their different ways, to draw me in. Molly is especially solicitous, serving me first, hoping I don't mind her using this dish or that plate, treating me like some sort of revered elderly relative who mustn't be annoyed. Finn watches me all the time, though if I catch his eye he looks away. Judith is nervous. She talks and laughs too much, then pauses and says, apropos of nothing, 'Sorry, Lou,' and there is a sudden silence, as though everyone is waiting for me to accept her apology. I don't bother saying, 'Sorry for what?' – I just nod. And as for Don, he smiles kindly at me. He has this infuriatingly patient air. He is waiting. His expression says he is waiting for me to come round and he is confident that I will.

I don't ask questions, but everyone else does. Don asks Molly about Africa and she fills him in on what she's been doing in Zambia and why she's in London. I've heard it all already, of course, but she tells it slightly differently to her father. It seems to me she is seeking his approval and wanting praise from him which she didn't want from me. Maybe she didn't need it from me, knowing that I supported her anyway. She described her training in Serenje, the town which has electricity and is considered luxurious compared to the village she went on to. She told him about the 'nshima' they ate, a kind of maize which has a mashed potato consistency but virtually no flavour. Then she emphasised, pointedly I thought, how family-orientated all the villages in Nambo are, with enough huts grouped together to take extended families so that within each village there are smaller villages of grass huts. Don asked how exactly the huts were built and she told him that only the roofs were grass but the walls were of hardened mud or sometimes locally fired brick. She lived with different families for a week each and was surprised how life varied according to the composition of each family. She blushed when Don said, 'Well done, you amaze me.' He takes care, too, to ask Finn how he's getting on without a hint now that he thinks this gardening thing a waste of time – polite questions, factual. Finn is suspicious that he is being patronised and is a little surly in his answers. But as the questions become more detailed he is becoming more convinced that his father really is interested and the surliness is evaporating.

All this information swilling about, the stuff of our lives while Don has been absent. At first, nobody asked him any questions, perhaps because they were afraid to, in case Don went back to how he had been when they were last with him, but gradually they made the odd enquiry. Don was ready for it. He was obviously glad to have the opportunity to explain where he'd been since his stay in hospital and told us of his movements in some detail. I tried not to listen. I really didn't want to know. I went into the sitting-room saying I had a call to make and I closed the kitchen door as I went out. Let him enthral them all with his tale of where he'd been and who he'd been with and then his fake eureka moment and the happy ending.

I rang Ruth. I asked if I could come and stay for the weekend. 'Perfect,' she said. She was going to be on her own; it would be lovely. She didn't ask me why I wanted to visit – I've never invited myself in all these years – just stressed how eager she was for me to come. Maybe she stressed it a little too strongly. She's not stupid, and must know something is wrong.

*

It's good to be staying in a proper house again. It's not just the sense of space but the privacy, the self-contained atmosphere, as though we're insulated from the world. Ruth's new house is detached and surrounded by a garden and, though other houses are near, they can't be seen from most of her windows. She has a conservatory opening out of her sitting-room and we loll there, on her bamboo sofas, drinking wine and looking out into the garden, at the bird table.

'This is lovely,' I said. 'We should have had a conservatory.'

'I could never understand why you let that house go,' Ruth said. 'Why did you?'

I didn't reply. I hardly understood myself. It was because I wanted, when it was all over, to start again and I couldn't do it there, in that house. I needed new territory. I had to have it, and to find it I needed money, so the house had to be sold. I told Ruth what I'd told her at the time: Don offered no resistance because he needed money too, for his investigations.

'Maybe, one day, you'll have a house again,' Ruth said.

'I doubt it,' was all I said. It wasn't just that. I needed 'new territory', but it was more than that. The house itself upset me. Nothing awful had happened in it, but it started to oppress me. It seemed to mock me in an odd sort of way. I'd go into rooms and feel overpowered by them, as though they did not belong to me – I'd stop, and stare at the furniture and belongings and wonder how they came to be there, and then I would hurry out into the garden where this peculiar feeling would lift, but not for long. It wasn't that Miranda haunted the house or anything ridiculous like that. I didn't connect any of this to Miranda. The problem was the house itself. It wasn't mine any more. It was another woman's, somebody I used to know but had lost touch with.

I tried, once, to explain this to Don, though I could hardly explain it to myself. It took a long time, and several attempts, to get his attention but by then I'd grown used to this. I knew I would have to shock him to make him listen. So I did. I started a fire, a small fire, perfectly controlled, of Miranda's old school exercise books. I'd looked through them and checked that they contained nothing worth preserving (except for some English exercise books with stories and poems in them, which I kept). I took them into the garden when Don was sitting on the terrace staring into space. He'd been there half an hour. I'd spoken to him several times but, as usual at that time, he hadn't replied or acknowledged me. So I marched out, arms full of exercise books, and piled them on top of some newspapers I'd brought out earlier and I started a fire. It didn't catch his attention immediately. The paper was burning well before he seemed to notice and then he got up and called out, 'What are you doing? Use the incinerator!' I ignored him and went on throwing books onto the blaze until he came towards me, his face more alive (with irritation) than it had been for months.

I think I may have laughed, though nothing was very funny. It was the feeling of triumph – that I had done something to make him notice me! He thought I was hysterical, and for a moment he was concerned. 'Stop, stop, what is this, Lou, what is this?' he cried. I said it was nothing, I just wanted to talk to him and he had refused to hear me. He said this wasn't true, what could I be thinking of? I could talk to him any time I wanted. He even embraced me, out there in the garden, the first hug for ages and ages.

The fire soon burned out. Don wasn't angry about the exercise books – they didn't matter to him any more than they mattered to me. Perhaps, surprisingly, he wasn't sentimental about such things. He said, 'Let's go into the house and talk.' That's when I told him the house was the trouble: it was what I wanted to talk to him about. So we stayed in the garden and I tried. At first, he listened intently, but as what I said grew more and more incoherent his attention wandered. 'You're depressed,' he said. 'It's natural. It's nothing to do with the house. It's you.' But I insisted that I wanted to leave, go somewhere new. He said he hadn't time to think about moving when he had so much to do. And that was when I said what I had never planned to say. I said I wanted to go somewhere without him. I wanted to be free of him and his grief as well as the house. I almost added that I had come to dread his presence, but I didn't say it.

I suppose I am ashamed of that episode, which certainly doesn't show me in a good light – such cruelty and melodrama sound pitiful now. I didn't tell Ruth any of this, of course, when she said that about having a house again. I simply told her that Don was staying with me and how hard I was finding this, nearly as hard as living with him in our house had been afterwards.

I went over how he'd turned up, and what he'd said. Ruth was searching my face while I talked and didn't say anything crass, or assume I must be delighted that 'he's back to normal'. She just said, 'You're upset,' and gave me a hug, and that was enough to set me off. Ruth was the one person I didn't mind seeing me like this. She didn't say anything till I'd stopped snivelling. I couldn't explain to her why I was so upset because I don't know myself. Do I really not want the old Don back? Wasn't that what I had wanted, when he was so demented? Wasn't it what I yearned for, that this stranger, this horrible madman would stop pretending to be the husband I loved? If

Don was now restored to the way he had been before, what was the problem? My reaction didn't make any kind of sense.

The first thing that Ruth said, when I'd blurted all this out, startled me. 'You're frightened,' she said. Frightened? How could she think that? What was I frightened of? She shrugged. She said she didn't know but that was what struck her when she saw me getting out of my car – I simply looked frightened. 'You looked,' she said, speaking very slowly, warily, 'a little like the way you looked the first time I saw you, after you'd heard, you know, the awful news about Miranda, as though you were afraid to believe what you'd been told.' But how could there be any comparison with the way I felt then, and now? Don returning, his quest over, his rage and resentment apparently gone, could not be, should not be, frightening. 'Maybe,' said Ruth, still stepping so very carefully, 'you don't love him any more. That would be frightening, wouldn't it? I mean, you loved the old Don, before what happened seemed to change him, so when he reappears you ought to be thrilled. And you're not. Is it because in the interval you've stopped loving him? That would be frightening.'

I denied it. I don't know any more what loving Don means. It's gone, my capacity to love him, as I used to love. Loving Molly, loving Finn – but loving Don?

*

Nearly the end of term. Glorious weather at the moment, hope it continues for the school holidays. The sky is an incredible blue all day long, and the sun clear and strong but not too scorchingly hot. The children look so *free* in their shorts and sleeveless tops and sandals, and it makes life so much easier when they don't have to struggle, as some of them do when it's cold, with buttons and fastenings on jackets and coats. They trot in just as they are. Except for the twins, who remain in long-sleeved garments, their legs still enclosed in trousers. But they don't seem uncomfortable. Probably to them this weather is not so hot.

171

We are considering friendship. I have to step carefully, though. Some of them have no obvious friend, some are everyone's friend. Friendship makes us happy, I tell them. Friends help each other. Friends play together. If we have no friends we are lonely. We must all try to be friends with each other. A simplistic set of statements, but the children approve, they all want to have friends and for everyone to be nice to each other. Paige says her best friend is her dog. Can dogs be friends? Of course, I say. Lola says her best friend is her cat, and others echo her. 'Who is your best friend, Miss?' asks Paige. I told her about Lynne, Pat, and Ruth. I said they were my best friends. But in fact I seem detached from them, not so pleased to hear from them as I used to be. Ruth wanted to make a date for our annual reunion but I made excuses, and she knew I was making them. I didn't go to last year's reunion either, though Lynne, at whose home it was held, was so persuasive, assuring me, as ever, that it would do me good, 'What are friends for?' she asked, and answered herself, 'To help get one through the bad times.' But I'm through them. It's over. Friends now should be for enjoying myself with. I think about what it would be like, to spend a weekend at Ruth's with her and Lynne and Pat. What would we do? Eat, drink, exchange news, and most of all reminisce. That is the part which is so important in our reunions, the going over of memories, the 'Do you remember?' bit when we all shriek and laugh at the ludicrous scenes of past embarrassments we conjure up. I've no enthusiasm for this any more. I don't feel connected to that past. I'm not going to go. Seeing them separately will have to do.

Of course, I hadn't answered Paige quite truthfully. Don was my best friend, always. Friendship led to love. But is he a friend now? If he is, why do I want him to leave me alone? And if he isn't, then what is he?

*

Don left today. I came home an hour ago and the flat was

172

empty. I'd gone straight from Ruth's to school this morning so I hadn't seen him since Friday. I thought at first he was just out, maybe at some job interview, maybe just walking, but then I saw the note propped up against the kettle. 'Gone to Judith's' it said. 'Will stay there till I've sorted something out. Thanks for everything. Keep in touch?' Judith will love having him, but how extraordinary that he has gone there. He used to say, after it all happened, that, much though he loves her, he couldn't spend another night under his sister's roof. She irritates him to the point of exasperation. He's always been ashamed of this, but he can't control his feelings for long. It's tiny things that set him off – the way she never stops talking and demanding responses. Judith has to have involvement all the time – it's 'Don't you think?' and 'Don't you agree?' and Don can't bring himself to give a simple yes or no. And she hums and sings as she moves about; she's noisy and he's quiet. She bangs doors like a teenager and moves around, he claims, like a baby elephant.

So, he's at Judith's. Good. Even if he's got over his unreasonable resentment of his sister, he will soon find her annoying again. Being there will force him to find a decent place to live as soon as possible. And it must mean he has accepted that I don't want him back in my life. He can't be completely out of my life, but I don't want him at the centre. I don't have to give reasons to myself. I don't have to examine my state of mind. It's enough that I want to go on living on my own. I feel comfortable here, in my flat. In this, my new life.

*

Don didn't tell Molly that he was moving out. She came expecting to find him here this evening and there was some confusion, because as she's been staying with Judith herself I assumed she would know. But she didn't. He wasn't at Judith's when she left this morning and nothing had been said about his arrival. Never mind, I said, he's there now, so if you want you can move back here. No, she said, I'll stay at Judith's. She's got plenty of room. No need for me to move back.

She said this so carelessly, but surely she must know how it hurts me. I want her to come back here. I want her to want to come back. She has such a short time left in London and since Don came I hardly seem to have had any time with her. But I said, 'Fine, fine, whatever suits you best.' She stared at me, chewing her bottom lip the way she always does when she's working up to saying something she isn't sure she should say.

'Yes?' I asked.

'Mum,' she said, 'what has happened to you?'

I said that was a big question. What exactly did she mean?

'The way you look at Dad,' she said, 'that's what I mean.'

'And how do I look at him?'

'As if he's a stranger you don't much like.'

'Well,' I said, 'that's what he became, remember? Afterwards? You agreed, you felt the same, and so did Finn.'

'Yes,' she said, 'but that's all over, he's himself again. You've got to forgive him, he couldn't help how he was, he couldn't help being obsessed, and he's sorry.'

'Sorry?'

'Yes. Sorry for what he put you through. What he put us all through. You can't go on holding it against him for ever. It's cruel. You're being cruel. Why? It's not like you ...'

Has Molly forgotten? Is it possible that she has forgotten? I wanted to remind her of what that first year was like, how her father became more and more distant, how we appeared to become of no concern to him, how we ended up almost afraid of him. Had she forgotten the day she broke her arm? How she was running down the stairs outside his study and tripped over her own undone shoelace and went crashing to the bottom? He was in his study, he must have heard the crash and her scream – I was at the bottom of the garden and heard the awful sound from there – but he didn't move. He was, he said, in the middle of an important phone call to Holland. Molly lay at the foot

174

of his stairs until I came running in and even then, when I shouted for him to ring for an ambulance *he finished the call first.* Of course, afterwards, he was remorseful. He apologised. But it was obvious to Molly and to me that his precious investigations took precedence. Had she forgotten all this?

I will never be able to talk to Molly about how I feel about her father. It is too intimate. It would feel like a betrayal. I can't tell her that I feel nothing for him any more. It's no good his telling me he is sorry. Something has been destroyed and I don't believe it was my doing. Don could argue it wasn't his either, it was what happened. But that's not a good enough answer. It's a question of priorities. Miranda's death pushed us all to the back of his mind. He didn't care enough about the living, and that has altered permanently the way I feel. I'm too tired, too emotionally worn out to start all over again. Molly and Finn are young. He can reclaim them, but not me. I'm glad for him that this seems to be possible.

So all I said to Molly was, 'Cruel? I hope not.' I didn't want to cry in front of her, but the longer she stood there accusing me of being cruel to her father the more likely it seemed that I might. 'It's the Book Group night,' I said, clearing my throat. 'I have to go. It's at Shirley's.'

'Go, then,' she said, and left the flat before me.

*

I couldn't concentrate of course. I'd liked the book – it was a biography of Katherine Mansfield and it had felt comforting to be absorbed in another woman's life – but I sat silent most of the time, thinking that never in a million years would I have expected the children to side with their father against me. Well, that is a silly way to put it, of course they are not doing anything of the sort. I am the one who is seeing the situation in those extreme terms. How can I blame them when, to them, it seems that Don is over his obsession, or as over it as he ever will be, and has come back to us, and that I am the one rejecting him and can't even articulate why. They see me as cruel, and that's what it looks like. He is forgiven for his behaviour but I am not. He was seen as not being in his right mind – and now I am the one not in my right mind. They want me back, and I can't find myself, that other Lou, that other mum I was before. This is afterwards, and it is how I am.

*

Judith rang just now. She wants me to come to a surprise birthday celebration for Molly – '… nothing much, a meal, that's all, and a cake, and all her family here.' I had to swallow hard. I should be the one organising a celebration. I am her *mother*. And I would have done, nearer the time. I had it planned in my head, not that Judith would believe it. I was going to invite everyone to dinner in a restaurant – hadn't decided which one. Now Judith has pre-empted this. I couldn't bear to argue and tell her it was my role to be inviting her – oh, let her do it. She loves it, she is in her element.

She said not to say a word to Molly, which is easy because I've hardly seen her this past week. She's busy, with so little time left before she leaves again for Africa, and of course she's staying at Judith's – so cosy they all are, the rest of my family under the same roof. She's popped in a couple of times, to collect things, but we've had only polite exchanges, nothing more. I asked if she was looking forward to going back, and she said yes, she was, she missed the landscape and she missed the children. 'I'll be back for good at the end of the year,' she said. 'I have to make the most of my time there.' I asked her then if she was going to take up her deferred place at Leeds, and she said she would, and then do a PGTC. That surprised me. 'You want to teach?' I said. 'Don't sound so shocked,' she said, 'you know when we were little we always wanted to be teachers, like you.'

She said it in an offhand way, and she was speaking in the past tense, but still, I was touched. It's true, of course, the bit about them both, when they were young, wanting to be teachers. They played schools all the time, taking it in turn to be the teacher. Molly was much stricter than Miranda. When she was the teacher I'd hear her shouting commands like a sergeant-major and she doled out punishments ferociously. I caught her once rapping Miranda's knuckles with a ruler, really hitting her hard. I remember stopping her and saying I never, ever, hit a child – where on earth had she got this horrible idea from? Books, she said. She was only about eight at the time and the books she read were very limited, but she'd just been reading some version of a Dickens novel adapted for children, with gruesome illustrations of pupils being beaten. The power of literature!

Later, though, I seem to remember they went off the idea. When they were teenagers, teaching as a career became anathema to them – too dreary and uncool. Conversely, Don's job grew in attraction. Advertising was cool, and they loved it when one of his adverts became popular and their friends quoted the copy back at them. Their father's working life seemed quite glamorous to them – they were impressed by his agency's offices in Marylebone – whereas my world was one they knew all too well and couldn't wait to escape from. 'Couldn't you have done something else, Mum?' Molly once asked me, and when I said I'd always wanted to be an infants' teacher she groaned. I did once try, timidly, to defend my job, pointing out the satisfaction of being able to help a child read and write, but I never succeeded in making teaching sound fascinating, which to me it was and is.

Molly might make a good teacher but she hasn't a temperament as suited to teaching as mine is. She is too bolshy. She'd find it a strain having to fit in with any rule or regulation of which she disapproved, and there will be plenty of those. And she has a temper, which she would have to control. In that one respect – temperament – Miranda would have made a better teacher. She doesn't – didn't – find it hard to accept direction.

That was her undoing, in a way. She was too … No point in going on with this train of thought.

*

Paige's mother asked to see me today. She hung about when she brought Paige, which was unusual – Paige isn't one of those children who really needs to be brought to the classroom door. She asked, could she have a word about something after school? Not in front of Paige, though, she'd take her home first and come back, if that was OK. We fixed a time. All day I was wondering what on earth Paige's mother wanted to see me about. Usually, when a parent requests 'a word' it is to complain and it isn't difficult to predict what it will be about, but in Paige's case I hadn't a clue. So when Mrs York came out with 'Paige is being bullied. She's started wetting the bed. It's that Haroun,' I was astonished and not at all ready for the accusation.

The wisest thing to do in these cases is calm the parent down, encourage them to get whatever it is out of their system. It's unwise to contest the truth of what you're being told. If you do, arguments begin which get nowhere and the exchange can get very heated. But I was *so* surprised – the allegation was patently absurd – that I laughed. 'Haroun?' I said, 'but he's half Paige's size!' That, it seemed, had nothing to do with it. A bully, said Mrs York, could be any size. There were more ways of bullying than through physical strength. Hastily, I agreed. I apologised for laughing, said that I'd just been so taken aback, and then I invited her to tell me what she thought had been going on. Paige was being mocked, she claimed. Haroun called her fat. He led a whispering campaign among the children. They hissed 'fatty' at her, all the time. Mrs York wasn't having it. Paige was tall, she was big-boned, she was well covered but she was *not* fat. She knew where this kind of thing led: Paige would become anorexic. She herself had suffered from this kind of taunt and she knew how it hurt and she wasn't having her daughter go through this kind of thing.

I was tempted to list for Mrs York the jibes I'd heard Paige hurl at Haroun, but I didn't. Instead I said that small children – I reminded her they were all five, or not quite five, in my class – were constantly saying mean things to each other. If I heard them, I stopped them, of course, but to a certain extent name-calling was part of the school experience and children learned how to deal with it. I wondered, tentatively, if maybe the bed-wetting was due to some other cause, if there might be something else troubling Paige ... But that got Mrs York started on her *own* problems, her marital troubles which I'd no wish to listen to but which successfully got her off the topic of Haroun's 'cruelty'. I ended up promising to keep a very close eye on Haroun and making sure he did not torment Paige.

After she left, I sat thinking of the only time I ever asked to see one of my children's teachers to complain about something. It wasn't about bullying, though I know Miranda was bullied at one stage and I almost asked for a meeting then. It was because Molly had been put in a different class from her twin and was crying about it at night. I'd been informed, of course, that this was going to happen, and I'd been given the reasons and had even agreed with them. Both girls would benefit from this kind of separation. And Miranda did, there was no question about it. But Molly didn't. She was upset, she wanted her twin at her side. Don was adamant that we should not interfere – the school knew best. But did it? Did they? It worried me. I didn't want to be one of those parents who complained, though I was not actually going to complain (so I told myself), but neither did I want Molly to go on being so miserable.

So I secretly went to see her teacher. It was an education, being on the other side. I realised that if I was not actually afraid of Molly's teacher I was certainly apprehensive and also embarrassed. The teacher, whose name I forget, was young, not even thirty, I remember calculating, but she was brisk and confident, as though she'd been teaching for many years. I was about thirty-five myself then, so not much older, but she made me feel younger than she was. I said my piece, about Molly being wretched, parted from her twin, and the teacher said, without any preamble or apology, 'She's very bossy. The other children don't like her.' I was furious. It seemed to me her response had nothing to do with what I'd come about and I resented both her description of Molly and the statement that followed. But I clearly recall not wanting to offend the teacher and make things worse for Molly. So I tried to suggest that it was not bossiness that Molly was displaying but the symptoms of missing her twin. As for the other children not liking her, I asked – politely, I thought – how the teacher could tell, and how she thought Molly might be helped to overcome their dislike. I thought I was being tactful, but the teacher brushed aside my tact. Molly, she said, had to learn that she could not dominate. That was her problem and being a twin had made it worse because she was so used to dominating Miranda.

That's the trouble with teachers – they have your child in their class for five minutes and hey presto, they know every-thing about her, much, much more than her own mother does. It was a warning to me, when I returned to teaching, and I tried always to remember it. Molly did not dominate Miranda. This was a fallacious theory. Molly helped her twin, who asked for that help, and she looked after her. Without Miranda there to need her, it was Molly who was at a loss. She was looking for a substitute, someone else who needed her strength, and she hadn't found anyone. I didn't say any of this to that teacher. I said I hoped she'd agree that Molly, if bossy, was a lively, active child, eager to do things, so could she perhaps give her little jobs in the classroom, give her some responsibility. She said she'd try, but I could tell that nothing was going to change her mind.

Still, maybe she took on board some of what I said. She did make Molly window monitor and gave her another series of simple jobs. At any rate, Molly settled down and stopped being

180

so miserable. I wished, all the same, that I hadn't gone to see her teacher. Don was right.

*

What can I give Molly for her birthday? Thinking about it, I realise that I haven't given her a real present since Miranda died. Her birthday has been too painful to celebrate. Last year she was in Africa and I only sent her a book of poems.

*

It has happened before and it will happen again and it never gets easier to deal with: I meet someone who truly does not know what happened to Miranda. This time it was a woman I'd been at teacher training college with, though I never knew her well, and I couldn't, when she came up to me in the National Portrait Gallery, remember her name. But I did recognise her, even after twenty-five years. 'Louise?' she said, 'Louise Findlay, isn't it?' I said, yes, warily, and then realised who it was, and tried to cover up the fact that I'd forgotten her name. She helped me out. 'Kitty,' she said, 'Kitty Clarke. I know all about you. Pat used to write to me and sent me snaps sometimes of your family. Guess what, I've got twin girls too. I haven't heard from Pat for ages now, two or three years, I think. How is she? Maybe she's lost my address. I emigrated, you know, to New Zealand. We're only over here because Andrew's mother's very ill ...'

On and on she went as I stood there, trapped. She suggested that we went down to the café, and I found myself going along with her. She chattered away, telling me all about her twins, both at university, one sporty and one not, one with a serious boyfriend and one without. Then, inevitably, apologising for talking so much, she asked about my twins, and the moment came. I dropped my head. I couldn't just pretend, I couldn't just walk away. Kitty is a perfectly nice woman. I used to like her, even if she always did talk too much. She wasn't like that Florence woman on holiday. Kitty sat across from me, smiling, eager to listen, friendly, and I really didn't need to feel defensive. What on earth was I defending myself against? I didn't know. Against a response I didn't want, I suppose – too much emotional reaction. Or too little. I can't bear, even now, people being too sympathetic or too appalled. And I can't bear them wanting to get away, either, because they are embarrassed by the tragedy and don't know how to cope with it. But I have to get over this dread, and so I chose to do it with Kitty. I said simply that one of my twins had drowned in a sailing accident. I made myself watch Kitty's face closely as I spoke. I saw the horror there, and then the empathy – yes, that was what it was, a melting of her face, a softening, then a tightening of her brow as she imagined herself in my position. For once, she didn't launch into another verbal stream but instead reached out and touched my clasped hands very lightly and said, 'Oh, Lou,' quietly. She didn't ask for details, thank God. She was silent, stunned, and I found myself saying, almost in a hearty fashion, 'Well, it was nearly three years ago,' and I added for good measure that cliché I particularly dislike, 'Life goes on.'

Kitty did ask a few questions after she'd recovered and before we parted, but none of them were about Miranda's death. She asked how Molly was coping and I told her about Africa but didn't volunteer any other insights. Then she asked about my husband, and that was another test. I failed it. I couldn't find the energy to describe how I felt about Don, especially at the moment. Kitty had never met him and she'd never known us as a married couple and it seemed irrelevant to start confessing that we were separated. So I just said he'd had a hard time coping but that he was much better now. 'And you, Lou?' she said. I felt it was time to go and suddenly remembered an appointment, which didn't fool Kitty for a moment. There was a hurried exchange of addresses and so on, and then we parted, promising to stay in touch.

I watched her walk away from the gallery towards Trafalgar Square and thought how she'd be feeling lucky, with both her twins alive and well. It's one of the benefits we bereaved bestow on other people – we make them feel lucky.

*

Back to fretting about what to buy Molly for her birthday. A camera, maybe, a digital camera. She's got a camera but it isn't digital and she does like taking photographs. Or a video camera, but she's always said she preferred still photographs. So, a digital camera. It will mean a trip to the kind of shop where I always feel at a complete loss, a target for those salesmen, who sense straight away that you're ignorant about such things. I will ask Finn to go with me. He'll know all about such cameras.

*

Don has bought Molly a digital camera already. Well, of course. His thinking would follow the same pattern as my own, so it is hardly surprising that we arrived at the same conclusion. 'Can't it be from both of you?' Finn said, and I said no far too quickly, it could not. 'There's no need for all this, you know, Mum,' he said. I didn't like the way he said it, and asked him what he meant. 'It's like you're rivals,' he said, 'you and Dad, fighting over everything, even nice things like a present for Molly.' I said we did not fight, we had never fought, and there was no rivalry between us over Molly's present or anything else. 'Oh, there is,' he said, with that annoyingly superior smile he's developed lately.

It will have to be either clothes or else some kind of special bag. She loves her old bag but she did say there were some holes in the corners and that the straps are wearing thin. I can try to find an exact copy in soft, good-quality leather. At least looking for something like that will take me to the kind of shops where I am comfortable and where Don would never be likely to go, if he plans to buy her anything else.

183

10

CHAOS AT school today. The new rules on security have come into operation and parents are now forbidden to come into the building to deliver their children to classroom doors. Only nursery children are allowed to be accompanied, but not the others. Parents have to leave their children in the playground and some of them were upset by this. They all like the idea of security being strict, so that no madman or bomber can enter, but they don't like the atmosphere this creates.

I don't like it myself. Meeting parents twice a day at my classroom door is a good way of getting to know them, and it helps to deal with any problems – it feels quite natural just to have a few words, and slip in bits of information without setting up meetings. So much can be easily put right in that way. As for security, haven't we gone far enough in that direction, with the school gates locked almost all the time and an intercom fitted? There hasn't been free and easy entry for several years now. The parents gather outside at 3.30 as though outside a prison.

It isn't far from the playground to the reception classroom, only along one corridor and then round the corner, but the way some of the children entered this morning you'd have thought they'd walked miles. Their parents are used to moving them along briskly, holding their hands and sometimes half-dragging them, desperate to deliver them to me so they can get off to work or back home. This morning, left to make their own way for the first time, some of my class ran but others trailed and looked lost and exhausted when they arrived. I sent Jeremy to check on the stragglers and he found Lola sobbing in the corner where the corridor turns. She says she didn't know which way to go. No good pointing out that she'd been coming to school for nearly nine months now and that in any case all she had to do was follow the others.

What, I wonder, will this do to the children? We have to give explanations for these security measures and I've heard some mothers, Paige's for example, talking about 'bad men' and what they might do if they got into the school. It's going to make the children nervous, and some of them are nervous enough anyway.

*

It's extraordinary the way ranting on to myself about security measures, as I did yesterday, can take my mind off things I don't want to have to think about – pure distraction, works a treat. Don never allows distraction. Sometimes, when he was in head-clutching mode over some problem at work, and couldn't think how to solve it, I'd tell him to listen to some music, or watch television – it'll distract you, I'd say, and the answer will come. But he didn't agree. Nothing must distract him till he'd concentrated his mighty mind and found the solution.

Today, I seek distraction but I haven't found it. The dinner for Molly is in two days. I can't think about anything except how I'm dreading it. I've got the bag. I've wrapped it. I've got the card. I've written it. I know what I am going to wear. I've made the decision to drive there, because I don't want to drink and I do want to be independent and able to leave when I like.

*

Message from Judith when I got home today. She wonders if I might like to come over early tomorrow, say about three or four, to help her get ready for the party. I could hear her, when

185

I listened to her message, straining to be casual, to avoid being patronising, to make it sound as if she needed help, which everyone knows she does not. I'd be condemned to carrying out orders, that's all. I won't accept, of course. I'll ring and say I've got to go and pick up something in the afternoon and can't make it, sorry to let her down. What a game this is.

*

Woke very early, inevitably. I always do, on their birthday. I wake just before the time Molly was born and then I lie there reminiscing in my head. Or I used to. The sentimental, indulgent trip down memory lane has been cancelled. I can't enjoy it any more. But I tried, this morning, to get some of the innocent pleasure back, and I managed to, a little. Then, as I lay there, the telephone rang, the sound harsh in the stillness of the room. It was only five o'clock. Who would it be? Was it another nuisance call? A wrong number? My heart raced a little, and my hand shook as I lifted the receiver and said hello.

'Hello,' Don said, very quietly. 'I knew you'd be awake. I just thought I'd say hello.' I didn't reply. 'I knew you'd be remembering,' he said, 'and I am too.' I still didn't say anything. Don cleared his throat. 'Lou, I really am remembering. They were happy days. That day, this day, especially. I remember every single second of it ...' 'Don,' I said, 'please don't. I'll see you this evening.' And I hung up. I got up then, and here I am, trying to make sense of his call. He wanted, I'm sure, to impress me. He wanted to show me that he was close to me whatever I thought. The message was: we have something to share, so let's share it. Memories. Good, happy memories which can't be destroyed and continue to bind us together whatever has happened. True. But what Don doesn't understand is that memories are not like elastic, and they don't stretch into the future. They pull us back and become dangerous. He can't trade on memories.

When the phone rang again I thought it was another call from Don and I almost didn't answer it. But then I thought that

186

if I didn't, he would keep on and on. It was Molly. 'Hi, Mum,' she said, sounding cheerful but as though she had a cold. I said happy birthday, and you're awake bright and early and have you got a cold, and there was silence and I realised she was crying. I couldn't bear her not to be beside me so that I could hug and comfort her. 'I'm coming straight round, early or not,' I said. But she stopped me, saying no, she was going to get dressed and run across the park to me. That was what she wanted to do.

I stood at the window, watching for her so that she wouldn't need to ring the bell. Still just after six and not much activity yet in the street. A lovely morning, slightly hazy, the leaves of the plane trees at the end of the street shimmering in the faint breeze and behind them the white-blue of the morning sky. Molly would be entering the park. She'd have run through the silent streets between it and Judith's house, maybe passing a milk float. She was running towards me as fast as she could and I was so grateful, so glad. I'm so lucky, I thought, to have her. Lucky, lucky, lucky.

*

It wasn't quite how I imagined it would be when she did arrive. I thought we'd both be emotional. I'd seen us embracing, clasping each other tightly, maybe crying as we did so. But none of that happened. I saw her turn the corner at the end of the street leading to the park and she looked up and saw me and waved, and I pressed the button to release the front door as she ran into the forecourt of our flats. Then I waited at my own door, expectant and eager, but when she arrived, panting, she ducked past me gasping 'shower' and was in the bathroom immediately. It made me uncertain, not knowing quite what to do. So I did the obvious, squeezed oranges to make her juice and put the coffee on. When she emerged, wrapped in my towelling robe, her hair dripping, she sat down at the table without a kiss or cuddle.

I said happy birthday again, and went to her side and kissed her forehead, and she returned my kiss with one of her own, but it was lightly given, almost an absent-minded gesture. Then she said, 'Mum, I've come to beg a favour. I've been awake nearly all night, thinking.' I said she could have any favour she liked, she knew that she only had to ask. 'Mum,' she said, 'I want you to be friends with Dad today. It's all I want for my birthday. I don't care about presents. I just want you two to be friends again.' I went round to the other side of the table and sat down. My face felt hot, so I suppose I was flushed. I felt reprimanded somehow, as though I was being told off for some bad behaviour. 'We are friends,' I said. 'We've never been anything else.' 'It doesn't look like it,' she said. 'It hasn't looked like it since he came back. You hardly seem able to bear being in the same room as him. You change when he's there, you go all distant and cold. You were nicer to him when he was mad.' 'Was I?' I said. 'That was kind of me, then.' I was being sarcastic but she took me seriously. 'You *are* kind,' Molly said. 'That's what's so weird. I don't get it, why suddenly you pretend you're not. Don't you love him any more? Don't you even *like* him? What is it? Is it all because of Miranda? If she knew ... That was what made me tearful this morning. Oh, Miranda, I was thinking, if you knew what happened *afterwards*, the fall-out, the wreckage. How has it happened, Mum? It's nearly as awful as Miranda dying. No, no, don't shake your head, don't hide your face, that's what it feels like to me. I can't bear it. I bore Miranda's death but I can't bear this thing between you and Dad. It shouldn't be like this. Nothing can make Miranda alive, nothing can be done about it, but something can be done about you and Dad. It's stupid and unbearable, this situation. He loves you. He always has. And you won't let him.'

She'd hardly drawn breath. As she talked, rapidly, her voice rising all the time, her distress, evident at first, turned into anger. With *me!* She was angry with me. I was being wilful, it seemed, childish, and I must be scolded and made to apologise, then everything would be all right. I said nothing for a long time. She shifted on her chair, drank the orange juice, banged the glass as she put it back down. It was a good idea for me to keep silent. I felt it slowly giving me an advantage. She began to look uncomfortable, and I risked reaching across the table and squeezing her hand. 'Molly,' I said at last, 'I can't explain what I don't understand myself, can I? I just feel ... I've felt ... I'm not the same, that's all. Something's gone, between me and your father. I can't seem to get it back. It's no good blaming me. And I don't blame him. But it doesn't mean you have to be miserable. You've got us both, even if not under the same roof. And I'll be fine with Don so long as he accepts that I can't go back to how we were. That's what you want, isn't it?' She nodded. 'It's what he wants, I know, and it's what I thought I wanted for so long afterwards, just for us to be as we were. But I don't want that any more. I want what I have instead, the life I've made.' 'But it is *no* sort of life!' Molly burst out. 'You know it isn't – this flat – everything – you're just pretending.' 'No,' I said. 'I'm not. But I can be friends with Don, if he'll settle for that. Good friends. Now he's better, he'll make a new life, you'll see.'

She didn't see, and of course saying that last bit was fatuous, and I regretted it. She got back into her running clothes, sweaty though they were, and prepared to go back to Judith's. 'Don't look so unhappy on your birthday,' I said. 'Please give me a smile, a little one, even if you think I'm a brute.' She said she didn't think that. What she thought was that the madness, which had affected Don for so long, had now passed over to me. '*You*'re mad now,' she said. 'You know you love him, you know you want to be with him.' I shook my head. 'I'll see you this evening,' I said, 'and I'll be very, very kind. To everyone. All right?'

Then, we did hug, but it was more of a consolation hug than anything else. I hated to see her so defeated, all the spirit and energy gone out of her. I wondered how long she'd practised saying what she'd said, and what she'd hoped the outcome would be. Certainly not this.

*

Half an hour to go, and I'm all ready. Who knows how this party will turn out? I don't know whether I'll be sitting here writing happily about it, or so depressed I won't be able to write at all. But if the purpose of these sessions, writing to myself, is to clear my head, and to try to get things in proportion, then I want to reassure myself that I am going to Judith's determined to try to give Molly what she wants. I will be friendly to Don. I will be as near to my old self as I can get. I will do nothing to mar the evening.

But I'm not sure that the way I am dressed is quite like the old self Molly wants, not that she meant anything as trivial as clothes. It matters, somehow, that I should look as attractive as possible, simply for my own self-esteem. That's why I called Lynne into service. I lied. I told her that I was going to a dinner for a colleague who was retiring and that it was to be held in a posh hotel. I said I wanted to look my best and that I had nothing in my wardrobe remotely suitable. Lynne was delighted to help, of course. 'You never have made the best of your looks, Lou,' she said. God knows what she thinks my looks are. I'm not sophisticated or stylish or smart, but I think I'm always what my mother called 'nicely dressed'. I don't follow fashion, but I'm not old-fashioned. Don always said I looked lovely, though it's true that he said this whatever I was wearing.

It turned out that what Lynne meant was that though I have what she calls 'a rounded figure' I don't emphasise the roundness. Well, I don't like things that cling. And she said that because I'm only 5 foot 4 I shouldn't wear mid-calf skirts – 'draggy on you' – which I tend to. So, I've ended up sitting here wearing trousers and a tight-fitting top and a short, loose jacket thing. Not me at all. The trousers and jacket are white, the top a sort of bronze colour. It's quite low, the top, and sleeveless, but I won't be taking the jacket off. I quite like the jacket. The material feels like satin but it isn't. I don't suppose any of this

190

outfit will wash, but it doesn't matter. I probably won't wear it again. There's a lot of neck showing, and a bit of cleavage, though not as much as Lynne advised. I've shortened the thin straps of the top so that the neckline is higher. And I'm wearing a necklace Miranda gave me, the last present before she ... Her last present to me.

Maybe I should change. There's still time. I can wear the blue dress I've always liked. It's only cotton, and far from party wear, but it suits me, I think, and I feel comfortable in it. If I turn up looking like this, then everyone will remark on it and read significance into the obvious transformation – why has it been made, what am I trying to say? And more than that, I'm not convinced that this *is* making the most of myself as Lynne alleges. I probably look like mutton dressed as lamb. That would be sad. At least I haven't been foolish enough to change my hair or my make-up, though Lynne was all for it. There's nothing wrong with my hair. No grey in it yet, it's still dark and curly and thick, and I don't have to do anything with it except brush it. I like my hair, and I like my skin, and I don't intend to do anything with that either.

I'm not going to go and do anything as silly and vain as stand and look at myself for ages in a full-length mirror in order to decide whether to stay as I am or not. I've already looked in a mirror. I know I look good. 'Good?' I look different, very groomed, dressed up, maybe too dressed up for a family dinner. Miranda, always interested in clothes, would have loved how I look, but will Molly?

*

Phone call there, just as I was deciding to get into the blue dress, from Finn. Can I pick him up? He has been on a job and his moped has broken down and he doesn't want to ask Dad or Molly or Judith (why not?). I haven't time to change now. So, as so often, the decision has been made for me, in an entirely random way.

191

One in the morning. I've been home half an hour. I should sleep, then write.

Why struggle to be chronological? But it is easier, starting at the beginning and working through until now. Isn't that what all this is about? Looking for hope in orderliness.

I drove to the house where Finn had been working. He was standing looking anxious on the kerb and had the passenger seat open almost before I had pulled up. He was filthy, of course. 'Thanks,' he said. I was driving, so naturally I wasn't looking at his face, but I could feel his surprise, I knew he was still looking at me. 'Why are you all dressed up?' he said. 'It's a party, Finn,' I said, 'remember?' 'Yeah, but ... I mean ... not that sort of party. It's just a family dinner.' I didn't reply. He sounded resentful, irritated, as though I had no right to be 'dressed up', as he put it. 'Very nice, anyway,' he said, eventually, and then, 'Dad will ...' and he stopped. I didn't ask him what he meant. 'What are you giving Molly?' I asked quickly. He groaned, said nothing much, he hadn't much money, so he'd bought her an illustrated book about birds in Africa which he'd got at a car boot sale, and he'd made a card. I laughed, and he laughed too and said yeah, it was a real sticky-glue-and-glitter job.

So we arrived at Judith's house smiling, but then when it came to getting out of my car and revealing myself in my new outfit, I felt awkward and embarrassed. I saw Finn looking me up and down, and I couldn't interpret his expression. 'Cool,' he said. 'Don't,' I said. He had a key, so at least I didn't have to wait for Judith to open the door, and I didn't have to endure an exaggerated reaction while I stood on the doorstep. We went in. There was a wonderful smell coming from the kitchen. Then Finn raced off up the stairs to shower and change and at that moment Don came out of the sitting-room and into the hall. It's hard to say who was more taken aback. Don was wearing a suit, a new suit. It was a light grey, immaculate, and he had a startlingly white shirt on and a tie patterned in grey, white and orange. We stood and looked at each other, transfixed. Who knows what we would have said or done if Judith had not come out of the kitchen, all hot and bothered, wiping her hands on her apron, and crying, 'Well! Look at you two! Ooh, you look lovely, both of you!'

It was like meeting a stranger. I felt for a crazy few minutes like asking his name, and what he did for a living, and did he have a family. But neither of us, in fact, said a word to each other as Judith, who luckily never stopped chattering on, urged us into the sitting-room. I prayed for Finn to be quick and come rushing in, but he was ages, and when Judith said she had to get back to see to her soufflé we were left together. 'You look … well, I can't think how to describe how you look,' Don said, 'apart from beautiful.' 'So do you,' I said. 'New suit, obviously. Suits you, sir.' He seemed relieved to laugh. 'Doesn't feel right, though,' he said. 'It isn't me, it never was, I'm not really a suit man.' Now, isn't that what you say to someone who doesn't know you? I think so. Getting Don into suits was always difficult and I dreaded the occasions when even he thought it necessary. He had to wear a suit for work only at the beginning of his career, and it was fuss, fuss every day – ironic, because he is one of those men who look best in a formal suit.

Judith had pointed us towards a jug of Pimm's she'd made, and Don poured us each a glass. 'Where's the birthday girl?' I asked. He said she was still getting ready. I went out on to the terrace – it was still sunny – and began wandering round the garden, dead-heading roses as I passed. Don followed me. I reminded myself that I was determined to be friendly and so, when we came to Judith's arbour, I said should we sit and wait for the children here? We sat side by side, drinking our Pimm's. It was quite strong, lots of gin in it, and I was glad, even though I'd planned not to drink. I needed that slight blurring of the senses alcohol always gave me. Neither of us spoke. We looked towards the house, and waited.

They came out together, Finn with his arm round Molly's shoulder, and stood on the terrace. He looked so tall beside her, and protective. It brought immediate tears to my eyes, but I fiercely ordered them not to fall. Don and I got up at the same time and went towards our children, holding our glasses aloft as though we were toasting them, and Don did say, when we reached them, 'Cheers!' I saw at once that Molly's eyes were red and heavy, though she was smiling, or trying to. We hugged each other, but gently, me hugging Molly first and then Finn, and then Don did the same. We all told each other we looked amazing, lovely, cool, though it was Don and I who had made the most effort, obviously. Finn did have clean jeans on, and a proper shirt instead of a T-shirt, but he hadn't exactly tried to dress up. And Molly – well, Molly looked strange.

She wasn't wearing trousers. I searched my memory and couldn't remember when I had last seen her in a skirt or dress – years ago, I'm sure. Miranda wore skirts as often as she wore trousers, but Molly from her teenage years onwards only wore trousers. Getting her into a skirt was like getting Don into a suit. But now she was wearing a skirt, very short and brightly coloured, and a thin white cotton top, which was tucked in at the waist with a beaded belt. Her arms and legs were bare. Her legs were very white because even in Africa she wore trousers. She looked sweet, younger than her years, but uncomfortable. None of us made any remarks or teased her about her skirt.

Our presents were on a table in the sitting-room and we trooped in for the grand opening, with Judith appearing again, her apron discarded. Judith had given Molly a pair of binoculars, small and light, which was a good present, because Molly had mentioned how fascinated she'd got by the birds in Africa. She was enthusiastic about all her presents, then Judith produced champagne for Don to open, though I didn't feel like it after the Pimm's. Judith's meal was a triumph, but then her meals always are, and while we were eating the conversation flowed easily. Molly sat between Don and me, Finn opposite, with Judith. Neither of her boys was in London, so it was just us, a small gathering of five people. There was a birthday cake, which Judith, naturally, had made and candles, and we all sang 'Happy Birthday'.

It was later that a sudden silence seemed to fall. It wasn't quite dark by then, and still very warm, so we went out to the terrace for coffee. I was glad to be there, outside, the light dim in spite of Judith's candles. I sat on the wooden bench, with Molly. I sat down first and she came and joined me. I was glad, not wanting Don to do so. 'Thanks, everyone,' Molly said, her voice husky. 'When is it you leave?' Judith asked. 'I keep forgetting. Is it next week?' 'This week,' Molly said. 'Four more days and I'm off.' It took Judith to ask the obvious 'Are you glad to be going?' – though it was what we all wanted to know. Molly paused. She was clearly choosing her words carefully. 'Sitting here now, with you all, I'm not glad. I mean, who would want to leave a happy family gathering?' Don caught my eye, but I looked away. 'But I'm looking forward to another few months, yes. I just worry, though, about what'll I come back to. When you're thousands of miles away you sort of want everything to stay the same back home. Coming back and finding ... well, it wasn't the same.'

Judith got up. 'I'm going to clear up. No, no, I don't want any help, thank you. You just sit and enjoy being a family.' I could have screamed – 'being a family' – for god's sake, Judith. So she trotted back into the house and we were left. 'Well, family,' Finn said, lightly, 'what shall we do? Scrabble, anyone?' We tried to laugh, but not very successfully. And that's when everything changed. The light-heartedness disappeared. Four gloomy people sat together staring into what was by then a dark garden. And I do need to sleep, before the next bit. I have to.

*

Sunday. Theoretically good, means I can recover from going to bed so late and getting little sleep. But I wish it were

Monday, and school to go to, and the children to fill my mind.

Still, I can flop, I needn't drive myself on to do anything. I can get this over first, have done with this foolishness. I can sit here in my dressing-gown at my desk and even though my body aches, as though it had run a marathon, and my head is heavy – but then I did drink, after all – it is not asking much of myself to finish what I started. It won't take long.

There we were, in the garden, Judith's candles flickering, lighting our faces kindly. They were those sort of scented candles – 'Passion', I saw one was called – set in tins. She had about a dozen of them – what do I mean, 'about', when I counted them over and over: she had exactly twelve candles on her terrace table, arranged all round the edge except for one, which was in the middle. The smell was overpowering and not entirely pleasant, but nobody said anything. We watched the candles as though they were fascinating. We watched each other. Finn kicked the table leg every now and again. He did it gently enough, but it became annoying. I saw Don longing to tell him to stop it but not wanting to risk an argument or Finn simply leaving the table. The candles shook. I didn't say anything either. It was Molly who said to him that he was going to knock the candles over if he went on kicking the table. He immediately got up to go, as both Don and I had known he would – he'd only been waiting for an excuse.

'Right,' he said, 'I'll be off. Have to be up early tomorrow, got a big job.'

'On Sunday?' Don said, but his tone mild.

'Yeah. We often have big jobs on Sundays.'

'Night, then,' said Molly. 'Thanks for the pressie. See you tomorrow night.'

He gave her a kiss, and then he hesitated before coming round to me and giving me one too. 'Night, Dad,' he said, and off he went. He really did go to bed. We saw the light go on upstairs in his room and then go off.

'And now there are three,' Molly said. 'Cosy, huh?'

'I'd better go myself,' I said.

'You can't,' Don said. 'You're driving, and you've drunk quite a bit.'

'I'm not in the least drunk.'

'No, but you've drunk quite a bit. Better wait a while, have some more coffee, and some water, Or stay here.'

'I can't stay here,' I said, quickly. 'I have to get home.'

'Why?' asked Molly. 'What's the urgency? There isn't any, is there? You just want to leave us, that's all, isn't it?'

'Don't put it like that,' I said. 'You know I don't want to leave you, not the way you make it sound.'

'What way, then?' Molly said. 'What other kind of leaving is there? You want to be on your own.'

'That doesn't mean shutting you out or ...'

'It does. It means exactly that.'

'Molly ...' began Don, and she turned on him so furiously it was frightening.

'You!' she said. 'You did it, you left us, oh you did, that's what all that rubbish about investigations amounts to, you left us when we needed you. And now you're back, well, I'm glad, I really am, and I forgive you, I do, but she's doing the leaving now, so don't "Molly" me. I'll say what I like, what I didn't say to you then and I should have done.'

And then she burst into tears.

*

Had to stop. Have had a long, hot bath. Washed my hair. Got into comfortable old clothes. Had some breakfast, and now here I am again, supposedly composed and ready to get it all out. I have to.

She wept, and we both jumped up and went to her, but she wouldn't let either of us touch her. 'No!' she shouted. 'No, no!' And then Judith came bustling out, asking whatever was the matter. 'Nothing,' Don said. 'Molly's just ...' But Molly cut in with, 'Everything, Judith, everything is wrong but they won't make it right.' Judith stood quite still, and spread her arms wide in a strangely comforting gesture, as though she was trying to embrace the air round us and fold our distress within it. 'Well,' she said, and again. 'Well.' 'Judy,' Don said, 'could you manage some more coffee, or shall I? ...' 'Of course,' Judith said, and went back into the house.

'Coffee isn't going to help, Dad,' Molly said, still wiping the tears away. 'Oh, my God! Coffee ... as if ...'

'It'll help your mother,' Don said. 'She's driving home.'

'Molly,' I said, 'if it would help, I'll stay here for tonight, but ...'

'No!' she said. 'I don't want you to, *you* don't want to. It would just be a farce. Get thee to your nunnery,' and then she started to laugh. At first I thought she was being hysterical, but then I realised it was a real laugh, and she couldn't stop. Don's face was heavily in shadow but I could tell he was smiling now. 'Oh,' Molly gasped, 'it must be the drink!' And then I joined in. It was one of my mother's sayings – if anyone behaved in a ridiculous fashion she used to say, in the most serious of tones, 'It must be the drink', even if there had been no alcohol anywhere.

Judith came out with the coffee. 'And now it's hysterics, is it?' she asked. We said no, no, just a joke. She said she was glad to hear we were on to jokes, because she was going to have to go to bed and she couldn't have gone if we'd still been in such a state. I said I was going too, as soon I'd drunk the coffee. 'You won't stay, Lou?' she said, quietly. 'No,' I said, 'I'm going back to my flat. But why don't you all come to me for lunch, and we could have a walk in the park.' 'All of us?' Molly said. 'All of you, of course,' I said.

Judith went to bed, and I drank my coffee. I felt perfectly capable of driving. I hugged and kissed Molly, who made an attempt to respond and do the same, but without much enthusiasm, and I said sorry, several times. She didn't ask what for, which was lucky, because I couldn't have said. Don said, 'I'll walk you to your car.' I was going to say there was no need, but I didn't, in case it would upset Molly. We went into the house, Don closing and locking the glass doors behind us, and then through to the hall, and Molly went off up the stairs. Don held the front door open for me, and Judith's cat slipped in. 'Got your keys?' he asked. I took them from my bag and dangled them. The gravel crunched noisily under our feet. All the lights in the house were off, but suddenly one went on and we looked up and saw Molly about to lower her blind. She waved. We waved back.

Then Don said, 'Can I kiss you good night, Lou?' Immediately, I felt the tears come. How long since he'd wanted to touch me? I didn't think I could bear it. I shook my head, and said I didn't think so, no. But he'd seen my tears. 'Wait,' he said, 'you can't drive when you're so upset.' I said I wasn't upset. I said it was late, and I wanted to get home, and sleep. I had to go. Once in the car, with the door closed, I felt better. He stood there, bathed in Judith's security lights, his hands in his pockets, shoulders hunched and it didn't seem right to leave him like that. What did I feel? What did I feel ... I don't know. Something. Something I was afraid to feel but which felt important. I lowered my window, and put my hand through. He rushed forward, and held it. 'Good night, Don,' I said. 'See you tomorrow.'

I haven't got much for lunch, but then none of us will be hungry after last night. I can make omelettes. At least I can make good omelettes, just as good as my sister-in-law's. God knows why I invited them all, though. It wasn't necessary. I could have done it another time. But it was for Molly's sake. I want her to see that I haven't left the family, even if I want to live on my own. I've never had any intention of leaving, in the real meaning of that word. I care deeply about all of them – even Don – don't they know that? I want to show her that her father and I can be friends, good friends, even if I disappoint her by not holding out hope of anything else. I can't just say to her that something broke, afterwards. Miranda died, and then, afterwards, with all that we went through, something else died.

We can't resurrect it, just as we can't resurrect Miranda. We can only start over again, endure the memories, wait for the pain to lessen. As it has, already. We don't want more pain, more grief. Molly would say that, by separating, Don and I have done exactly that, caused more pain, more grief, but I have to convince her that she is wrong.

First, I have to convince myself. It's time to put this away. There's no more sense to be made of what has happened since 30 July 2003 – I mean, what has happened once it was all over. I want to move into the future, let my thoughts lead me there. I don't want to look at the children in my class and see disaster ahead for them, drownings and bombings, and the other terrible random events that will almost certainly await some of them. It's an awful way to live, shuddering endlessly at life's tragedies, waiting for them to happen. I will not live like that. I want to be able to say, in ten years or so, that afterwards, a long time afterwards, I recovered. I don't want people to say of me that my life was blighted by Miranda's death. I don't want my life to be defined by it. I have recovered a little, I will recover more. So will Finn, so will Don, and so will Molly. What might happen then, I don't know.